Amy Cross is the author of more than 100 horror, paranormal, fantasy and thriller novels.

OTHER TITLES BY AMY CROSS INCLUDE

American Coven
Annie's Room
The Ash House
Asylum
B&B
Better the Devil
The Bride of Ashbyrn House
The Camera Man
The Curse of Wetherley House
The Devil, the Witch and the Whore
Devil's Briar
The Dog
Eli's Town
The Farm
The Ghost of Molly Holt
The Ghosts of Lakeforth Hotel
The Girl Who Never Came Back
Haunted
The Haunting of Blackwych Grange
The Haunting of Marshall Heights
Like Stones on a Crow's Back
The Night Girl
Perfect Little Monsters & Other Stories
Stephen
The Shades
The Soul Auction
Tenderling
Ward Z

Days 9 to 16

AMY CROSS

First published by Dark Season Books,
United Kingdom, 2018

Copyright © 2018 Amy Cross

First published in November 2013 as *Mass Extinction Event: The Complete Second Series*. This edition originally published in July 2018

All rights reserved. This book is a work of fiction. Names, characters, places, incidents and businesses are the product of the author's imagination or are used fictitiously. Any resemblance to actual persons, living or dead, or to actual events or locations, is entirely coincidental.

ISBN: 9781718012257

Also available in e-book format.

www.amycross.com

CONTENTS

PROLOGUE
PAGE 13

DAY NINE
PAGE 23

DAY TEN
PAGE 85

DAY ELEVEN
PAGE 147

DAY TWELVE
PAGE 207

DAY THIRTEEN
PAGE 249

DAY FOURTEEN
PAGE 295

DAY FIFTEEN
PAGE 331

DAY SIXTEEN
PAGE 382

EPILOGUE
PAGE 425

DAYS
9 TO 16

PROLOGUE

"IT'S THIS COUGH," the guy says, his voice sounding strained. "It's just not going away. I swear, I've never had anything like it."

Sitting a few seats away on the bus, Joseph can't help but smile. The two men near the front have been discussing their health problems for a few minutes now, and one of them in particular seems to be struggling with a cough that he just can't keep under control. Ordinarily, Joseph would have moved to the back of the bus in order to avoid the chance he might catch something, but this time he has no such worries. He knows exactly what's happening, and he knows that he already has the same infection. Well, 'infection' is a strong word. To everyone else on the planet, it's an infection, but to Joseph, it's just... life.

"If you're coughing blood," the guy's friend says, "you should go see a doctor. That shit's serious."

"It was only a few specks," the first guy replies. "I've been coughing so much, I've probably just torn something in the back of my throat. You know how it is." He pauses to cough again. "You hear that?" he adds eventually. "It's fucking deep on my chest, man. It's not fun. I was starting to think it might be pneumonia, but it's not. It's just a fucking kick-ass cold."

"Better be," his friends says. "I don't want to catch anything."

"I'm not sneezing *on* you, am I?"

"It's in the air, man. It's like, when you cough and sneeze, all these little droplets are left hanging for hours, and they're all over everything. When you're sick, you should go to bed and stay there instead of coming out and infecting people. It's selfish!"

"Whatever."

"I'm serious! You come out here, coughing and spluttering and all that shit, and you're infecting everyone in your path! It's pretty bad, man. Can't you just ride it out at home? This kind of stuff spreads like wildfire. God knows how many people you've infected already. All the people on this bus are probably messed up, for one thing."

Joseph looks out the window. He knows

exactly what's going to happen over the next few days, and he knows that these men are going to be utterly unable to do anything about it. His most recent calculations suggest that the spread will be at least 99.5%, if not more, and it's already clear that these two specimens are going to be among the first to die. There's a part of him that would like to warn them, but Joseph knows that the best thing is just to let everything proceed as planned. It's tempting to think that maybe he could turn back, but even if he was having true second thoughts, he couldn't undo anything. The wheels are in motion, and the plan is unstoppable. The spread must be massive by now, traveling not only through the streets of the city, but also extending its reach all around the world. He can't help but think of all the people moving through airports, unaware that they're spreading the seed of their own destruction.

"You okay?" asks a voice nearby.

Turning, Joseph finds that a woman is staring at him with a concerned expression. She looks like a typical busy-body, the kind of person Joseph hates. In fact, she reminds him of his grandmother, the woman who raised him and ruined his life, turning him into a miserable, bullied child. He has to remind himself to stay calm, because there's a part of him that would dearly like to grab the old bitch and cause her some proper pain. For a moment, he allows himself to fantasize about bouncing her face off the back of the seat, smashing her skull and then watching as the blood flows all over the floor.

"I asked if you're okay," the woman continues. "Can you hear me?"

"I'm fine," he replies gruffly.

"You know you've got a nose-bleed, don't you?" she asks. "It's, like..." She pauses, staring at him.

Wiping his upper lip, Joseph finds that there is, indeed, a trickle of blood. Pulling a tissue from his pocket, he gives it a quick wipe. He hadn't expected to get so many symptoms himself, and he's a little surprised that he didn't manage to notice the blood moving down his face, but he figures he's just been distracted lately.

"You got a fever?" the woman continues, peering at him with a hint of suspicion. "You don't look well. Are you sweating? You got a high temperature?"

"No," Joseph snaps at her. "Of course I haven't got a fever. Have *you* got a fever?"

"I was just asking -"

"Why?" Joseph asks. "Why is my health any of your business? You should be more worried about yourself. Seriously, do you have any idea what's coming? Or are you so stupid, you can't even piece together all the signs? Are you just another typical human idiot?"

The woman stares at him.

"Of course you are," he sneers. "You're just like all of them. No-one's gonna give a damn about you. You're no more intelligent than a cow or a pig. You're the perfect example of why I..." He catches himself just in time, realizing that he was close to telling her the truth. She'd never have believed him, of course, but still, he figures he doesn't need to add any complications. "Forget it," he says eventually. "Just... leave me alone and go back to whatever you were doing, huh? Get on with your mundane fucking life, while you still can."

Raising an eyebrow, the woman sits back, clearly not impressed by Joseph's tone. He doesn't care, though. All that matters to him, right now, is getting back to his apartment so that he can await the end. After building up to this moment for so long, he's becoming impatient, and he figures he's probably allowed himself to come out into the world a little too much lately. He should have cocooned himself away much sooner and relied on twenty-four hour news channels to keep him updated. It's as mistake he won't make again. As he turns to look back out the window, he watches the world and tries to imagine how things will be in a couple of weeks. There'll be a few survivors, of course, but he's confident that they'll be mopped up soon enough. They'll be the unlucky ones, in a way, because their deaths will take longer, and because they'll have some understanding of what's happening. He looks forward to speaking to them, from the other side.

***

The cough gets worse on the second day. *Much* worse.

Standing by the window, Joseph looks out at the playground near his apartment. It's getting late, but there are still some children playing on the swings. As he continues to cough, Joseph can't stop watching the children, wondering what they might have grown up to become. Politicians? Civic leaders? Inventors? Criminals? He figures they'd probably be a random mix, but there's a part of him that regrets taking any their chance to find out for themselves. Watching them, he realizes that they'll never be anything more than a group of children. They'll never grow up and have their own families. They'll never get old. In a way, they'll be frozen in time. He's never thought about the children before, but now he realizes that he's doomed them all.

He pauses to cough again.

When he was a child, Joseph had plenty of friends. The problem was that they were all idiots, at least as far as he was concerned. He used to play with them only because he knew it was expected of him, and because he didn't want to let anyone know that he hated other people. Even at a young age, he had a strong streak of self-preservation, and he was fully aware that the slightest hint of weirdness would most likely lead to him being booked in for counseling sessions. He'd known a boy named Bobby who, after going to various sessions, had been pulled from school and sent off to some special academy for 'troubled' children. Joseph most certainly didn't want to meet the same fate, so he'd learned to be a chameleon and blend in. For many years now, it had been a successful strategy.

The only problem, in the old days, was his family. There weren't many of them, but they definitely seemed to suspect that something was wrong with him, even if they never came right out and said anything. He'd notice them occasionally, glancing at him as if they expected him to be doing something strange or unusual. Over the years, these moments had merely reinforced Joseph's belief that he was 'weird' and 'special'. He'd tried to keep out of their way as much as possible, even though he knew that this, in itself, probably reinforced their suspicions. Eventually, he just gave up caring what they thought, and he accepted that he and his family would never get along. Now, on the brink of his greatest victory, he pauses to imagine what they'd all think if they could see him now, if they knew that he would be the man who'd bring the world to its knees and then force it to be reborn in a powerful new form.

Coughing again, he looks at his hand and sees a few specks of blood. He'd never expected to be affected like this, but he's still sure that the virus won't kill him. After all, viruses don't tend to cannibalize their own kind. He figures the virus is adapting and learning, and that it'll take a little while before it recognizes its master. In a day or two, his symptoms will clear up, just as everyone else is getting worse and worse, and that's how he'll finally be certain that his plan has worked. He's already looking forward to the moment of victory, and he knows it'll taste all the sweeter if it comes after a period of suffering. Letting out another cough, he can't help but laugh as he thinks of the virus spreading across the world, carrying its unique genetic make-up everywhere it goes. Never before, in the history of mankind, has such an empire been built; never before, he reasons, has one man been in control of such a powerful army. Most other would-be rulers tried to gather men to fight for them; Joseph, on the other hand, came up with a much better idea, and he's seeing the fruits of his work right now. They're everywhere.

He watches as the children turn and head inside. He hopes that their last night of life will be something particularly enjoyable, although he figures that they'll just waste their time with video games and other pointless activities. He knows, deep down, that while he might enjoy pretending that these children would grow up to be something great, the reality is that they'd most likely drift through life on a cloud of distaste and boredom. Although he's keen not to award himself too many accolades, he can't help but feel that in a way he's improving the world by ridding it of all these pointless people. He knows that his victims will never see it that way, but he remains convinced that eventually, after a few weeks, maybe a month or two, the transformation will be complete. Once the main phase is over, he'll be able to pick off the survivors, and then he'll be able to step back and admire his proud new world.

Turning from the window, he walks slowly across the gloomy apartment, stopping eventually to look at the silent TV screen. A news show is reporting on some kind of car crash on the interstate, and for a moment Joseph is dazzled by the images. The camera shows twisted metal frames being lifted by cranes, while police and fire officers stand around. There are a few ambulances parked nearby, and a strap-line along the bottom of the screen notes that three people have already died in the accident while another two have been taken to hospital. Seconds later, the image changes to become a shot of the news anchor, and Joseph leans closer to the TV, examining the pixels that constitute the man's mouth. Slowly, almost without thinking about what he's doing, Joseph starts to mouth the words he imagines the news anchor saying. Placing his eye as close to the screen as possible, he eventually sees the pixels for what they really are: little dancing patches of light, like a virus heaving and throbbing as it changes and grows. Eventually, a smile starts to spread across Joseph's face.

DAY 9

AMY CROSS

ELIZABETH

New York

TURNING, I LOOK BACK at the city. With the sun starting to rise above the horizon, Manhattan has a kind of deathly thrall, and a low mist hangs between the buildings. It looks almost like a toy town, made to be populated by little plastic figures of men and women. It's hard to believe that this place was once my home.

I buried Henry in Central Park. Although I considered leaving him where he fell, another part of my mind took over, telling me to keep busy. I found a shovel and a wheelbarrow in Bob's tool room and I managed to get my brother's dead body through the dark streets, finally reaching Central Park just a few hours ago. Digging a grave was the hardest physical labor I've ever had to endure, but I was determined to get it right. I dug long and I dug deep, emptying my mind and just focusing on the pure sensation of the soil being ripped from the ground. To be honest, I probably dug further than six feet, and I think I kind of ended up on some kind of auto-pilot. Finally, snapping out of my daze, I realized the grave was ready, so I climbed out and rolled Henry's body into the pit. When he landed at the bottom, there was a snapping sound, which I guess means one of his bones broke. I said a little made-up prayer and then I shoveled all the soil back into the pit, and I broke off some branches and made a very basic makeshift cross. Hell, I'm not even religious, but I made a cross. I don't really know why.

And then I left.

Now I'm out here on one of the long roads that leads away from the city. I'm heading northwest, I think, following the signs for Chicago. I've got a vague plan to look for Mallory and the others, although they must be way ahead by now and I guess the odds of ever meeting them again are low. Still, I have to try something. Trudging along the road, with a couple of Bob's rifles slung over my shoulder, I keep well away from any cars that I happen to pass. It's strange, but I feel incredibly calm. I guess the full impact of the past twenty-four hours - hell, the past nine days - hasn't really hit me yet. I haven't properly thought about what happened to Henry, or about those final moments with Bob. I'm just focused on the empty horizon and the prospect of one day finding somewhere new. I guess I'll cry and get upset when I reach a new home. Until then, I have to stay strong. And blank.

The truth is, I haven't even cried. Not properly. My own brother died, and although I can feel the tears behind my eyes, I can't get them out. What does that make me? Am I in shock, or am I just some kind of monster?

In the distance, I can see the airport. To the best of my knowledge, that's where my parents were when this whole thing started. For the past week, I've been desperate to go out there and look for them, but now I feel the opposite: I don't even like seeing the place. I mean, the odds of finding them alive are miniscule, and the terminal buildings are probably just a bunch of tombs. Stopping for a moment and taking a swig from a bottle of water, I stare at the distant airport and realize that there's no movement at all. In fact, as I turn in a complete circle, I realize that there's no movement anywhere. It's as if, as far as the eye can see, I'm the only living thing.

And then I hear a noise.

Turning, I look at the road ahead. Maybe I'm going crazy, but I *heard* something. It was just a kind of scrabbling sound, like feet on rough ground, but there's no way I'm going to take any unnecessary risks. Slipping one of the rifles off my shoulder, I stay completely still, staring at the half dozen cars skewed on the tarmac. My heart's racing as I wait for some kind of sign, some indication of what caused that noise. Slowly, I take a couple of steps forward, hoping to get a better view, but there's still nothing. Taking a deep breath, I realize I can't handle the uncertainty. If there's something nearby, even if it's something bad, I want to know right now.

"Hey!" I call out, my voice cutting through the vast silence. "Over here!"

No reply.

I take a couple of steps forward.

"If you want me," I shout, "come and get me!"

Nothing.

"There's no -" I continue, before stopping as I hear the noise again. Somehow it seems further away, almost as if it's coming from beyond the edge of the road. I guess I could just hurry along and hope that, whatever it is, it doesn't cause me any bother. Still, I feel as if I want to know exactly what I'm up against. Despite the fact that I know I'm taking an unnecessary risk, I walk cautiously over to the other side of the road, keeping the rifle pointed forward as I approach the barrier that runs along the edge of the carriageway. Finally, I look down the side of the road, at the section of grassy scrub-land that runs between this road and the next.

There's a girl.

Stumbling through the grass, she looks to be about my age, maybe slightly older. Her clothes are ragged and torn, and from the way she's walking, it looks like she's injured, but at the same time her skin looks normal, so I don't think she's like that creature we saw back in the city. She's stumbling away from the city, but she doesn't seem to have noticed me. It's as if she's just making her way slowly through the grass, ignoring the world around her.

"Hey!" I call out.

She doesn't respond. She just keeps walking.

"Hey! I call out again.

She stops, and slowly she turns to look at me. She's pretty, with long blonde hair and large blue eyes, but she seems a little confused, as if she's not entirely sure about me. I guess that's understandable. As she shields her eyes from the rising sun behind me, she must be pretty confused by me as I stand here with a bag over one shoulder and a rifle over the other, with another rifle in my hands.

"Are you okay?" I ask, lowering the rifle but keeping my finger near the trigger, just in case. Even though she doesn't look like one of the creatures, I can't be too careful.

She just stares at me.

Looking over my shoulder, I make sure that there's no-one nearby before I turn back to the girl and climb over the metal barrier. I'm still not certain that this girl is safe, but I can't just ignore her. After all, if she's smart and unhurt, we might be able to help each other.

"My name's Elizabeth," I say, taking a couple of steps forward. "What's yours?"

She stares at me, still shielding her eyes from the light of the sun as it rises behind me.

"I came from the city," I continue. "I've been there since..." I pause, and then I look down and see that I've still got some of Henry's blood on my clothes. My first reaction is shock, but after a moment I realize that I'm just going to have to keep going like this. I can't go back to the city for different clothes, and I can't walk naked. Damn it, I should have changed before I left, but I was so shocked by everything that happened, somehow I didn't realize. "This isn't my blood," I say, looking over at the girl. "It's my brother's. He died. I tried to save him." I wait for an answer, but she just continues to stare at me. "I didn't kill him," I add. "Someone else did. I killed *that* guy, though. I left his body in the apartment."

No reply.

"My name's Elizabeth Marter," I continue, stepping closer to her. "Can you tell me your name?"

We stand in silence for a moment.

"Dawn," she says eventually, her voice trembling as she continues to stare wide-eyed at me.

"Dawn?"

"Dawn," she says again.

"Elizabeth," I reply. "Are you... Were you in the city?"

She stares at me.

"Where are you going?" I ask.

She turns and looks toward the horizon, as if she's going the same way that I'm going.

"Do you want to walk together?" I ask. "Have you got any stuff with you? Food? Water?"

She turns to look back at me, and from the blank look on her face, it's almost as if she doesn't understand the question. I'm not entirely sure what's wrong with her, but she seems to be struggling with even the most basic questions.

"Here," I say, lowering the rifle before grabbing a bottle of water from my bag. "I haven't got much to spare, but..." I hold the bottle out to her. "It's yours if you want it."

Slowly, cautiously, she takes the bottle and unscrews the lid, before taking a few sips. It's almost as if she suspects that I'm planning to hurt her, but I guess the past few days have probably taught her to be cautious. After all, it's kind of a miracle that anyone got out of that city, especially with people like Bob wandering around.

"You should probably save some," I continue, as Dawn finishes the last of the water. "Like I said, I don't really have any to spare."

She drops the plastic bottle.

"No!" I say, stepping forward and picking the bottle back up. I brush dirt from the neck before taking the lid back from Dawn and screwing it back on. "I'm saving these," I tell her. "I brought a funnel with me, and when it rains, I'm gonna try to refill it. I figure rain water's okay to drink. I mean, if rain water's poisoned, then we're all just completely screwed, right?"

After carefully putting the empty bottle back in my bag, I turn to Dawn and see that she's still just staring at me. I swear, it's as if she's doesn't really understand what I'm saying.

"You're in shock, huh?" I ask. "That's okay. I think I am too, but in a different kind of way. I'm heading toward Lake Ontario. It's, like, four hundred miles north or north-west. I don't have a map, but there are loads of street signs, and I think I have to just kind of follow the road to Chicago for a while." I wait for a reply, but she's still just staring at me. "I figure I can walk thirty miles a day," I continue, hoping to eventually prompt some kind of reaction, "so it's gonna take me the best part of a month, when you add in time to stop and get some supplies, and maybe the road isn't totally straight, and I might get lost. I'm hoping to catch up to some other people, but I'm not sure..." My voice trails off as I realize that Dawn doesn't seem to understand what I'm telling her.

I sigh, trying to work out what I should do next.

"You're welcome to come with me," I continue, "but I have to get going." The truth is, although I want to stay and help this girl, I know I don't have the luxury of time, and I can't put myself in extra danger just to help someone who doesn't seem to even really know that I'm here. "Okay, so I'm gonna start walking now," I tell her. "If you want to come, just follow me, okay?"

With that, I turn and start walking along the grass, before climbing over the metal barrier and resuming my journey along the road. There was definitely something pretty weird about that Dawn girl, even if I couldn't quite work out what was wrong with her, but while I'd like to have someone with me, I guess that maybe she'd just hold me back. I keep walking until finally I stop and turn, and to my surprise I see that Dawn is stumbling along, about twenty meters behind me, having apparently followed me up onto the road. She stops when she sees that I've stopped, and she clearly doesn't want to walk right next to me, but it seems that she's decided to come with me, at least for now. Turning, I keep going, and although it feels weird to know that there's someone walking behind me, I figure that maybe it'll work out. I mean, she has to start talking eventually.

# THOMAS

Missouri

"JOE!" I SHOUT AS I climb out of the truck and hurry around to the back. Having driven all night, barely able to even make out the road in the light of the moon, I've finally decided to stop now that the sun's coming up. I'm running on pure adrenalin as I lift the tarpaulin and see, to my horror, that Joe's a bloodied, motionless mess.

I stand in silence.

"Joe?" I say cautiously.

No response.

I'm not ready to give up just yet. Sure, it looks bad, but there has to be help somewhere around here. All during the night, I was convinced that we'd eventually find someone or something, but there's been nothing but mile after mile of empty road. About an hour ago, we passed a street sign that welcomed us to Missouri, but I just kept my foot down because I figured there was a chance that maybe, outside of Oklahoma, things might be better.

"Joe?" I say again. Reaching out, I place a hand on his shoulder. "Please don't be dead," I continue. "Please don't -"

Suddenly he moves. It's not much, but it's enough to let me know that he's alive. A faint groan comes from his lips, and although he's clearly still unconscious, I can't help but be overjoyed at the realization that he survived the night. I guess the tourniquets I tied around his wounds must have at least helped slightly. Climbing up onto the back of the truck, I reach down and place two fingers against his wrist, and I can just about make out a faint pulse. He's alive, but he's still in a bad way, and I still need to get us some help.

"Can you hear me?" I ask, looking down at his blood-stained face. "Joe, are you there?"

He groans again, which I guess is a good sign. After all, the groan seemed to be a response to what I said to him.

"Okay," I continue, "I don't know if you can understand what I'm saying, but we're in Missouri. We drove all night. I don't really know what happened back there, but something was totally wrong in Scottsville. There were these things, and they nearly... I pause as I realize how dumb the whole thing sounds. Then again, I know it's all true. I can still remember the look on Clyde's face when he thought he'd got us cornered. "I had to get us out of there," I continue, "and then there was this really loud boom, and then this guy with a feather."

I sit in silence for a moment.

"I meant to head west," I say eventually. "I don't know how we ended up going east. I guess I'm not very good at navigation, but I did my best. Anyway, east isn't so bad, is it? At least we're headed toward Washington. Maybe that's where they're gonna start putting things right and fixing this mess, huh? Do you think, Joe? Is that the best place to go?" I wait for him to reply, desperately hoping that somehow he might wake up and help me. Right now, I have no idea what to do. I've never been out of Oklahoma before, and I have no idea whether going to Washington would actually be useful. Maybe, instead, we should just hunker down somewhere and hope that the world gets sorted out.

I wait.

"Joe?" I ask.

Silence.

My biggest fear over the past day has been that he might just die suddenly, without any warning. The truth is, Joe's injuries are probably way worse than I've accepted, and I figure there's going to come a time when I'll have to make a decision. That time isn't here yet, though, and for now I have to focus on keeping him alive. I need to stay strong. If I allow myself to become weak, even for a moment, I might lose my brother forever.

He groans.

Leaning closer, I see that one entire side of his upper chest has been badly damaged, crushed by the car that collapsed directly on top of him. The heavy bleeding seems to have stopped, but it's clear that he's not going to simply heal up. The fact that he's even alive at all right now, in a way, seems like a miracle. The damage must have affected his lungs, maybe even his heart, and he's been steadily losing blood for twenty-four hours. It's getting to the point that I'm not even sure if a fully-equipped hospital would be able to do much for him.

"We're going to keep driving," I say eventually. "We have to get to some place eventually, right? Somewhere we can find help? All we have to do is just stay strong. Can you do that, Joe? Can you just hold on for a few more hours?"

I wait for a reply.

Silence.

"Shit!" I mutter, realizing that things are getting desperate. "You have to stay alive!" I shout eventually, even though I know it's not going to help. "You can't die! Everyone else died, Joe! You're the only one left! Do you hear me?" For a moment, I'm filled with anger as I contemplate the possibility that my brother might finally bail on me, just like the rest of my family. The thought of being left alone in the world is too much to bear. After all, the only person who might possibly still be alive is Martha, but she's back in California. For a moment, it occurs to me that maybe I should turn the truck around and head back west. If I can find Martha, she'd know what to do. She'd *have* to help.

Joe groans, but it's not even clear whether he's conscious.

"We're going east," I say finally. "There's no argument. We'll go east until we find someone who can help, and maybe we'll eventually end up in Washington, but at some point we have to run into someone. Maybe the army's already helping out. They're gonna help Washington and New York first, aren't they? Then they'll start heading this way. If we head toward them, we'll find them sooner." I take a deep breath as I realize that this plan, although it's somewhat insane, is better than just sitting around doing nothing. It's our only chance.

Climbing down from the back of the truck, I hurry to the driver's cab and get back inside. By the time I've got the engine running again, I've managed to put aside my doubts. This plan is going to work. We *are* going to get help, and Joe *is* going to survive. Any other outcome is just too terrifying to even think about right now. The world might be in a mess, but it's not going to end.

DAYS 9 TO 16

ELIZABETH

New York

THE BACK OF THE plane is all burned out, so it's hard to make out the name of the airline company, but the front end is relatively unscathed. The problem is, it's right across the road, and taking a route around the edge is going to be difficult since the gaps between the roads out here are getting increasingly overgrown. It's as if someone intentionally dropped the thing right in the middle of the road, with the specific aim of stopping people from getting past. Sighing, I stand and stare at the downed plane, and finally I turn to look back at Dawn, who has stopped about ten meters behind me.

"What do you think?" I ask.

She stares at me.

"No thoughts, huh?" I reply, before turning to look at the plane. I've seen other planes in the distance since I left Manhattan, but they all seem to have burned after they hit the ground. I don't know why this one is mostly intact, but since we're quite close to the airport, I figure that maybe it had barely left the ground when the trouble hit. With the main fuselage tilted to one side, I can see that the landing gear is sticking out, but although I'm not too keen on going any closer, I figure that if the fuel tanks were going to explode, it would have happened by now. The fire seems to be out, at least, and now the plane is just a vast monument to the world that existed before all this craziness happened. It's only been just over a week, but already it seems hard to believe that humans were ever able to get such huge machines into the air. I wonder if there's anyone left alive who knows how to fly one of these things.

"We're gonna go around the front," I say, hoping that Dawn can hear me. It's weird to be taking charge like this, but it's not as if Dawn seems to have much of an opinion on anything. "We're just gonna get past this thing, and keep going, okay?" I turn to her, but of course she's still just staring blankly at me. "All you have to do is follow," I continue. "Think you can do that?"

No reply.

"Of course you can," I mutter, turning back

to the plane and finally starting to walk over to the side of the road.

Climbing over the barrier isn't the difficult part. The difficult part is getting down the grass verge that leads to the trench that runs between the roads. The last thing I can afford is to get any kind of injury, so I make my way very carefully down the side of the embankment until, finally, I'm in the shoulder-high grass that runs along the bottom. Looking up, I see the nose of the plane looming above me, and I'm careful not to look too closely at the cockpit windows, just in case I might spot something I'd rather not see. After all, there are probably a hundred or more dead bodies in there, and they've had eight full days to fester.

Looking back, I see that Dawn is slowly making her way down after me.

"Good girl," I say, figuring that she's basically following me like a dog.

Although the grass is long, it's not too hard to walk through, and soon we're both past the plane. Figuring that I'd rather be up on the road, I start climbing back up the side and eventually I haul myself over the barrier.

"Jesus!" I shout, almost falling straight back down as I see that there's a dead body just a few meters away. I steady myself, but I can't take my eyes off the corpse. It looks like a guy, face down on the tarmac, with a whole load of flies buzzing in the air above him, and what appears to be a piece of shrapnel in his back, as if he was felled by some flying debris. I can't see his face, but one of his arms is stretched out, the skin looking discolored and with something crawling through the flesh. I guess the flies and maggots have well and truly got to him, but at least he's not like the guy back in the city, who seemed to be alive despite the fact that his body was dead. Taking a deep breath, I force myself to remember that this is unlikely to be the last dead body I encounter during this journey. Still, it brings back memories of the scene back at the apartment building when I was kneeling next to Henry.

Turning, I see that Dawn has reached the barrier. As she climbs over to join me, she seems totally unfazed by the dead body, and instead she simply stands next to me, as if she's waiting for me to lead the way again. Damn it, I wish she'd actually talk to me. It'd be good to have someone I could talk to about these things, but she just seems totally blank, as if there's barely a thought in her head. I guess this is her way of dealing with what's happened, and hopefully she'll emerge from her sense of shock eventually.

"It's okay," I say, stepping past the corpse. "Let's just keep going."

As I walk away, I find it hard to believe that I'm able to deal with all of this. I should be breaking down in tears, but instead I'm managing to keep everything under control. I guess the tears and the sobbing will come later, when I can *afford* to relax, but for now -

Suddenly I stop dead in my tracks as I hear a dull banging sound nearby. Turning, I see that Dawn has also stopped, but the banging sound is continuing and after a moment I realize that it's coming from inside the downed plane. I stare up at the windows along the side of the fuselage, but there's no doubt: someone's in there, banging on the metal and trying to get our attention. It's a chilling though to imagine someone in the plane, staring out through one of the little windows and looking straight at us.

"Leave it," I say to Dawn. "We can't rescue them. We..." I pause as I spot movement in one of the dark little windows. It's impossible to make out the person's features, but they've clearly seen us, and now the banging is becoming increasingly furious, almost manic.

I take a deep breath. What if this was the plane my parents were on? As a cold shiver passes through my body, I remember that my mother called from the airport, which means that she and my father were already off the plane. Allowing myself to relax, I try to remind myself that there's no point torturing myself unnecessarily by trying to imagine everything that could possibly have happened to them. They're gone. I accept that now, and it's time to move on. I just have to keep going.

"There can't be a survivor," I continue eventually. "It's been more than a week. Even if they had enough food, the disease from the other bodies." I pause to imagine what it would be like to end up trapped in a long metal tube with scores of corpses. Finally, I realize that although it might technically be possible that someone survived for this long, the more likely explanation is that it's another of the creatures that Henry and I saw in the car. After all, a survivor would probably have been able to open the door or find some other way out of the plane, whereas the creature seemed unable to even open the car door. Whatever they are, they don't seem too smart, so I guess this is just another of them, banging on the inside of the plane in a vain attempt to get out. I'd like to think that I won't encounter any more of them, but I know that's a forlorn hope. At some point, I'm going to have to work out what to do, but right now I just need to focus on getting to Lake Ontario. Maybe Mallory and the others have some ideas.

"Come on," I say to Dawn, before I turn and walk away. "We can't stop." I glance over my shoulder and see that she's still staring up at the plane. "Dawn!" I shout. "Come on!" I keep walking, and finally I hear her footsteps behind me.

THOMAS

Missouri

THE HOUSE LOOKS DESERTED, but as I park the truck a few hundred meters away, I realize I can't afford to take any risks. Those creatures could be anywhere, and with Joe out of action, I can't be certain of keeping us safe. Then again, we need some fresh supplies, so I figure I might as well take a look.

"It's okay," I say as I hurry around to the back of the truck. Joe looks bad, maybe even worse than before, and it looks like there's some fresh blood coming from his wounds. The roads around here are pretty rough, and I'm pretty sure that the constant travel isn't much good for Joe's injuries, but I barely even have time to think at the moment.

As I grab our only remaining rifle, I tell myself that we have to keep moving. If we stop, we're going to die, both of us.

"I'm just gonna take a look inside," I say as I double check that the rifle is loaded. "They might have some medicine."

Turning to the house, I pause for a moment, waiting for any sign that there's someone inside. It's a fairly small wooden house, but although it's out here in the middle of nowhere, it looks to have been fairly well maintained. There are some piles of wood over by the door, and a nearby fence looks as if it was painted quite recently. In a way, it reminds me of my family's house back home, although this place is quite a bit smaller. Still, what really matters is that we seem to be miles from anywhere, which means there's a good chance that this house and all the land is completely cut off from everything that's been happening in the world.

"Hello?" I call out, walking cautiously toward the door. "Is anyone home?"

No reply.

Deciding that it might be too dangerous to try the door, I head to one of the windows. It's dark inside, but I can just about make out a kitchen. The place looks clean and tidy, although I'm remaining cautious for now. Walking over to the door, I give it a gentle push but find that it's locked. I look back over at the truck and see Joe's blooded form on the back shelf, and I realize that even though I hate the idea of breaking into this place, I've got no choice. Besides, no-one's answering me, so I figure the occupants of this place must have either died or left. Taking a step back, I pick up a large rock from the ground, and then I throw it at the window before I have a chance to think twice.

The glass shatters, and I hurry over to get a better look inside. The first thing I notice, to my relief, is that the place doesn't smell bad. I'm not expert, but I'd have thought that after a week of rotting, a dead body would stink pretty bad, so hopefully this means there's no-one inside. I guess the occupants must have been out of the house when disaster struck, or maybe they set off to get help. After all, there's no car anywhere around. Using the butt of the rifle, I clear away the rest of the glass and then I slowly, cautiously climb inside.

It takes me a few minutes to check all the rooms, but finally I realize that there's definitely not a body here. I don't know where the people went, but right now I don't care: all that matters is finding some more supplies, and hopefully getting hold of some medical equipment that might help Joe. I hurry through to the bathroom and go through the cabinet, but I don't find much more than some pain-killers and a few prescription tablets that I've never heard of before. I pocket them anyway, while reminding myself that at times of emergency, this isn't so much stealing as sharing things around. I hated it when Joe robbed that gas station last week, but this is different: this is a life or death situation. Joe might have some moral gray areas, but I'm certain that I've made the right decision here.

Once I'm certain that there's no more medicine left, I head through to the kitchen and start going through the fridge. There's no electricity, of course, but I find a few old tins of beans, which I figure could be useful. To my surprise, I also find what appears to be some kind of animal, arranged on a plate with its fur still on; I look closer and realize it seems to be a skunk. Taking a step back, I tell myself that while things are bad, I'm not quite at the point yet where I'm going to eat skunk meat. Closing the fridge, I walk over to the sink and try the taps, but of course there's no water. That's my biggest concern, I guess. We've only got enough water to last a couple more days, and that's before you factor in the need to keep Joe's wounds clean.

Hearing a noise outside, I duck down for a moment. I wait, but the whole place is silent again. Still, I know I heard something, like a brief shuffling, scratching sound. I take a deep breath and tell myself that there's no option other than to go and take a look. I doubt the occupants of the house have come back, and hopefully none of those creatures have got this far, so I guess the most likely thing is that there's just some animal out there.

I walk over to the window and take a look outside. There's no sign of anything, so I quickly climb out and then, keeping the gun pointing straight ahead, I hurry over to the truck.

"Fuck!" Joe says, reaching up and trying to grab something from the other side of the flat-bed shelf.

"Hey!" I call out, as I realize that Joe must have been the cause of the noise I heard. "Are you awake?"

"Give me that!" he mutters, trying to get hold of a small wood ax that's resting in the back of the truck. "Are you fucking deaf? Give it to me!"

Climbing onto the back of the truck, I reach out to grab the ax, before turning to Joe. "What do you want it for?" I ask.

"What do you think?" he replies breathlessly.

"I don't know," I say.

"Just fucking give it to me," he splutters, "and then drag me out a bit into the woods."

"Why?" I ask.

"Do I have to fucking spell it out to you?" he shouts, before coughing up a small amount of blood. "Look at me," he continues. "I'm dying. There's no fucking point trying to pretend I'm not."

"You're not gonna kill yourself," I tell him, feeling a cold chill pass through my body.

"Fuck you," he says, trying but failing to grab the ax from my hand.

"No way," I say, moving away from him. "You're gonna get better."

"It hurts!" he shouts, his bloodshot eyes filled with anger and fear. Reaching his shoulder, he pulls away the sheets that have been covering him, revealing the full extent of his injuries. One entire side of his upper chest has been badly crushed, with fresh blood seeping from wounds that have started to turn a kind of yellowy-black color. "Look at it!" he continues. "This is so fucking far beyond anything, Thomas! It's infected and shit!"

"I'm gonna get you to a hospital," I tell him.

"There's no fucking hospital," he continues. "There's no fucking anything." He tries to get up, but the pain is clearly too much and he lets out an agonized scream as he falls back to the floor.

"You can't give up," I say, terrified of the thought that I might lose him.

"Please," he whispers, with tears in his eyes. "Do you have any fucking idea how much it hurts to die like this?"

I shake my head.

"You know it's gonna happen," he continues. "You're not a fucking doctor, you fucking dip-shit. Even if you try to keep me alive, it's just gonna be one, two days max of fucking agony. Fuck, I'm sweating already. And what if..." He pauses. "What if I've got whatever turned those other people into..." His voice trails off for a moment. "You need to save yourself," he adds eventually. "I've never given a damn about anyone else, but right now, I want you to save yourself. You're the only one of us left, so just leave me here and get going. If you haven't got the guts to kill me, just leave me behind with an ax and drive off, and I'll sort myself out. But I don't want you dying just 'cause you think you can save me. You can't."

"I'm not leaving you," I tell him.

"Are you really that fucking stupid?" he asks.

"I'm not leaving you," I say again, tossing some food at him before I grab one of our last bottles of water and roll it toward him; he pushes it all back to me.

"Don't waste that shit on me," he says firmly. "Come on, Thomas. You're *not* this dumb. I know it."

I stare at him for a moment, trying to decide what to do, and then finally I make a decision. Shuffling off the back of the truck, I start walking toward the house.

"Thomas!" Joe calls after me. "Get back here! Thomas!"

ELIZABETH

New York

"OKAY," I SAY, stopping and leaning against the barrier that runs along the side of the road, "I need to take a break." Having been walking more or less non-stop since the middle of the night, I'm starting to realize that maybe I'm not in very good shape, and it's not as if I'm exactly well-nourished right now. It's been a couple of days since I ate anything that would really count as a full meal, and I'm starting to feel weak. For the first time, I'm actually starting to wonder whether I can manage this four hundred mile walk.

Looking back the way we came, I see that Dawn has stopped nearby. I swear, she just seems to copy me all the time, almost as if she can't make any decisions of her own. I can't help thinking that she seems to be having a hard time dealing with everything that's happened. After all, so far I've seen several people die, I've witnessed some kind of creature trapped in a car, I've killed a man in self-defense and I've buried my younger brother. I guess Dawn has probably gone through some pretty crazy stuff herself. It's weird to think of myself as a strong person, because I've always felt like I'm fairly sensitive and emotional, but right now it seems that I'm dealing with things fairly well. I just wish that Dawn would talk a little, to keep me company.

"So what happened to you?" I ask eventually, hoping to engage her in conversation. "After all this stuff started, I mean. Were you in the city?"

She doesn't reply. She just stands there, staring at me.

"What about your family?" I continue, as I take an energy bar from my bag. I don't really have the resources to start sharing stuff, but I figure I can't exactly let her starve. Opening the packet, I break off half the bar and hold it out to her. "You need to eat," I say, but she doesn't respond. "It's food," I tell her. "Yeah, it's not a steak, but it's still food. Maybe some time, we can catch a cow and..." I pause. "I don't quite know what we'd do next. Milk it, I guess, and then try to cut some meat off its body."

No reply.

"Let me know if you change your mind," I mutter, before I start to eat the bar. Once I'm done, I put the empty wrapper back in my bag, just in case it turns out to be useful some time. "I was with my brother," I say. "We were alone in our apartment building, but then this guy kind of took control. His name was Bob. He was a total asshole, and eventually..." I pause as I realize that I don't really want to put this into words, not yet. "Bob's gone," I say eventually, "and so's my brother. Things didn't work out too well."

Silence.

"You know," I continue, "if you just -"

Before I can finish, I hear a distant noise, and I turn to see a camper van driving along one of the other roads nearby. I stare for a moment, unable to really comprehend what I'm seeing, and although my first thought is that maybe it's time to hide, I quickly realize that there's no way one of those creatures could be driving a vehicle. This must be people. Actual, live people, and they have a vehicle.

"Hey!" I shout, waving my arms as I run along the road. "Over here!"

The van keeps driving.

"Hey!" I scream, desperately hoping that they might see us. "Stop!"

After a moment, the van seems to slow down, and finally it comes to a halt. There's a pause, before the door opens and a figure steps out. The vehicle's too far away for me to make out any details about the person apart from the fact that it appears to be a man, and he's definitely noticed us. I'm not sure what to do at first, but finally I figure this is an opportunity I can't pass up. I'd assumed I wouldn't meet anyone during the journey, but now there's a real life person with an actual vehicle. This could be the difference between life and death.

"Come on!" I shout to Dawn, before I start running along the road. I quickly clamber over one of the barriers and rush through the grass, before climbing up onto another road. The camper van has stopped on a section of road that passes over a bridge, but sheer adrenalin pushes me to keep running until finally I get close to the van and see that the person standing next to the driver's door is a youngish guy with a big curly mop of black hair, a leather jacket, and a cigarette. He seems relaxed enough, and he has the casual demeanor of someone who can probably look after himself just fine.

"Hey," I say breathlessly as I finally get close enough. Glancing over my shoulder, I see that Dawn is following, although instead of running she seems to be simply walking after me. I turn back to look at the guy next to the van, and finally I notice that there's a woman sitting in the passenger seat.

"Hey," the guy says, before taking a drag on his cigarette. "You lost out here?"

"I don't know," I say. "I mean, we're just walking."

He pauses. "Where to?" he asks eventually.

"Lake Ontario."

He raises an eyebrow. "Why are you going to Lake fucking Ontario?"

"I know some people," I explain, still a little short of breath. "They went there a few days ago, so I figure I'm going to try to catch up. They've got a plan."

"Huh," he replies, seemingly a little unimpressed. "Lake Ontario. Never thought about that."

"I think they want to be next to the water," I say.

He sniffs, before looking down at my shoes. "You gonna walk five hundred odd miles in those?"

"Why?" I ask.

"You've got some spares, haven't you?"

Sighing, I realize what he means. In my rush to get going, it never occurred to me that this single pair of sneakers might not be up to the job. If they wear out, I'll have to walk in my socks, and after that I'll be barefoot all the day. I thought I'd got everything covered, but I guess I missed a few things.

"You got sun cream?" he asks.

"No," I reply bitterly.

We stand in silence for a moment.

"I suppose you want a ride," the guy says eventually. "I mean, seeing as you're not remotely equipped for a long journey."

"I..." Pausing, I see that the woman in the passenger seat doesn't look too friendly. She's staring at me as if she's annoyed, which I guess means that she didn't want to stop. "Which way are you going?" I ask.

"West," the guy replies. "That's kind of all we've got right now. We've got some friends who own a farm about a hundred miles from here, so I was thinking we could head there for a bit, check up on them. At the very least, there might be some food. Other than that, we could kind of use a destination." He pauses. "Erikson," he says eventually. "That's my name. Carl Erikson, but everyone just calls me Erikson. Or they did, before..." His voice trails off.

"Elizabeth," I tell him. "Elizabeth Mercer. I'm from New York."

"Hello Elizabeth Mercer from New York," he replies, before looking over at Dawn, who's still quite a way behind. "Who's your friend?"

"Her name's Dawn," I reply. "She's not really my friend. I just kind of found her, and she's following me."

He takes another drag on his cigarette. "She looks weird. What's wrong with her?"

"Nothing," I say. "I think she's just in

shock."

"No," he replies, squinting as he watches her getting closer and closer. "Something's wrong with her. The way she's walking, the look on her face. Something's not right."

"No, really," I continue, "she's just kind of spaced out. She doesn't really talk much, but she's okay. She keeps herself to herself most of the time. I don't know what happened to her, but I'm pretty sure she's traumatized. I'm just waiting for her to snap out of it."

"Huh." After a moment, he stubs out the cigarette before carefully placing the butt in his jacket pocket and then leaning back into the camper van. "Come on," he says to the woman, "we could use some extra people. If we keep going by ourselves, we're gonna go crazy."

"They got any food?" the woman asks.

"You got any food?" Erikson calls out to me.

I nod.

"She's got guns, too," he says to the woman. "They're just kids. I think we can trust them, and if we can't, we'll just ditch them somewhere." He turns to me. "No offense. You're safe with us, unless you try to pull any shit. You do that, we won't be friends anymore. Got it?"

I nod.

"I'm serious," he continues. "You need to pull your weight, too. We're not a charity."

I stare at the woman, and it's clear that she's not keen on the idea. She looks to be kind of young, maybe in her early twenties, with raven black hair and eyes that seem to be staring straight into my soul. Since I've barely had a chance to speak, I can only assume that it's the *idea* of me that she doesn't like, rather than anything personal.

"Fine," she says eventually. "They can come."

"This is my girlfriend," Erikson says as he pushes the driver's side door shut and turns to me. "Her name's Shauna. There's not enough room in the front for you two, so you'll have to ride in the back." He walks around to the side of the van and slides the door open. "It's not exactly tidy, but I figure it'll do. Beggars can't be choosers, right? We were out camping when all the shit came down."

I walk over and take a look inside. The place is kind of dark and cramped, but there are seats and a table, and piles of old newspapers on the floor, along with various bags that seem to be stuffed with food. The air smells a little stale, but it's a lot better than continuing on foot.

"We robbed a convenience store or two," Erikson says. "I'm not proud of it, but we figured no-one else was gonna take the stuff. We never, ever would have done anything like that before all this shit came down. You two are the first people we've seen since we set out a couple of days ago.

The way things are, I reckon it's finders keepers from now on. Law of the jungle, you know? Survival of the fucking fittest."

"You have to eat your own damn food!" Shauna shouts from the passenger seat. "You're not allowed any of ours! Tell them they can't have our food!"

"You heard the lady," Erikson says with a faint smile.

I nod.

"Can you drive?" he asks.

"No," I reply.

"Well," he continues, "I guess I'll teach you some time. Don't go thinking you've found a couple of chauffeurs, okay? Just..." He leans closer. "Don't mind Shauna," he whispers. "She's always been kind of the jealous, crazy type, but just cut her some slack and you'll get on just fine. Okay?"

"Okay," I reply.

"What are you whispering about?" Shauna shouts.

"Nothing!" Erikson tells her, as Dawn finally reaches us.

"This is Carl Erikson," I say, turning to her, "and his girlfriend Shauna. They've offered to let us go with them. They're heading west, and I figure we might as well all go together. Do you want to come, Dawn?"

She stares at me.

"You don't say much, do you?" Erikson says with a smile.

Dawn turns and stares at him.

"Don't mind Dawn," I continue, climbing into the back of the van and taking a moment to carefully stow my bag and the guns. "She won't be any trouble. I promise." Sure enough, just as I'd expected, Dawn climbs into the van and sits over on the chair by the other side of the table. I honestly don't know whether I should be glad that she's so little trouble, or annoyed that she just seems to think she can wander along and expect me to fix everything. I joked to myself earlier that she's like a dog, but actually she seems to have less intelligence than any dog I've ever met. She just seems to be totally placid and calm.

"You alright, then?" Erikson asks, staring at Dawn.

Slowly, she turns to stare at him.

"Well," he says with a cautious smile, "I guess we're all gonna get to know each other a little better once we're underway, but for now I'll just say that I hope you ladies enjoy your time with us. We're not so bad, once you get to know us. Even Shauna."

"Fuck you," Shauna mutters.

"She's a peach," he continues. "We're gonna keep driving until sundown, and then we'll probably pull over and have some food and settle for the night. I don't quite know how things are gonna work out, but I guess we'll deal with any issues as we come across them." He pauses. "You seem like nice girls, but I want to make one thing clear. This is my van. Well, mine and Shauna's. We decide where we go. If you don't like it, just let us know and we'll drop you off by the side of the road, but there's not gonna be any debate. This is *not* a democracy. It's a camper van." With that, he slides the door shut.

"Nice to meet you," I say, turning to Shauna. "I'm Elizabeth."

"I heard," she replies, before shifting in her seat so that she's looking out the side window. It's pretty clear that not only does she not like me, but she wants to make sure that I *know* she doesn't like me. I guess I can understand her point of view in a way. After all, it's hard to know who to trust, and as Erikson climbs into the driver's seat, I realize that I have no idea whether these two people are telling the truth about their identities or their intentions. Glancing back over at the two rifles I brought from Manhattan, I figure that at least I have a way to defend us if we get into trouble. As the van starts up and we start moving along the road, I turn and look out the window. After a few minutes, Manhattan is barely visible in the distance and finally the city disappears completely beyond the horizon. I don't know when I'll be coming back, but I *will* be back one day. When all of this is sorted out, I'm going to come and put some flowers on Henry's grave.

THOMAS

Missouri

HE KEEPS SHOUTING FOR a few hours, calling me all the names under the sun and cursing me out, but I'm not budging. Sitting at the table in the little kitchen, I stare straight ahead and try to work out what I should do next. The truth is, deep down, I know that what Joe said makes sense: I *should* leave him behind, and if he was anyone else, I *would* dump him off the back of the truck and leave him here. But he's my brother, and he's probably the only family I've got left, so I figure I need to come up with another idea.

    The problem is, I'm not smart enough. I've never been very intelligent, although often I've been smarter than the rest of my family. Still, I'm not the kind of person who's always coming up with good ideas or working out ways to get out of bad situations. I'm no good at trying to survive, and on top of that, I'm pretty weak. My father always had a way of knowing what to do, and doing it even if he didn't like the idea; my mother, also, was able to just force herself to get on with stuff. As for me, I guess I'm more like Joe than I want to admit. I've always avoided making tough decisions, and this is no exception. I have no idea what's right, and I have no idea what I'm supposed to do.

Eventually, as Joe finally stops calling out to me, I decide to do something I haven't done for many years. It's kind of desperate, but it's my only choice.

Getting down onto my knees, I close my eyes and put my hands together. There's an ominous kind of silence all around me, as if the world is waiting for me to say something. I'd like to think that God is waiting for me to speak, but in truth, I don't even know if I believe that he exists. Still, I've got to try something, and this is the only idea I've got at the moment.

"Dear Lord," I whisper eventually, "I know I haven't exactly been to church much, and I know my family's been pretty much the same, except my mother, she wanted to go but my father wouldn't drive her. Anyway, I know you know all this already, 'cause you know everything, but I'm just letting you know that *I* know it's wrong." I pause, trying to work out how to phrase this. "We need a miracle. I don't know what's happening, and I don't know how much of the world has been affected, but right now, Lord, we need a miracle. I need you to make me smart enough so I can come up with a way to save my brother. He's really bad right now, and I don't even know if he'll make it through the night, so I need you to give me the extra intelligence so I can work out what to do. Or give us some other kind of miracle."

From outside, there's the sound of Joe starting to moan again. He sounds like he's in a bad way, worse than before.

"Can't you hear that, Lord?" I ask. "I know you can, so won't you do something? We need a miracle to help us get to somewhere safe, and we need another miracle to bring us someone who knows how to help my brother and fix him up. I know he's hurt bad, but you can do something about that, can't you? You can make it so he doesn't get infected, and -"

I pause as Joe's pained moan becomes louder. Although I try to block the sound from my mind, it's impossible. He sounds like he's suffering all the pain in the world.

"You can make it so he gets better," I continue, squeezing my eyes even tighter shut. "You can fix him, so... fix him. I need him alive. I don't know why you made it so that the truck dropped on him in the first place, but whatever it was, he's learned his lesson. I know he's been a bad person in the past, but he's not the only one. We've all been bad. Don't punish him for robbing that gas station or for getting drunk or for anything else. Give him a miracle and let him live, and let the pain all go away so that he doesn't have to suffer. Can't you hear him?"

I pause, and the only sound comes from Joe's agonized cries for help.

"Please, Lord," I whisper, clasping my hands together so tight, it's starting to hurt.

I wait.

"Just one miracle," I continue. "Can't you spare *one* miracle to help us?"

Again, I wait.

Nothing.

And then...

With Joe still calling out for help, I open my eyes. Maybe it's insane, but I'm sure I can feel something moving through my body, giving me strength. All my doubts and fears seem to be falling away, and there's a new kind of strength rising inside me, telling me what I have to do. Part of me's scared, but part of me knows that this is the only way I can make things right. I don't know if it's a miracle, exactly, but it's something new in me, something that's giving me more strength that I ever knew I could possess. I know what I have to do, and I know I can do it. With a heavy heart, I get to my feet and walk toward the door.

ELIZABETH

New York

"PISS BREAK!" ERIKSON SHOUTS as he brings the van to a halt by the side of the road. It's almost sunset, with the light starting to fade, and I guess we'll be looking for someone to stay the night soon. Climbing out, he starts walking into the nearby bushes, leaving me sitting in the back of the vehicle with Dawn. We've been driving for hours, and he still hasn't really responded to me. She just seems content to sit and stare in the distance, letting her body jolt about as the van speeds along these uneven roads.

"You need the bathroom?" I ask, worried that she might lack the necessary gumption to work out what she's supposed to do. I'm still a little cautious about her, and I'm starting to wonder if she's more than just traumatized. What if she's got a proper problem, maybe something that existed before all of this happened? Still, I feel kind of protective of her, almost like she's a stray dog I found in the middle of nowhere.

"Jesus Christ," Shauna says as she gets out of the truck, "can't the bitch even decide when to take a leak?"

I stare at Dawn, hoping to see some flicker of recognition, but she still seems blank. Without saying anything, I lean across and slide the door open before getting out of the van. To my surprise, when Shauna comes waddling around from the other side, I see that she's pregnant. Like, seven or eight months gone, with a big bump.

"Yeah," she mutters as she walks past me. "Good timing, huh?"

I turn and watch as she makes her way into the undergrowth. To be honest, I can't even begin to imagine what she's going to do with that baby. I mean, obviously she's going to give birth and try to raise it, but with the world in such turmoil, how the hell is that child ever going to have a chance? Suddenly I realize that I understand why she seems so angry with the world, and there's a part of me that wants to go and offer her some help. Then again, I guess she'll come to me if she needs anything.

"You girls drink?" Erikson asks as he emerges from the bushes, pulling up the zipper on the front of his trousers. "We've got quite a lot of beer, so if you fancy one, help yourselves. Only one, mind."

"I'm fine, thanks," I tell him, before making my way into the undergrowth. It takes me a few minutes to find a quiet, private spot, but eventually I manage to pee before cleaning myself and heading back toward the camper van. By the time I get there, I find that Erikson has pulled out some bottles of water from a box, and he's placed one on the table in front of Dawn, who's still sitting inside the vehicle.

"Your friend doesn't seem to want drink," he says.

"Dawn," I say, walking over to the door, "you really need to drink. I know you might not realize it, and I know you might not feel like it, but you've got to keep yourself healthy. You can't just shut down and stop living."

She turns and stares at me.

"You understand me, don't you?" I continue. "Dawn, you *do* speak English, don't you?"

She frowns.

"Give me a sign," I say. "Just nod if you understand."

Slowly, she nods.

"Good," I say, before taking a swig of water.

"I really think you should have a drink. It doesn't have to be much, but you could die if you don't. No matter how bad you feel, you'll feel ten times worse if you let yourself get dehydrated." I wait for her to answer, but she seems lost in a daze, unable to do anything other than stare blankly at me. "Dawn, come on," I continue. "Don't be dumb. Just unscrew the top of the bottle and drink a little. Enough to keep you going, at least."

Finally, as if somehow my words have slowly managed to work their way through her mind, she picks up the bottle and does exactly what I told her to do. She seems more than a little confused, and I can't help but glance over at Erikson, who's watching this all unfold with a puzzled look on his face. I can see that he's basically thinking what I'm thinking, which is that whatever's wrong with Dawn, it's way more than just trauma or shock.

"Are we gonna get going, then?" Shauna shouts as she emerges from the undergrowth.

"Wait!" Erikson hisses at her.

Slowly, almost as if it hurts, Dawn puts the bottle to her mouth and takes a brief sip, before lowering it again.

"You need to drink more," I tell her, feeling a tightening sensation in my chest. Something's wrong here, and there's a look of fear in Dawn's eyes that makes me wonder if I made a big mistake by letting her tag along.

After a pause, she raises the bottle again, and this time she starts to drink all the water. As she tilts her head further back, however, I suddenly realize that most of the water is just pouring out the back of her skull, and dribbling down onto the floor.

"What the fuck?" Erikson says, taking a step back.

Dawn continues to 'drink', until the bottle is empty and the rest of the water has finished pouring through her head. Finally, she puts the bottle on the table and gets to her feet, shuffling out of the van and walking straight past me. As she goes, I see that there's water all over her back, mixed with what appears to be blood.

"What's wrong with her?" Shauna asks.

Before I can reply, Dawn stops and then drops to her knees, before toppling over and landing face-first in the dirt. My heart still racing, I walk cautiously over to her, and finally I spot something sticking out from under the hair that covers the back of her neck, glinting in the sun. Taking a deep breath, and fighting the urge to run, I kneel next to her and move the hair aside to reveal what appears to be a large piece of metal embedded in the back of her skull. Wedged deep, the metal must be stuck in her brain, which I guess explain the fact that she was so blank and unresponsive. It's hard to believe that she was even able to walk around, but I guess somehow the injury left her motor skills intact.

"Jesus," Erikson says, turning away. "What the fuck happened to her?"

"I have no idea," I say, feeling a cool sense of fear and sorrow rising through my body.

"Fuck," he continues. "She must be, like, brain dead or something."

"She's properly dead," I say, looking down at Dawn's face and seeing that her eyes are wide open, and she's not even responding to the specks of dirt and dust on her eyeball. Cautiously, I reach down and put my fingers against the side of her neck, and sure enough there's no pulse. "She's dead," I say again, before turning to the others. "I had no idea," I say, as I realize that my hands are shaking. "I swear to God, I thought she was just shocked."

"I told you not to pick them up!" Shauna screams.

"This isn't her fault!" Erikson replies, unable to stop staring at Dawn's body.

"I told you!" Shauna says, waddling around to the passenger side of the van. "Leave them here! They're not coming with us!"

"I'm sorry," I say quietly.

"We have to leave her," Erikson says. "You can come, Elizabeth, but she's dead. We can't take her body, and we don't have time to stop and bury her."

"She needs a grave," I reply.

"If you want to dig her a grave," he continues, "you can, but we're not going to wait for you." With that, he hurries back to the van.

"I'm sorry," I say, looking down at Dawn. "I have to go. I'm so sorry I couldn't..." My voice trails off as I realize that there's no way she can hear me. At least she's dead now, so the suffering is over. Getting to my feet, I hurry back to the van and climb inside.

"What's she doing here?" Shauna shouts.

"We can't leave her here," Erikson replies firmly. "She'll die."

"So?" Shauna continues, turning to me. "You've got *no* right to be here, you crazy fucking bitch! Get back out there with your fucked-up friend!"

"She's coming with us!" Erikson says, starting the engine and hitting the gas pedal. As the van lurches into motion, I lean across and slide the door shut, before turning and looking out the back window and watching as Dawn's body disappears into the distance.

"I swear to God," Shauna says, staring straight ahead, "this is a fucking mistake."

Sitting in the back of the van, I realize there are tears in my eyes. It's crazy, but while I still haven't properly cried about Henry, I'm soon in floods of tears as I think about what happened to Dawn. I knew her for less than a day, and now I'm not even sure if I 'knew' her at all. Was she even capable of thought, or did she just follow me around in her brain-damaged state? I find it hard to believe that there was no hint of her mind in there somewhere, but with tears pouring down my face, I can't help trying to imagine what she must have been going through. Suddenly, as I look out the window and see the sun starting to dip below the horizon, a thought strikes me. When I first met Dawn, I was standing with the rising sun behind me; I remember the way she squinted and shielded her eyes from the sun. I take a deep breath as I realize that the only word she ever said to me, 'dawn', wasn't her name at all. She was just saying what she could see behind me.

    I never knew her real name at all.

THOMAS

Missouri

"HEY," I SAY, STANDING next to the back of the truck.

Joe's in no condition to reply. During the few hours I was inside the house, his condition has got way worse, to the point that he seems to be kind of delirious. There's fresh blood coming from his injuries, combined with white and yellow pus, and in his attempts to crawl away, he's ended up smearing everything all over his face and body. Before, I would have convinced myself that there's a way to fix all of this, but right now I've got this new kind of strength that's telling me I have to do the right thing. Not the easy thing, and not the thing I want, but the thing that's right and moral and good.

I have to be a good brother.

"Can you hear me?" I ask, climbing up onto the back of the truck. "Joe, can you hear me?"

He doesn't reply. He looks fevered, and although he lets out a low, guttural groan, it's clearly not a response to anything I've said. He's like a rabid animal. I don't even know if the real Joe is in there anymore. In a way, I want to know that he can hear me, to know that he understands what I'm doing, but at the same time I guess it'd be better if his mind has left his body completely, leaving behind nothing that can really feel pain. This isn't Joe; this is just his body, writhing and gasping before the inevitable end. All I need to do is find a little more inner strength, stop seeing things as if I'm still a child, and do what's necessary. I need to be a man.

"Okay," I say, taking a deep breath, "I'm gonna do what you asked, but I'm gonna do it in a way that stops your pain as fast as possible." Deciding that there's no point delaying things, I grab the tarpaulin and lay it over Joe's body, leaving just his face clear for a moment. "If you can hear me," I continue, looking down at his bloodied, fevered features, "I hope you know that I'm just doing what you wanted. God gave me this strength, you see, and he made me realize that I've got to do what's right. So I'm..." I pause, as tears start falling down my cheeks. "So I'm gonna make it real quick, and painless, or as painless as possible. You won't feel anything, and then you'll be on the other side. Like, in paradise. You'll be up there in heaven, looking down at me."

No reply. He just continues to let out a groan.

"You're gonna see everyone again," I continue. "Everyone from back home. You're the lucky one here. You understand that, right? You're the one who gets to go to a better place and be with everyone. I've got to stay here and deal with..." I pause as I realize that I'm in danger of getting too focused on myself. This is about Joe. "You've been the best brother I could ever have had," I continue, "and I know we disagreed about a lot of stuff, but I know you were there for me when it mattered, just like I'm here for you. I'm sorry I couldn't make things work out better, but at least I can take away your pain." I open my mouth to say something else, but finally I realize that I'm just prolonging his agony. There's nothing else I can say, nothing else I can do, so I simply take the edge of the tarpaulin and move it over his face.

Stepping back, I grab the rifle and check that it's properly loaded. I can still hear Joe moaning from beneath the tarpaulin, and there's a part of me that wants to just get in the front of the truck and start driving again, hoping against hope that some miracle might deliver us to people who can help. I know that's not the right thing to do, however, and I know that I'd just be condemning Joe to a long, drawn-out and painful death. If I love my brother, I have to kill him. He's clearly in some much pain, it's agonizing to listen to him. Slowly, I raise the rifle and aim it at the part of the tarpaulin that's covering his head.

Everything around me seems to fall quiet. The forest, the house, Joe's moans, my own heartbeat.

I take a deep breath.

I steady my shaking hands.

Finally, I pull the trigger. The body under the tarpaulin jerks once, but falls completely still before the echo of the gunshot has even stopped ringing through the trees. I'm left staring at the hole in the tarpaulin, and then at the large pool of blood that's starting to soak through. For a moment, it's as if my mind has gone completely blank. I can't even process the reality of what just happened, of the fact that I shot my brother, but eventually I realize that the silence all around me is also the silence of Joe's passing. All his pain is over, and I just hope that in his final moments, he understood that I was doing the right thing. Despite everything else, I know deep down in my heart that it would have been wrong to let him live with such agony. It would have made me feel better, in the short term, not to have had to make this decision, but in the end I chose to sacrifice my peace of mind in order to look after Joe.

Climbing down from the back of the truck, I prop the rifle against the side of the vehicle before walking a couple of paces toward the house. I know I need to clean up, to dig a grave and bury Joe, but right now I feel as if I'm going to collapse. My knees feel weak, and I can't stop replaying the past few minutes in my mind. Did I make a mistake? Did I do a terrible thing? As I reach the house, I pause for a moment and take a series of deep, calm breaths. It's as if the world is spinning, and I have to force myself to remain calm. I'll get over this. I'll find a way to stop thinking about everything that happened, and somehow I'll carry on. For Joe's sake, and for my parents' sakes, I'll keep fighting.

"Turn around slowly," says a man's voice from nearby.

I freeze. I hadn't heard anyone approaching, and my first thought is that maybe it's one of those creatures.

"Did you hear me?" the man continues. "Turn around very slowly and put your hands where I can see them."

Barely able to string two thoughts together, I raise my hands and slowly turn to see that there's a middle-aged man standing over by the trees, aiming a rifle straight at me.

"On your knees," he says.

I stare at him.

"On your knees," he says again, more firmly this time.

Slowly, I get down on my knees, and I watch as he takes a couple of steps closer.

"Okay," he continues, closing one eye as he steadies his aim at my head. "Now why don't you tell me who you are, and why you just shot a man in cold blood outside my house?"

# DAY 10

ELIZABETH

Pennsylvania

I'M SLOWLY JOLTED AWAKE by the motion of the van as it bumps and bounces along some kind of gravel road. Blinking a couple of times, I realize that somehow I must have eventually fallen asleep, and now the warm light of dawn is flickering through the passing trees.

"Wakey wakey," Erikson calls back from the driver's seat. "How you doing back there, Elizabeth? You manage to get your head down?"

"Yeah," I mutter, still feeling kind of groggy. It takes a couple more seconds before I remember everything that happened yesterday with Dawn, or whatever her name was, and finally I look out the window and see that we seem to be way off the beaten track. "Where are we?" I ask.

"Pennsylvania," Erikson says.

"Seriously?"

"I've got a friend out this way," he continues. "Haven't heard from him for a while, but last time I talked to him, he was living on a couple of acres of land, raising chickens and..." He pauses. "Well, I don't quite know *what* he was doing, to be honest, but he seemed to like coming out to the country and getting away from things." He turns to his girlfriend, who so far seems to be conspicuously ignoring me. "Shauna, do you remember what the hell Toad was doing out here?"

"No fucking idea," she mutters.

"Toad?" I say, a little shocked by the name.

"It's what we called him at school," Erikson continues. "He's just... well, you'll see, but despite his appearance, he's a great guy. Actually, that's not fair. He's just kinda earthy, if you know what I mean. He's got no style. These days, the guy's usually to be found covered in fucking soil, digging some kind of garden or whatever the fuck he spends his time doing." Up ahead of us, a large farmhouse comes into view. "He's very friendly. We'll just stop here for a couple of days before we get going again. Maybe scrounge some supplies, if he's in a good mood. I don't know if -"

Before he can finish the sentence, there's a loud pinging sound, as if something has ricocheted off the metal frame of the van. We keep going for a moment, before there's another loud bang and the entire windscreen shatters into a thousand pieces, spraying us all with glass and causing Erikson to swerve the van until it comes to a halt straight across the road.

"Get down!" he shouts.

Just as I duck down under the table, there's another loud bang, and this time it's clear that someone's shooting at us. My heart's racing as I crawl across the floor of the van, trying to get behind one of the chairs, but moments later there's a loud bang as a bullet bursts through the door and hits one of the bags over near the other seat.

"Fucking asshole!" Erikson shouts from the foot-well of the driver's seat. "Anyone hurt?"

"Get us out of here!" Shauna screams.

"Elizabeth!" Erikson calls out. "You okay back there?"

"Yeah!" I shout back. "But why's he shooting at us? I thought you said he was a friend!"

"I also said he's a bit weird!" he replies, as another bullet strikes the van, followed by the ominous hissing sound of a slowly deflating tire. "Fuck! Now what are we supposed to do?"

"Are those blanks?" Shauna asks, just as there's another shot, blasting a hole near the back of the vehicle.

"Do they seem like blanks to you?" Erikson

screams.

"Doesn't he know it's you?" I ask. "Doesn't he recognize the van?"

"I doubt it," Erikson says. "We kind of... liberated this baby from the guy who owned it before us. He was dead, though, so I figure it doesn't really matter. We cleaned it out and everything! There's no reason to worry."

"We're going to die!" Shauna screams. "This is fucking insane! That asshole's going to kill us if you don't get us out of here!"

Reaching up, Erikson tries to start the van again, but something seems to be wrong. He tries a couple more times, with no luck.

"You're going to flood the engine!" Shauna hisses.

"I know what I'm doing!" he replies.

"I knew we should never have come here," Shauna continues, her voice filled with panic. "You're gonna die, and I'm gonna die, and this baby's gonna die before it ever has a chance to see the world. We never should have come to see this asshole, and we never should have picked those girls up! You know what we should have done, Einstein? We should have stayed the fuck where we were. We should have just stayed in place and waited for everything to go back to normal. Instead, you insisted on having us drive out here to see some psychotic loner who thinks the best option is to blow our fucking heads off!"

"Calm down," Erikson replies, "I'm gonna fix this! Toad's not a bad guy, he's just scared. He probably thinks we're coming to rob him, that's all." He pauses. "At least we know he's alive. And he's stopped shooting, which is probably a good sign."

"It just means he thinks we're already dead," Shauna mutters. "He'll wait a while, and then he'll come out to pick over what's left, and when he finds us, he'll blow our fucking heads off."

"I'm gonna go out there," Erikson says after a moment.

"No fucking way!" she replies.

"Once he sees it's me," he continues, "he'll be fine! He's probably got binoculars or something lined up on us, so he just needs to see my face and everything'll be okay. He's not gonna shoot me! We go way back! We're friends! Honestly, there's just been a bit of a misunderstanding, but it'll all get smoothed out!"

"Send her," Shauna says, looking back at me.

"Why the fuck would we send *her*?" Erikson asks.

"You know what Toad's like," she continues. "He likes the ladies. Show him a girl, he'll come running out of that place with his tongue hanging to his knees."

"No way," I say. "He'll shoot me!"

"No," Erikson says, turning to me, "Shauna's right. He *probably* wouldn't shoot me, but he *definitely* wouldn't shoot you. I mean, Toad's a fucking sucker for the ladies. He sees you, there's no way he'll shoot a hot girl when he thinks he can -"

"Shut up!" Shauna shouts, slamming his head against the seat. "She's not hot, but she's a girl, so she'll do!" She turns to me. "No offense, but you get the idea. The guy has an eye for the ladies, and in my current condition, I don't really fit the bill. You might as well make yourself useful. Just go out there, wave at the house, and wait for him to come out. As soon as you can talk to him, tell him that Carl Erikson and Shauna Bennett are in this vehicle and tell him to stop being an ass!"

I shake my head. There's no way I'm going to get out of this van while there's some maniac with a gun anywhere nearby, and I don't see why Erikson and Shauna really think I could be much help. I guess they just figure I'm expendable, and that it wouldn't be the end of the world for them if they miscalculated and I ended up with a bullet in the head. So far, this 'Toad' guy seems to be pretty trigger-happy, and I can't help thinking that they're underestimating his willingness to fire off some more shots.

"Push her out," Shauna says after a moment.
"No!" I shout.

"Push her!" she says firmly. "Just do it!"

"I'm not pushing anyone," Erikson replies.

"So you'd rather put your own unborn child at risk?" she says. "I swear to God, if you don't push that little streak of piss out right now, I'll get out myself. Is that what you want? You want me to put myself in danger instead of her? That's nice to know, Carl. Really fucking nice!"

"Maybe a pregnant woman would be the best one to go out," I mutter.

They both turn and stare at me.

"He's not going to shoot a pregnant woman, is he?" I continue.

"Maybe I should be the one to go out there after all," Erikson says.

"Fuck you," Shauna replies, reaching out to open the door on her side.

"No!" Erikson shouts, grabbing her arm. He turns to me. "Listen, Elizabeth, you're the best option here. I've known Toad for a long time, and he's not going to shoot at you, okay? He's just not. The guy was just firing a few warning shots, but he's not insane. He'll at least hear what you have to say first, so just make sure he understands that you're here with us." He pauses. "Seriously, by the end of the day, we'll all be laughing about this. We'll be sitting around, chatting about the old days and generally having a good old natter, probably over some of that home-brewed beer Toad's always going on about."

I open my mouth to say that I won't do it, but after a moment I realize that maybe I don't have a choice. From the way Shauna's staring at me, I genuinely believe that she'd be willing to physically throw me out, and it's not as if we can just stay in the van indefinitely, especially with a blown tire. Sooner or later, one of us has to go out there and talk to this guy. I just don't see why they're so convinced that *I'm* the best candidate for the job. Surely this Toad guy would react much better if he saw that his friends were here than if he spotted some random girl he's never seen before?

"Isn't there some other way?" I ask. "Maybe we could make a sign and hold it up for him to see? Maybe we could make a white flag and wave it out the side of the van?"

"Trust me," Erikson says firmly. "I know you don't really know me, but I wouldn't send you out there if I wasn't absolutely certain that you'll be safe." He pauses. "We're in this together, Elizabeth. We let you come into our van, we probably saved your life, and now it's your turn to do something. Yeah, it's risky, and yeah, it's pretty fucked up, but in the current circumstances, it's something that needs doing. You're not gonna let us down, are you?" He waits for me to answer. "Hand on my heart, I swear to God he's not going to hurt you."

Sighing, I look over at the door, which still

has a small bullet hole in the side.

"He *won't* shoot once he sees you," Erikson says again.

"You seem very sure about that," I say bitterly.

"I am," he continues. "I know Toad. I mean, it's been a couple of years since I last saw him, but I know this guy and I know how his head works. People don't change, not *that* much. He's fundamentally a good and honest man."

"Does he normally shoot at people when they're coming along his driveway?" I ask.

"Strange times," Erikson replies with a hint of melancholy. "Strange fucking times."

Without saying anything, I crawl over to the door, before reaching up and sliding it open. If the guy with the gun is in the farmhouse, he won't be able to see me until I get all the way out and walk forward a few meters, past the driver's door. My heart's racing, but I seem to be gaining some degree of strength that I never knew I possessed. Taking a deep breath, and forcing myself not to think about this too much, I climb out of the van, hold my hands up in the air, and walk around to the front. I'm pretty sure that this is the craziest thing I've ever done in my life, but I figure I've got no choice. I just hope that Erikson was right when he said his friend Toad would never shoot me.

The farmhouse is about fifty meters away. I

can't see anyone, but I'm assuming that this Toad guy is watching me from one of the windows. Unless he's an absolute monster, he hopefully won't open fire on someone who's clearly unarmed, although the fact that his nickname is Toad doesn't give me much confidence. As I take a couple of steps forward, I realize that it's a good sign that he hasn't fired so far, so I keep walking, making sure to hold my hands up where he can see them at all times. So far, so good, but I won't be able to relax until he comes outside and I can see that there's no longer a gun pointing at me. I just have to trust that Erikson was right when he said that Toad wouldn't open fire, otherwise I'm an easy target.

"Hello!" I shout eventually, although I figure I'm probably still too far away for him to be able to hear me properly.

Silence.

I turn and look back at the van. There's no sign of Erikson or Shauna, who are still down in the foot-wells, hiding from any potential stray bullets. I guess this is all very easy for them, and there's a part of me that wants to go and grab them, and then drag them out so that this 'Toad' guy can see us all.

Realizing I have no choice but to keep going, I turn back toward the farmhouse and start walking again. I still can't work out where this Toad guy might be hiding, but I can't help imagining that he's got the crosshairs of his rifle aimed straight at my face.

"Hello!" I shout once I'm a little closer. "My name's Elizabeth! I'm here with Carl Erikson and Shauna!"

Silence.

"They say they know you!" I continue, taking another step forward. "They sent me out here to tell you that -"

Before I can finish, there's a loud gunshot, and I'm knocked clear off my feet as a powerful force smashes into my shoulder and sends me crashing to the ground.

THOMAS

Missouri

"HEY!" I SCREAM, banging on the door. "Let me out of here! You've got no right to do this!"

Taking a step back, I listen out for any sign that the guy is coming back. It's been eight or nine hours since he led me, at gunpoint, down here into the basement of his house, and since then there's been no sign of him. It's dark down here, but the rising sun has begun to show through a small window at the far end of the dark, dank room.

Silence.

"Hey!" I shout again, pulling on the door handle, to no avail. Turning, I hurry across the basement, looking for something, anything I can use to force my way out of here. I've already spent a couple of hours trying the window, but it seems to be made out of reinforced glass and I couldn't even make a dent. Unfortunately, the entire basement seems to be completely empty, almost as if the guy deliberately removed anything that I could have used to get out. I'm starting to feel as if I'm completely at his mercy, and that's a feeling I really don't like.

Heading back to the window, I take another look outside. Now that there's some light, I realize I can see the truck over by the trees, with the tarpaulin still covering Joe's body. I feel a dull, heavy sensation in my chest as I think back to what happened yesterday. The truth is, since I was brought down into the basement, I've been able to distract myself by focusing on me efforts to get the hell out of here, but every so often I'm forced to think back to the moment when I pulled that trigger. I feel like in some way, all my feelings have been bundled up in a bag and pushed to one side, but at some point I'm gonna have to deal with what I did.

Just... not now.

Hearing a noise over by the door, I freeze, and after a moment I realize that there's a key in the lock. Before I can come up with a plan, the door swings open and I see the guy standing with a rifle pointed straight at me.

I wait.

"You hungry?" he asks, his voice sounding

old and gnarled.

I stare, my heart racing as I try to work out what to do next. There's a part of me that thinks the best option would be to just take a run at him. After all, he's pretty old and I doubt his reaction times are too hot. At the same time, he's got a gun pointed straight at me, and this isn't the kind of situation where I can afford to make a mistake. Out here in the middle of nowhere, with no likelihood of any cops ever turning up, it wouldn't be difficult for this old guy to blow my head off and get away with it. I guess things are kinda lawless right now.

"It's a simple enough question," he continues. "You hungry or not? If you are, you can have some food. If not, you can stay down here a while longer."

Cautiously, I walk over to the door, unable to take my eyes off the barrel of the rifle. The man makes his way into the basement, keeping the gun pointed at me as he moves around until he's behind me.

"You go first," he says. "Any funny business, anything at all, and I'll shoot. You got that? I've shot a man before, so don't think I'll hesitate. It's up to you whether or not you wanna live, but I've got this thing pointed right at the back of your chest. It's pellets, too, so it'll rip you up pretty bad."

"I don't wanna hurt you," I tell him. "I just

found this place by accident -"

"You broke my window."

"Yeah, but -"

"And you shot a man," he continues. "Shot him dead in the back of that truck. Don't try to deny it. I saw you."

"That was -" I pause, but I can't get the words out. I can't let myself think about what happened with Joe. Not yet.

"You want food, you walk out that door, but remember I've got your back in my sights." He pauses. "There's a few rules we need to establish around here. I'm not gonna let some murdering little thief have the run of the place."

"I'm not -"

"Get upstairs," he says gruffly.

Figuring I should do what he says, I turn and walk toward the door. Although the guy's clearly getting on, in his sixties or seventies, he seems pretty threatening. I guess I just need to talk to him and explain exactly how I ended up here. As I start walking up the stairs that leads to the main part of the house, I can hear him following close behind, and I want to turn and explain everything, to make everything okay.

"Stop," he says suddenly as I get to the top of the stairs. "Two steps forward."

I do exactly what I'm told. Although I'm trying not to show it, I'm pretty terrified right now, and I'm convinced that this old guy means business. Then again, he's getting on, so he can't keep an eye on me all the time. He'll make a mistake sooner or later, and that's when I'll get him. I feel bad for plotting to hurt him, but he's not giving me a choice.

"Okay," he continues. "I'm gonna have to do something to make sure we both know where we stand. You got that?"

I open my mouth to reply, but I have no idea what to say. This whole situation is so bizarre and messed-up, I don't even know where to begin. For one thing, I have no idea whether this guy is genuinely crazy, or just scared. I'd understand if he was scared, but at the same time I'm getting a pretty weird vibe from him, as if maybe he's got a few screws loose.

"Fine," he says.

"I -" I start to say in reply, but before I can finish, there's a heavy thud at the back of my head and I'm instantly knocked unconscious.

ELIZABETH

Pennsylvania

THE ROOM IS DARK, with curtains drawn to keep out as much of the day's light as possible. For a moment, I feel completely lost. I keep expecting to find myself back in my family's New York apartment, with the windows shattered and cold air blowing into the room; I can't help but feel that Henry might burst in at any moment and tell me some crazy story about Bob. Finally, however, I start to remember that those days are gone. My mind races through more recent events, right up to the moment when I was standing facing the farmhouse and...

    I pause.
    I was shot?

When I try to sit up, I immediately feel a sharp pain in my left shoulder. I take a deep breath, but the pain won't go away, and finally I grit my teeth and force myself up. Damn it, I always thought I had a high pain threshold, but this grinding sensation in my shoulder is too much to handle. It's almost as if two damaged bones are pressing against one another. I manage to sit up properly in the end, but the pain is intense and I let out an agonized gasp.

"You're awake," says a female voice nearby.

I freeze. Did I imagine that?

Moments later, there's the sound of someone moving across the room, before a silhouette appears in front of the window and finally the curtains are pulled apart. I have to shield my eyes for a moment as I get used to the light, but eventually I realize that there's a middle-aged woman walking slowly toward the bed, with a faint smile on her face. She has short brown hair, and she's one of those people who look effortlessly friendly, which immediately makes me worry that she might be dangerous.

"How are you feeling?" she asks.

I stare at her.

"You should be fine," she continues. "It was only a flesh wound, really. The bullet didn't do any serious damage. You passed out through shock more than anything else. You're going to have some soreness, some stiffness, and some pain, but the wound isn't infected and it'll heal over eventually. There'll be a scar, obviously, but I'm afraid plastic surgery is a little beyond my skill-set right now, especially with the rather limited resources we've got here. Still, at least you'll have a good story to tell people in future. You can tell them you were gunned down by a psychopath when you strayed onto his property shortly after the end of the world began." She sits on the side of the bed and reaches out a hand for me to shake. "Dr. Patricia Connors," she adds. "Pleased to meet you."

I swallow hard, trying to work out what's happening.

"I understand why you might be a little dubious," she continues, reaching into her pocket and pulling out a twisted, black piece of metal. "This is the bullet that hit you. It actually went straight through, but it glanced a piece of bone so there were some pieces of shrapnel that needed to come out. Again, I want to stress that it wasn't anything too serious. You lost some blood, but you'll produce some more soon enough. You were lucky, though. A few inches further toward your neck, or down toward your collarbone, and it would have been much harder to get you through this. In fact, I don't know if I'd have been able to do it, so you should be thankful that you were shot by someone with a good aim."

I look over at the window.

"Your friends are downstairs," she adds. "After the little misunderstanding, everything was worked out. Toad apologized to them, but the truth is that we can't afford to take any risks. There aren't many of us here, and we've already seen the consequences of making a mistake. We had to be absolutely certain that you were who you claimed to be, otherwise the results could have been catastrophic. I know this probably doesn't make too much sense to you right now, but I promise, soon you'll understand." She pauses. "Are you hungry? Thirsty? There's no reason for you to stay in bed. In fact, it might be good if you get up and get a bit of a stretch. You can come downstairs and meet everyone -"

"Everyone?" I ask, interrupting her.

She smiles. "I'm afraid there are a few of us here. Toad's very kindly agreed to let us stay for a while, although he's being a little grumpy about it. From what Carl said, I get the impression that you haven't actually met Toad yet, have you?"

I shake my head.

"He's..." She pauses. "How can I put this? He's a complete ass. Seriously. Just keep out of his way as much as possible. He's not around too much, anyway. He tends to go off into the woods at first light, and he comes back late with his catches. He doesn't say much, and most people have learned to leave him be. Don't be offended if he basically just ignores you. Human interaction isn't really his strong point. The rest of us are friendly enough. We don't bite, although we *do* expect people to pull their weight around here. You'll get cut a little slack because of your injuries, but fundamentally, if you don't pitch in, you'll be asked to leave. Is that clear?" She waits for me to reply. "I'm serious. No freeloaders are allowed around here. You do your share, or you fuck off."

"I only came here because Erikson and Shauna brought me," I tell her, feeling as if I'm being talked down to a little. "I'm on my way to Lake Ontario."

"Lake Ontario?" She frowns. "Why the hell are you going there?"

"I just..." I start to say, before I realize that maybe she's got a point. Once I accepted that there was nothing left for me in New York, I just assumed that Lake Ontario was my only option, since that's where Mallory and the others went. Now, however, I'm starting to wonder whether there might be a better option somewhere else. I mean, I can't even be sure that they ever made it all the way over there. There's a chance that they changed course, or maybe they ran into trouble. For all I know, they might be dead, and even if I make it all the way up there, I might never find them. "I don't know," I continue after a moment. "I'm still trying to work things out."

"You got any family left alive?"

I shake my head. "I don't think so," I add.

"That's rough," she replies. "Everyone's lost someone. Most people have lost everyone. That's just how it's been going lately. You're in good company, kid. We're not sure how many people are dead, but it seems to be north of 99%, maybe 99.5% or higher. You know what that means?" She waits for me to answer. "It means there might be just a few hundred people left in the entire country, or even in the entire world. I don't know if that makes us lucky or unlucky, but I can tell you one thing for certain. You're not the only one who's alone. Everyone here has lost loved ones, family members, friends... And that's before you even get to some of the other craziness that's been going on."

"Like what?" I ask, still feeling as if I don't really understand what's going on here.

"You not seen them?" she asks.

I stare at her.

"You're lucky," she continues. "There's something going on. Something we haven't managed to figure out yet, but it's the reason you ended up with a bullet in your shoulder. There are creatures... things... They're dead people, but they're a danger. They're not zombies, before you start getting too excited. They're something else, and there aren't many of them, but they're dangerous and we think they might be massing slowly."

"I've seen one," I tell her.

"Where?"

"In New York. In a car. My brother and I found one. We killed it."

"You did, huh?" She pauses. "Where's your brother now?"

"Dead," I tell her.

"Did the creature get her?"

I shake my head.

"Accident?" she asks.

"He was shot," I continue, "by a guy in our apartment building."

"Sorry," she replies.

"It's okay," I say, hauling my legs over the side of the bed and slowly getting to my feet. I have to ignore the sharp pain in my shoulder, but eventually I feel as if I can at least get about. The last thing I want to do is sit here and have some kind of deep conversation about Henry, so I figure I need to change the subject. "Are you sure you took everything out?" I ask, convinced that there's more metal in my shoulder. "It feels like there's something sharp in there."

"It's clear," she says. "Don't worry, it's just a small amount of damage from where the bullet grazed some bone. If we had a proper hospital, I'd have fixed that too, but in the circumstances I couldn't help. You'll get used to it eventually, and it'll pass in a week or two. Until then, if you want my advice, try not to complain too much. People around here won't like it too much if you act like a martyr. That might sound harsh, but the truth is, everyone's carrying aches and pains, so you're hardly special in that regard."

"I got shot," I point out.

"And you're going to be fine," she replies as she walks across the room and opens the door. "Trust me, there are people here who *aren't* going to be fine. Not at all. Toad, for example, has seen some things. He doesn't talk about it, but I know something traumatized him. He used to be better at talking, but he's started to withdraw into his shell, and now he barely manages to communicate. Some things cause a lot more damage than a bullet. I guess we're all dealing with shock in our own way, right?"

"This Toad guy," I say, walking over to join her at the door. "He's the one who shot me, right?"

"Oh, no," she replies with a faint smile. "Sorry. That was me. I shot you." With that, she heads out of the room, leaving me standing alone for a moment. Taking a deep breath, I realize that whether I like it or not, I've ended up in some kind of group situation, which is exactly what I wanted to avoid after everything that happened back in New York. Figuring that I just need to be polite and start planning my next move, I head out the door and follow Patricia downstairs.

THOMAS

Missouri

WHEN I WAKE UP, the first thing I notice is that my head is pounding. There's a heavy, sharp pain right on the back of my skull, and when I feel around to check, I realize that the skin is broken and sticky with blood. I take a deep breath, and for a moment everything seems kind of dizzy, before finally I take a deep breath and decide that my only option is to get to my feet. As soon as I try to sit up, however, I realize that there's something wrong with my legs, and when I look down at my feet, I see that my ankles are chained together.

"That's to stop you running," says the man from nearby.

Turning, I see that he's sitting in a chair on

the other side of the kitchen, with the rifle laid across his knees.

"I don't want you getting the jump on me," he continues, "and since I'm getting on, I figure I need to give you something of an unfair disadvantage. Don't be angry. It's just the breaks." He pauses. "I also don't want you running off any time. Just remember, if you cause any trouble, it's easier for me to just blow your goddamn head off."

I reach down and pull at the chains, but they're attached too tight, and there's some kind of manacle around each ankle.

"You won't get them off," the guy says. "No point trying."

"You don't need to do this," I say, trying to get the manacles loose. They seem pretty old and rusty, so I'm hoping that maybe they're not as strong as they look, although so far I'm definitely not having much luck. "I just came here to look for help. My brother was hurt."

"So you shot him."

I take a deep breath, trying to stay calm.

"I took a look under that tarpaulin," he continues. "You got him good, right in the face."

"He was dying," I say bitterly. "You don't understand."

"Maybe," he replies, "and maybe not. All I know is that I saw you shoot a man, and that makes you kinda untrustworthy in my eyes, especially since you also broke a window in my place. Tell me, what am I supposed to think, huh? You're a murderer and a thief, so how do I know you're not a liar too?"

"I'm not a murderer!" I shout, getting to my feet.

"You're not?" he asks, smiling as he aims the rifle at me. "Well, it seems to me that you shot a man in the face when he was still alive, and I don't think he was begging you to kill him, was he? You're not an executioner, are you?"

"He was in pain!" I shout, feeling as if I want to go over and beat the crap out of this guy.

"Take one step closer," he replies, "and I'll pull the trigger."

I stare at him, and after a moment I realize that he's almost certainly telling the truth. There's just something about him that seems kinda crazy, as if he'd have no hesitation in killing me in cold blood. For one thing, he's got small, beady eyes that seem to be fixed on me at all times; for another, it's increasingly clear that he's got some kind of weird set-up out here in the middle of nowhere, as if he's one of those people who like to live far away from everyone else.

"You have to listen to me," I continue. "My brother and I, we're driving from Oklahoma. We're getting away from the stuff that's happened there."

"What stuff?" he asks.

"The stuff. Everything!" I pause, and finally I realize that if this guy has been living out here in the middle of nowhere, maybe he doesn't know. "There's been some kind of emergency," I tell him. "All the power's down. Planes crashing, phones not working, it's like the whole world has just gone insane. No-one knows what's happening, but there's this virus or illness or something that makes people sick."

"There is, huh?" he replies.

"You have to believe me," I continue. "I've seen it. It makes people get really ill and then they die, except some of them turn some other way and they start walking again. They become, like, these creatures that talk in this weird way, and some of them seem to not really have minds of their own, and some of them are people you might even know!"

"Dead people walking?" he asks, raising an eyebrow.

"I've seen it," I say. "With my own eyes. We were in Scottsville, in Oklahoma, and there were all these things. I don't know how many there are, but they were everywhere, and they were talking. My brother got hurt, but we managed to escape, and then we just drove and drove but we didn't see anyone and finally we got to this place, so we took a look around and..." I pause, realizing that I'm not ready to tell the next part. "Please," I continue, "you've got to understand. It's like the whole world's just gone wrong."

"Like an apocalypse?" he asks. "Like the Lord has finally seen fit to wash the sin and horror from the surface of this miserable world?"

"I don't know," I reply. "Like... I saw this woman explode. She got all sick and festering, and then her body burst. And my own mother, and my father too. And then my brother got crushed by a truck, and he was in agony, and..." My voice trails off as I realize how insane the past week has been. "This is day ten," I say eventually. "I think, anyway. I've been counting. It started ten days ago. Maybe it hasn't reached you out here yet, but I swear to God, it's happening."

He stares at me, as if he can't quite believe what I'm saying.

"It's true," I tell him.

"Maybe," he replies, frowning, "and maybe not. It's certainly an eye-opener, boy, but I really don't know if I can trust you. You wouldn't come up here and try to trick an old man, would you? I've never done anything to you, so I hope to God that you wouldn't think I'm an idiot. If you're lying to me, I'll see through it. I'll get to understanding what you're doing and I'll punish you, don't think I won't."

"It's all true," I insist. "Why else do you think my brother and I ended up out here?"

He pauses. "Few days ago," he says eventually, "I noticed something weird. I used to see jets going through the sky, over to the north. Then they stopped, maybe about a week ago."

"That's because of everything that's happened," I tell him. "I saw a whole jet just come crashing down last week. I bet they all just fell out of the sky when the power stopped working and people got sick."

He smiles. "I guess I'm lucky none of them landed on my head, huh?"

"It's not a joke," I say firmly. "People are dying."

"Sinners," he mutters.

"Everyone," I reply. "Not just bad people. Good people too. My parents died."

"Then they must've been sinners too."

I stare at him. The old guy seems so resolutely stuck in his ways, it's hard to see how I can ever convince him to see the world any other way.

"I've been expecting something like this," he continues. "Some kind of change. I never thought I'd live to see the day, but it seems I've finally been shown that I was right. God *does* listen, and he *does* punish those who've lived unholy lives."

"God isn't like this," I reply. "This isn't God's doing. God helps people. God's going to put all of this right. He didn't start it."

"That's the modern world for you," he continues, with a hint of a smile still on his lips. "Everyone pretends that God is some great big teddy bear who's going to make everything fair and just. Sometimes I wonder if anyone's ever really read the Bible at all. Doesn't matter much to me, though I've gotta say, I saw it coming. I actually read the text, you see, and I understood a long time ago that the real God, the one who exists, is much more vengeful." He pauses. "The question is, what are we gonna do about it? Assuming it's all true, of course. I mean, it doesn't change the fact that you're a murderer and a thief, does it?" He raises the rifle, aiming straight at my head. "Do you know what we do with murderers and thieves around here, boy?"

ELIZABETH

Pennsylvania

"YOU'RE LOOKING PRETTY GOOD for someone who got shot today!"

As I step out through the double-doors, onto the wooden porch that runs alongside the front of the farmhouse, I find Erikson sitting with a bottle of beer.

"Isn't this luxury, huh?" he asks, lifting the bottle. "Toad's been home-brewing, so he's got a fair old stash. Doles 'em out, one a week for everyone. Who'd've thought that one beer a week could taste better than one beer an hour? You want one?"

I shake my head.

"Sorry about what happened," he continues,

smiling awkwardly. "I guess I over-estimated Toad's sanity when it came to defending his castle."

"Toad didn't shoot her," says Patricia, stepping past me and walking over to join Erikson at the table. "I shot her. I'd do it again, too. Around here, we can't be too careful." She takes a seat and turns to look out across the fields that spread out into the distance. "We don't have a way of verifying new arrivals yet," she continues. "Fortunately, the symptoms seem pretty hard to miss, so once we get a good look at you, it's possible to be certain. There seems to be a latent resistance to the strain in a small section of the population, but it's hard to really be sure who's resistant and who just hasn't been exposed yet."

"You're a doctor?" I ask, loitering by the door.

"Don't get too excited," she replies. "This kind of thing isn't my specialty, not by a long shot. I can take out bullets and deliver a baby when the time comes, but I'm not going to be much use when it comes to trying to work out what the hell's going on." She pauses. "I'm pretty good with a sterilized needle and some thread, though."

"We're gonna stick around for a few weeks," Erikson adds. "I've spoken to Toad, and he's fine with it. Well, maybe 'fine' isn't the right word, but he's gonna let us stay. Patty's a doctor, so we figure it'll be useful to have the baby here, just in case there are any complications." He pauses. "You're welcome to get going by yourself, but if you want to wait for us, we're still probably gonna take the van eventually. It's just gonna be delayed, that's all."

"Where's this Toad guy?" I ask. "I haven't met him yet."

"Out in the woods," Patricia replies. "Some of the others go off foraging during the day. Most of them come back empty-handed, but Toad knows the land. He always finds something, and he's pretty good at setting traps. He knows which mushrooms are safe to eat, and berries, and he's already been cultivating some patches of land for a while. In a way, he's the only person I've met so far who seems remotely equipped to deal with this situation. He's got a huge stash of canned food in his basement, too, and pitchers for collecting rain-water."

"Toad was a survivalist," Erikson continues. "Sort of, anyway. He moved out here and started going a little peculiar. You know, one of those people who decide to go and live alone in the sticks and become totally self-sufficient, because they think the end of the world's coming."

"To be fair," Patricia says, with a half-hearted smile, "he might have had a point."

"I guess maybe it was a good idea after all," Erikson mutters. "I mean, he's sure saved our asses." He pauses. "But this isn't the end of the world. No fucking way. This is just a little pause while everything goes nuts. It's a correction. Things'll be back to normal soon."

"You'll meet Toad later," Patricia adds. "Just don't go expecting much in the way of conversation. He keeps himself to himself."

"Not in a good way, either," Erikson says, before taking another swig from his bottle of beer. "In a potential serial killer kind of way. The guy's totally fucked up." Getting to his feet, he comes over to join me at the door. "I know it's against the rules, but seeing as Toad's out, I figure I might go down and get one more beer."

"That's stealing!" Patricia says firmly.

"I think the world owes me one fucking beer," Erikson replies. "After everything that's happened in the past week, one beer isn't too much to ask for!"

"Toad doesn't owe you anything," Patricia says.

"It's just a beer," he mutters, stepping past me and heading inside. "Just one time. Keep your mouths shut. I'm celebrating the imminent birth of a baby. I'll skip my beer next week or something."

"He's an idiot," Patricia says after a moment, fixing me with a curious stare. "Please tell me he's not actually a friend of yours."

"I met him yesterday," I reply.

"That's better," she says. "I've met men like him before. They're no good, in the long run. I pity that poor bitch who's carrying his baby. Christ, I can't imagine letting such a waste of space into my bed, but I guess it's different strokes for different folks." She pauses. "Can you fire a shotgun, Elizabeth?"

"Me?" I stare at her for a moment. "I guess so."

"Wrong answer," she replies. "Either you can or you can't. If you can't, it's fine, but you need to be honest so we can teach you." She stares at me for a moment. "That's a good general rule around here. Don't try to cover up anything. If you can't do something, just say so, and someone'll teach you."

"I can't fire a shotgun," I admit. "I mean, I've never tried."

"I'll teach you this afternoon," she says. "You'll have a hell of a bruise from the kickback after the first couple of times."

"Why do I need to be able to fire a shotgun?" I ask.

"Two reasons. First, you need to be able to shoot at random people who drive up to the house." She pauses. "That was a joke. But seriously, those creatures we talked about, they're real and they're bad news. The policy here is to shoot on sight. No questions, just get a couple of shots off. Fortunately, they seem to drop pretty easily. Blam, if you're a good shot, you can get 'em down. Blam *blam* if you're not so steady. Anyway, once one's been killed, you keep the hell away from it. Someone's always on watch, twenty-four-seven, which is why we're happy to have a few new arrivals. You're gonna have to take your turn, Elizabeth, and the first couple of times are pretty damn spooky."

"You mean they come here?" I ask, shocked at the idea of those things suddenly appearing on the horizon. I turn and look out at the field, but there's no sign of anything so far.

"We've only had two so far," she replies. "Actually, one was before I got here, and the other was two days ago. Still, they were both headed straight for the farmhouse, which has got us a little spooked. It's almost as if they're drawn here, like moths to a flame. I'm assuming it's either scent-based or they're attracted to heat. Granted, we don't know what they'd do if they actually got here, but none of us wants to find out."

"They talk," I say.

She raises an eyebrow.

"The one in New York talked," I continue. "It didn't really make much sense. It seems confused, but it seemed kind of lucid. Like it was taunting us."

"I didn't know they could talk," she replies, visibly a little shocked. "That's gonna make shooting them a little more interesting."

Feeling as if my legs might give way, I walk across the porch and take a seat. The enormity of this situation has suddenly become very apparent to me, and I can't help thinking that maybe we should just keep running. After all, if those creatures are attracted to this place, we're clearly not safe.

"It's okay," Patricia says after a moment. "It's going to be fine."

"What is?" I ask.

"This. The world. I don't know how or when, but it's going to get fixed. This is just a temporary emergency."

I stare at her. "Who's going to fix it?" I ask, thinking back to a few days ago when I told Henry more or less the same thing, only to be proved wrong when Bob opened fire.

"You don't think the government's out there, working on something?" she asks, taking a cigarette packet from her shirt pocket and removing a single cigarette. "This is my last one," she continues, turning the little paper tube around and around between her fingers. "Fuck, I'm gonna miss it when it's gone. It's the one damn thing Toad hasn't been bothering to grow himself. No tobacco. It's gonna be a problem when I've finally smoked this one, but I'm saving it for a special occasion." She pauses, and it's clear that she's genuinely struggling to refrain from lighting up. "I just hope there's a special occasion before..." Her voice trails off, before she slips the cigarette back into the packet and puts the whole thing back in her shirt pocket.

"I think Erikson might have some cigarettes," I say after a moment.

She shakes her head. "He smoked his last one earlier. Don't think I don't know he's got his eye on mine, either. There's no way he's getting it, though." She pauses. "So, Elizabeth, I guess we should start training you up on one of the rifles. There's no point sitting around wasting time." She turns and looks out at the horizon. "We don't know when another of those things might turn up around here, but it could come at any moment, and I figure it's better to hit them while they're still fairly far out." Getting to her feet, she turns to me and smiles. "Come on. It's not that scary, really. Once you know how to use a gun properly, you'll feel a hell of a lot safer."

Before I can say anything, there's a distant rumbling sound and the whole world seems to shake for a moment, rattling the house before the tremor subsides.

"Not the first time," Patricia says, staring at me with a look of fear in her eyes. "You felt that before too, right?"

I nod.

She pauses. "Whatever it is," she continues eventually, "I don't like it. It doesn't feel natural."

THOMAS

Missouri

"FASTER!" THE GUY SHOUTS, standing at the top of the hill and watching as I struggle with the barrel of water I'm supposed to be dragging to the house. "We haven't got all day!" he continues. "I want this done before it gets dark! There's still a few more jobs I need doing!"

"It'd be easier if my legs weren't chained together," I mutter.

"What was that?" he calls out.

"Nothing!" I shout, giving the barrel another heave as I finally get it onto the level ground that surrounds the house. It's taken me almost half an hour to get the damn thing up a slope that seemed at times to be running at a forty or fifty per cent incline. Given that the barrel is completely full of rain water, I guess I shouldn't be surprised that I almost collapsed several times. "Why do you keep this thing down by the road, anyway?" I ask, out of breath and generally feeling as if I might black out at any moment. I swear to God, with the late afternoon sun beating down on me, I'm sweating like a pig, and there's no sign of any let-up.

"None of your business," he replies, raising the rifle so that the barrel is once again pointed at me. "You're not done yet. I want this thing over by the door. It's the best clean water source we've got right now. I don't know how long I'll be having you around, boy, but I might as well make use of you while you're here."

Figuring that there's no point trying to argue, I start rolling the barrel toward the house. There's a part of me that wants to just make a run at the old bastard and try to knock him down. Sure, he *might* manage to get a shot off and blow my head to pieces, but on the other hand I might just manage to get to him. It's not that I want to kill him, but I sure as hell don't plan to let him keep pushing me around like this. I've already got some kind of plan worked out: I'm going to lull him into a false sense of security, make him think he can trust me a little, and then I'm going to bash his head against a rock.

"This is what happens to murderers," he says, watching me for a few meters away. "Thieves, too. You're gonna have to work off your sins, and I intend to make sure that you do just that. God wouldn't want it any other way."

"This isn't anything to do with God!" I say, but before I can add anything else, there's a kind of rumbling sound, and for a moment everything starts shaking. I look over at the guy, and I'm just about to make a lunge for the gun when the trembling stops and everything goes back to normal.

"See?" he says. "That's what God thinks about you. He's sending a message. You've sinned, boy, and you've got to make it right. There's no point pretending otherwise."

"That wasn't God," I tell him.

"Who else can make the ground shake?" he asks. "Who else can make the whole world tremble? You'd do well to remember that the Lord's watching you, boy. He can see everything you do, and he knows what's in your heart. He's everywhere. Don't they teach you kids anything these days? Don't you even know what God is and what he can do to you?"

Setting the barrel in position next to the door, I take a step back. I've always thought that I'm in pretty good shape, but that was by far the hardest job I've ever had to do in my life, and right now I feel as if I need to rest. It's pretty clear that this guy is going to keep pushing me until I drop.

"Grab a shovel," the guy says.

I turn to him.

"Do I have to say everything twice?" he asks. "Get a shovel. There's plenty resting over by the side of the house. Just grab one. Doesn't matter which, as long as it's sturdy. You're gonna be using it for a few hours, though, so make sure it's one you can grip properly. Don't get the biggest one. It's too big for you."

Sighing, I walk over and pick up the nearest shovel. It's clear that this guy, whose name I don't even know, has decided that I'm going to be his general, all-purpose slave, and while he's holding that rifle, there's no way I can even hope to get the hell out of here. Still, he's pretty old and frail, so I'm sure I can overpower him once I've managed to get close enough, so once again it's clear that my best option is to find a way to make him think that I'm harmless. I need to spend a few days, maybe even a week, being obedient and well-behaved, and then I need to watch out for the right moment to strike.

"Come on!" he calls out. "The longer you delay, the later you'll be working!"

Carrying the shovel back over to him, I follow as he leads me over to the trees. We walk a few hundred meters into the forest, before finally he stops and turns to me. As usual, the rifle is pointed straight at my head, and I have no doubt that he'd use it if he thought I was going to try anything. I can only hope that his trigger finger isn't twitchy.

"Dig," he says firmly.

"Here?"

"Here."

I look down at the dry ground. "Why?" I ask.

"Why do you think?" He smiles. "You don't think we're gonna leave that corpse just sitting in the back of that truck, do you? Jesus Christ, boy, what kind of idiot are you? There's disease and all sorts of reasons why we've gotta get rid of it. You dig a hole, and dig it deep. There's a reason churches put bodies six feet under. It's to make it so wild animals can't dig people up. So get at least six feet down, maybe seven. I don't want any mistakes being made here. If in doubt, go a little deeper. Doesn't have to be too wide, though. It's not like we've got anything fancy like a coffin."

"A grave?" I say, my heart racing as I realize what he wants me to do. "For my brother?"

"He's liable to start stinking," the guy continues, with that big smile still plastered across his face. "There'll be flies and everything if we don't get moving, so I figure there's no time like the present." He pauses for a moment. "What are you waiting for, boy? Dig!"

ELIZABETH

Pennsylvania

DINNER AT THE FARMHOUSE is a strange event. There's a guy named Bridger who seems to be in charge of cooking, and everyone else seems content to let him stir the pot. Patricia, meanwhile, seems pretty nervous, and I can't help but notice that she takes her last cigarette out a few times and twirls it between her fingers, but she always puts it back in the packet after a few minutes. With Shauna having decided to stay in bed upstairs, Erikson seems kind of relaxed, although I'm suspicious that he might have taken more than one extra beer. There's also a guy named Thor, from Sweden, who seems polite but quiet, and it's his job this evening to keep an eye on the horizon and watch out for any unwelcome visitors. As we sit at the large kitchen table, there's not much conversation, and everyone seems intently focused on their food, as if it's the most important thing in the world.

"So what do you guys think Toad'll bring back tonight?" Patricia asks eventually, as she finishes her bowl of meat soup. She turns to Bridger. "What was in this tonight, anyway? Please don't tell me it was rat meat."

"We're not on the rat meat yet," Bridger replies with a half-smile. "I thought we agreed that there'd be a don't ask, don't tell policy regarding the food. Believe me, if we have to sit around here much longer, you guys are *definitely* not gonna want to know what starts going into the pot."

"Come on, just tell us," Patricia says. "We might as well know."

Bridger pauses. "Beef," he says eventually.

"Beef?" Patricia replies, as if she can't quite believe it. "Seriously?"

"Beef," Bridger says again, with a shrug. "I'm using up some frozen beef that's been thawing in the basement. Don't get too used to it. It's gonna be all gone within a week. *That's* when we might have to start thinking about the rat meat. There's plenty of rats around here." He glances over at me. "So how were things in New York? After the shit hit the fan, I mean."

"It was pretty empty," I reply, realizing that

everyone's turned to stare at me. "Not much going on."

"Sirens and stuff?" Bridger asks. "I've been wondering ever since this started, how it went down in the major population centers. Was there looting and stuff?"

I shake my head. "Everyone seemed to kind of vanish. I think people felt ill overnight and mostly went home. There were bodies in some of the cars, though."

"But no marauding gangs?" he continues.

"A few psychos," I reply, trying hard not to picture Bob's demented grin. "There were some planes that came down."

"Fuck," Bridger says, unable to hide a smile. "I bet that was a sight."

I smile awkwardly, not really wanting to get into the details. Even though it's only been just over a week since this whole disaster started, I feel as if I'm no longer even on the same planet as New York. Two days ago, I was still in the city with Henry and Bob, and now here I am, a thousand miles from nowhere and sitting in a room with a bunch of people I'd never even met when I set out from the city yesterday morning. Everything's moving so fast.

"Did they, like, just drop from the sky likes fucking stones?" Bridger asks. "Were there explosions?"

I nod.

"She probably doesn't want to talk about it," Patricia says, interrupting the conversation. "I imagine it was a pretty traumatic time."

"Yeah, but -"

"Bridger!" she says firmly. "Maybe leave it, yeah? Think about what it must have been like out there. I'm glad I happened to be out here in the sticks when it happened. The cities must have been hell."

"Toad's back," Thor says suddenly, looking out the window. It's almost dark outside, but there's still a little light, and seconds later I hear footsteps on the porch before a distant door opens and someone enters a different part of the house.

"Told you he's anti-social," Patricia says, turning to me. "Still, you should probably go and introduce yourself. It's only polite."

I stare at her, trying to work out whether or not she's joking. I guess I'm *hoping* that I won't actually have to go and meet Toad, at least not tonight. After everything that people have been saying about the guy, they've kind of built him up to be some kind of freak, and the last thing I want to do is meet another guy like Bob. Maybe I'm just being paranoid, but it feels as if the events of the past week have brought out the worst in some people.

"Go on!" Patricia continues, grinning. "Get

through to the pantry and just say hi, thank him for letting you stay, and tell him food's on the table. He won't say much, but he'll probably appreciate it, deep down. And then, just come back through. You'll still be in one piece, I promise."

"If he doesn't get you first," Bridger says with a smile.

"Shut up," Patricia says, turning to him.

"What?" he replies, acting shocked. "It's true!" He turns to me. "I don't mean to scare you too much, but Toad's a bit of a monster. I mean, why else do you think we call him Toad? If the world was normal, there's no way any of us would be out here with him, but right now he's pretty useful. He's the kind of guy who really should just be alone. Totally, completely alone forever. He knows it, too. He doesn't like having people around. That's why he spends so long out foraging each day. The guy barely even talks to any of us."

"It's true," Erikson says from the other end of the table. "He's always been a bit odd. I'm not sure, but I think maybe there's something a bit loose in his head, if you know what I mean. He's not quite wired properly. I used to think maybe he was, like, partially autistic or something like that, but now I think it's something else. I don't know, though." He smiles. "I'm sorry, I guess I'm probably scaring you. There's no reason to be nervous. He's actually a real teddy bear."

"Go on," Patricia says, leaning over and nudging my elbow. "Don't let these ungrateful assholes put you off. Just go and introduce yourself."

Smiling awkwardly, I get to my feet. The floorboards creak as I walk around the table, and I can tell that everyone's watching me. I don't know exactly what's wrong with this Toad guy, but it's as if the others are setting me up for some big fall. I reach the door and look out into the gloomy hallway, and I can hear someone moving about in the pantry. Glancing back into the room, I see that the others are all still watching me, and with a sigh I turn and start walking along the hallway, hyper-aware that my every step is causing the wooden floor to creak and groan. Eventually, I reach the door that leads into the pantry, and I spot a figure in the shadows at the far end of the room, working on the contents of some kind of large bag. In this light, it's hard to make out much detail, and I feel as if I'm in danger of interrupting some private moment. Still, I figure I have to at least introduce myself.

"Hi," I say eventually.

He pauses for a moment, but he doesn't turn to me, and he doesn't say anything. After a few seconds, he gets back to work.

"I'm Elizabeth," I continue, trying not to sound scared. "Elizabeth Marter. I arrived earlier with Erikson and Shauna. I..." I pause, watching as

Toad pulls some kind of dead animal from the bag and sets it on a nearby table. "I just wanted to thank you," I add, "for letting me stay."

He pulls another dead animal from his bag.

"The food was really nice," I say after a moment. "The others said to tell you that there's some waiting for you."

He pulls out a third dead animal.

"Okay," I continue eventually. "I don't want to disturb you, so -"

Before I can finish, Toad turns and carries his bag over to a nearby table, and finally I get a proper look at him. To my surprise, I see that he's young, maybe late twenties at most, and although he's covered in dirt and grime, and despite the fact that his dark hair is matted and unruly, there's something about him that immediately makes me feel as if I've been punched in the gut. His dark eyes glance at me briefly before he starts pulling some mushrooms out of his cloth bag and setting them in a bowl. As I watch him work, I can't help but notice that he seems quietly confident, and I stare at his hands as they start sorting through the mushrooms. Whereas everyone else here at the farmhouse seems out of place, this guy appears to be in his element, as if he belongs here.

"You're Toad, right?" I ask after a moment, worried that maybe I've made a mistake.

He glances at me for a moment, before

getting on with his work, and it's clear that this is definitely the right guy.

"Do you mind if I ask..." I pause. "What's your real name?"

With the mushrooms sorted into two bowls, he takes the bag over to a nearby sink and finally he empties out a tumble of what appear to be blueberries. I already feel as if maybe I've made a mistake and insulted him, so I'm not sure what to do next. I guess I should just turn around and go back through to the others.

"You can come with me tomorrow," he says suddenly, his voice sounding dark and smoky.

I stare at him, worried that maybe I just imagined that sentence.

"You need to help out," he adds, sorting through some jars from a nearby cupboard instead of looking at me. "If you come with me, you can help carry, and maybe you'll learn something. No offense, but you don't strike me as someone who's already brimming with transferable skills. We need to get you up to speed as fast as possible."

I open my mouth to reply, but I'm not sure what to say.

"Or you can stay here and learn to shoot," he adds.

"I'll come with you," I tell him.

"Be out front at sunrise," he continues. "Should be about 7am." With that, he starts cleaning out some jars, and after a couple of minutes I realize that the conversation is over. Quietly, feeling a little stunned, I turn and head out of the room. I can hear the others talking and laughing in the kitchen at the other end of the house, and I guess I should go back and join them. Still, I can't help thinking about tomorrow, and about the idea of going out into the wilderness with this Toad guy. I pause for a moment, loitering in the hallway as I try to get my thoughts together, and then finally I take a deep breath and decide that tomorrow's another day and I'll deal with things as they come. Bracing myself for the inevitable jokes, I eventually, reluctantly, go back into the kitchen to join the others.

THOMAS

Missouri

"YOU'RE WEAK, BOY," THE guy says, watching as I continue to haul Joe's body across the forest floor. "A man shouldn't kill another man if he hasn't got the strength to haul the corpse to a proper grave. Then again, I don't suppose you're a man at all, are you? Not really. The modern world breeds infants and children, not proper men."

I want to turn and bash the bastard's head against a tree, but I manage to hold off. With that gun pointed at me, he'd have no trouble picking me off before I got near him, and I'm not going to give him the satisfaction of thinking God wanted me dead. For now, I just need to focus on the task at hand, which means getting Joe into the grave I spent five hours digging. So far, having tucked the tarpaulin around Joe's ankles, I've managed to get him this far without having to see his actual body. I guess it's probably a good idea to bury him, anyway; the last thing I want is for wild animals to start picking him apart.

"You ready?" the guy asks, sounding amused by the whole situation.

"There's not much to be ready for," I reply, as I reach the graveside and prepare to push Joe's body down into the pit. I guess there's not much point standing on ceremony, but I still feel as if I should do or say something to mark the moment. In the old days, there would've been a proper funeral, but over the past week it's seemed as if people are just dying and being left where they fell. No more funerals. No more priests or proper burials.

"Wait!" the guy calls out.

Sighing, I turn to him.

"It's not that simple, boy," he continues. "You have to look upon the truth of what you did. You have to be a man and face up to your responsibility." He pauses. "When I was a kid, I saw plenty of stuff that'd make your stomach churn. Turned me into the man I am today. So you're gonna pull that tarpaulin aside and take a proper look. That's what you're gonna do, whether you like it or not." He raises the gun, as if to remind me that he's got me in his sights. "Then, and only then, are you gonna bury your brother."

"No," I say, feeling a cold shiver pass through my body. "I'm not looking at him."

"You wanna join him in the grave?"

Turning back to face Joe's body, I realize that I've got no choice. I take a deep breath, before reaching down and pulling the tarpaulin aside. When I finally see his face, shattered by the bullet I fired straight between his eyes, I immediately feel blank, before a strange kind of white anger starts to rise through my body. I want to rip the world apart for putting me in a position where I had to shoot my own brother. I stare at his broken skin and at the fragments of bone that are sticking out from beneath the flesh. His eyes, dead and unblinking, are looking straight back at me, and I can't help wondering if, at the last moment, he understood that I was sparing him from any further pain. I hope so. I hope he knew, right at the end, that I was a good brother.

"Okay," the guy calls out. "Let's get this show on the road."

"Give me a minute," I reply, unable to stop staring at Joe's broken face.

"It's too late for regrets," the guy continues. "I'm just making you look at the consequences of what you've done. If that's really your brother, the only reason he's dead is because you put a gun in his face and pulled the trigger. To my way of thinking, that's a sin. Only God gets to decide when and how someone dies. Maybe God directed you and made you his agent, but somehow I think this was caused by your own foolishness. Still, at least I know that God witnessed what you did, so he'll undoubtedly deal with you when the time comes. It's going to get dark soon, though, so we need to get back to the house. Finish this mess up!"

I take a deep breath, refusing to answer.

"I said finish this mess up!" he shouts. "Or do I have to put a bullet in the back of your head and send you down there with your brother? Is that how you want to go?"

Reaching down, I grab Joe's shoulder and roll him into the pit. I watch as his body tumbles down to the soil deep below, and then I stand and stare for a moment. This is the last time I'm ever going to see him. All my life, Joe's been around, often bugging me but always a part of the world. Sure, he could be a total jerk, and there were times lately when I really came to hate him, but it's hard to believe that this is the end. I wish I could go back in time just a week and fix things, and make it so that he didn't have to die. If we'd never gone to Scottsville, and if we'd never met Clyde, things would have been different. Together, we might have stood a chance. As it stands, I have no idea where I'm going to go, even *if* I manage to get away from this gun-toting madman.

"That's enough standing around," the guy says after a moment. "Fill the grave back in. It'll be dark soon."

Without saying a word, I get to work. Every shovel's worth of dirt feels like it's weighed down, and at first I'm not even sure that I can finish the job. Eventually, however, I've managed to get most of the dirt back into the hole, and I'm left standing next to Joe's final resting place.

"I need to put a marker here," I say. "Something so that people know where he's buried."

"Forget it," the guy replies, "no-one cares. Get back to the house."

"There has to be a marker," I say, turning to him. "It's only right. I'll get some wood and make a cross."

"Waste of energy," the guy says. "Get walking."

"But -"

"Jesus Christ, kid," the guy continues, "are you gonna argue about every little decision? I'm the one holding the gun, so I'm the one who gets to say what happens, okay? It's called democracy, and you need to get used to it. One gun, one vote. It'd be a shame to kill you when a perfectly good grave's just been filled in, but I won't hold back. You're only useful to me if you keep your mouth shut and stop arguing. In case you didn't notice, I was getting on just fine before you showed up, so I can easily go back to how things used to be." He pauses. "Come on. Let's get going."

The journey back to the house is slow, especially since the chains around my ankles are only nine or ten inches long, preventing me from taking anything long than baby steps. I can't help looking over my shoulder every now and then, to check whether the guy still has his gun pointed at me, but of course he's far too wily to let his guard down, even for a second. It's pretty clear that I'm going to have to wait a while before I get a chance to make a break, but I'm determined to get the hell out of here. There's no way I'm going to let this bastard think that he's won. Even if it's the last thing I ever do, I'm going to make him regret the day he started treating me like this.

"Here," the guy says as we get into the kitchen. He grabs some stale bread and tosses it at me. "That's your dinner. There's a cup by the sink. Fill it with water and take it downstairs with you, and make sure you get some sleep. You'll be working again in the morning."

Sighing, I do as I'm told before heading down to the dark, fusty-smelling basement. I turn and watch as the door is slammed shut, and I hear him turning the key in the lock. Standing alone down here, I realize that I can't take this much longer. Bread isn't going to keep me going, so I figure the old man is planning to work me until I drop dead. As I listen to the sound of his footsteps in the room directly above the basement, I decide that there's no way I can wait a week to get out of here. I don't know how I'm going to do it yet, but I have to find a way out of here as soon as possible. Taking a deep breath, I figure I'm going to have to escape tomorrow. Either that, or I'll die trying.

DAY 11

DAYS 9 TO 16

ELIZABETH

Pennsylvania

WAKING FROM A RESTLESS dream, I open my eyes and see that the first rays of morning sun are staring to show through the window. I blink a couple of times, watching as dust drifts through the air, and for a fraction of a second the world seems to be at peace. It's as if everything is calm and quiet, and there's no reason to worry. I turn and look around the room, half-expecting to see my brother somewhere, but there's no sign of him and at first I can't work out where he could have gone.

And then I remember.

Sitting bolt upright, I look around the bare, makeshift room and realize that I was supposed to meet that Toad guy at sunrise. I get out of bed and quickly get dressed, still feeling a little groggy as I stumble to the door and step out into the corridor. The floorboards creak beneath my feet, and the whole house seems to be totally quiet as I hurry to the top of the stairs and then down to the ground floor. I check the dining room, and then the front room, and finally I burst into the kitchen, where I find Thor, the Swedish guy, rolling some dough. Glancing over at me, he smiles, but he quickly returns to work.

"Where is he?" I ask, standing in the doorway.

"Who?"

"Toad. I'm supposed to meet him."

He stares at me. "Why would *you* be meeting Toad?"

"He said I could go into the forest with him today," I reply, starting to panic as I realize that I might be too late. "He told me to meet him at sunrise."

"Sunrise was twenty minutes ago," Thor replies, continuing to knead the dough. "I noticed him hanging around for a few minutes longer than normal. He's normally gone by the time first light shows, but this morning he was taking his time. I thought it was pretty strange, to be honest. Not his usual kind of behavior. I guess he gave you time to show up, but Toad's not the kind of guy who gives second chances." He pauses. "Then again, he's not the kind of guy who invites people to go with him. What gives? Did you promise to give him a little something in return?"

"Which way did he go?" I ask, hurrying to the window. Damn it, I was determine to wake up on time, but it's difficult when you haven't got an alarm clock. I was hoping that the sunlight itself would get me up, but I guess I was more tired than I realized.

"No way of telling," Thor says. "I think he's

got a set routine, but I've never paid much attention. Toad's the kind of guy who just gets on with things and doesn't make too much of a fuss. It's not as if he leaves an itinerary pinned to the wall. In fact, I don't think he's ever allowed anyone to go with him out into the sticks, at least not as long as I've been here." He pauses. "Face it, you're too late. Seeing as you're up, though, you might as well give me a hand."

"I'm going to catch up to him," I say, heading over to the door.

"Not so fast," he says, grabbing my arm and pulling me close. "What did you offer old Toad, huh?" He presses himself against me, and there's a leery grin on his face. "Whatever it was, maybe you'd like to do the same for me?"

"He invited me," I say, trying to get free from Thor's grip. "That's all."

"Pretty young woman like you," he replies, putting a hand on my waist. "Are you seriously saying Thor invited you out there for your conversation skills, or your ability to survive in the wild? We both know what he wanted. Seeing as he ditched you, why not do to me whatever you were going to do to him? It wouldn't hurt, would it? Just a little friendly interaction, if you know what I mean. Everyone else is asleep, so we could slip into the pantry for a few minutes."

"Get off me!" I say, trying harder and harder

to get away from him.

"Or what?" he asks. "You gonna scream?"

"If you touch me," I reply, trying to sound as if I'm not scared, "I'll hurt you. I'll scream, but also I'll hurt you, and I'll make sure that everyone knows what you're like."

"Come on," he says, pressing himself more firmly against me, "what's the harm? It's not like I'm asking you to marry me. We're in a bad place. You never know when we might die, so why not be nice to each other? Why not share the fun? Or do you wanna be Toad's girl? Do you think you can get better favors from him? I'm the cook around here, remember. Toad catches things, but I make them edible. If you're gonna cozy up to anyone, it should be me."

"Leave her alone," says a voice nearby.

Turning, I see that Patricia Connors is watching from the doorway.

"We were just messing around," Thor says, letting go and taking a step back. "It's good to keep the spirits up with a little banter, you know? I thought she looked sad, so I wanted to think of some way to put a smile back on her face."

"I thought you were going with Toad today," Patricia says, turning to me. She clearly doesn't believe a word that Thor just said.

"I was a few minutes late."

"Toad won't like that," she replies with a

smile. "Still, he can't have got too far. Go catch up."

I look over at Thor.

"Leave him to me," Patricia adds. "Thor and I need to have a little word. Elizabeth, you need to go and find Toad. Show him he can rely on you. If he decides you're not pulling your weight, he might decide there's no point letting you stay."

Without replying, I run out of the room, and finally I get out into the yard at the front of the farmhouse. I glance over my shoulder, making sure that Thor hasn't tried to follow me, and then I turn and stare out at the horizon. With the sun so low in the sky, it's hard to make too much out; there are trees in the distance, running to the crest of a hill that borders one side of the dirt road, but there's no way of telling if Toad went that way. Running around the house, my heart racing, I look toward the wide open fields that stretch as far as the horizon. There's still no sign of him, though, and it's starting to look as if I've messed up. All I had to do was get up in time, and instead I slept too long, wrapped up in a dream about my brother.

"Damn it," I mutter, turning and glancing toward the trees again. At the last moment, just as I'm about to give up, I spot movement a few hundred meters away. Sure enough, there's a figure walking into the forest, heading away from the farm. Without hesitating, I start to hurry after him. I don't really know the way, and I'm aware that there's a danger of other creatures turning up in the forest, but right now I'm only focused on the need to catch up and fulfill my promise to help out. After all, I want to be useful, and since this whole farm belongs to Toad, I figure he's the one I need to impress. I don't know how long I'm going to be stuck in this place, but I don't want to be seen as someone who doesn't work hard.

After a few minutes, I realize that although I'm slowly getting closer, he's moving pretty fast. Out of shape and out of breath, I pause for a moment, trying to work up the strength to keep going. Living in Manhattan all my life, I never really had to run anywhere. I mean, it's not that I'm hopelessly unfit, but being out here in the wilderness is a totally different lifestyle. I'm used to flat, firm sidewalks, but even the ground here is uneven and a little soft. It takes me a couple of minutes, but finally I get my breath back and I start running again, determined to catch up to Toad. Finally, when he's no more than a hundred meters away, I stop and decide to call after him, hoping that he'll wait once he realizes I'm here.

"Hey!" I shout, waving my arms in the air. "Wait!"

Up ahead, he stops and turns to look back at me. After a moment, however, he turns and keeps walking.

"Hey!" I shout, starting to run after him

again. I'm starting to realize that I'm totally under-prepared for this trip. For one thing, I'm wearing jeans and a t-shirt, and I'm already feeling cold; for another, these shoes are meant for walking around the streets of Manhattan, not running across boggy fields, and my feet are already wet. If Toad thought that I'd be unsuited to this trip, I'm about to prove him right, but there's no way I'm going to surrender just yet.

"Wait for me!" I yell, as I finally reach Toad. The ground is soft and uneven, and I almost fall over several times, but finally I catch up and come to a halt next to him. He doesn't look particularly pleased to see me; in fact, there's a look of mild displeasure on his face, as if he'd been hoping that I wouldn't show up. Suddenly I feel like some kind of child, and although I'd hoped to get to know this guy, it looks as if things have started pretty badly.

"You were supposed to meet me at dawn," he says cautiously. "You were late."

"I'm sorry," I reply, still a little out of breath. "I didn't wake up in time, but I'm here now."

He stares at me. It's hard to believe that someone nicknamed Toad could be so handsome, but he has the kind of rugged good looks that seem to belong out here in the wilderness.

"I won't wait for you again," he says. "If you can't keep up, you might as well just go back to the farm."

"I can keep up," I say firmly.

"We'll see," he replies, and it's clear that he doesn't think too much of me.

I open my mouth to reply, but he quickly turns and carries on walking. For a moment, I consider heading back to the farm. After all, the last thing I want is to spend the day with someone who clearly doesn't have a very high opinion of me. Then again, I guess I could still try to prove myself to him. Taking a deep breath, I start walking after him. He doesn't look back, but I'm pretty sure he knows that I'm here. He seems like he's pretty arrogant so far, but there's no way I'm going to give up and let him think that he's right. Even if he doesn't say another word to me all day, I'm going to stick it out, and if he thinks I'm some kind of city girl who can't handle the real world, I'll prove him wrong.

THOMAS

Missouri

"HEY!" I SHOUT, BANGING on the door. "Let me out!"

Silence.

"I'm hungry!" I shout, hoping that he might finally have pity. "I need the toilet! What am I supposed to do? Go down here?"

I wait.

No reply.

"What the fuck's wrong with you?" I shout, taking a step back before slamming my shoulder into the door as hard as possible, which isn't easy since my ankles are chained together. "What am I supposed to do down here?"

Reaching down, I try yet again to pull the

ankle chains loose, but there's no hope. I've been trying to get loose all night, and all I've managed to do is wear away my skin.

"Please!" I shout, close to tears. There's no way the old man can't hear me. This isn't a big house, so he can't be far away.

Realizing that there's no way he's ever going to reply, I look up at the low basement ceiling and wait for a sound. Is the old bastard even up there? It's been hours since I heard even the faintest of noises coming from anywhere in the house. The last time I heard the old man's voice, he told me to take some stale bread and get some sleep, and that I'd be working again in the morning. I guess he'll come and get me once the sun has come up. For now, though, this whole place is as quiet as a cemetery. I've been trying to get his attention all night, but it's not working. He's ignoring me, and I'm powerless to change anything. I guess he's ignoring me for a reason, maybe so that he can prove to me that he's in control.

"Get me out of here," I whisper, staring into the darkness. "Please God, get me out of here. I don't know why you've put me here, but let me go. I'll do anything, but let me go."

Silence.

I can't help thinking about my brother. It's only been a few days since he was injured, and I keep reliving the moment when I killed him. There's a part of me that wonders whether I should have tried to keep him alive, even though he was in pain. The truth, though, is that there was nothing I could have done. I'm not a doctor, and his injuries were too bad. He was probably praying that I'd finish him off. That's the kind of guy Joe was, really; he'd have hated being weak. At least he's in a better place now, and no-one else can hurt him. He used to drive me crazy sometimes, but it felt good to have him around, and I'm not sure how I'm going to manage now that he's gone.

Exhausted, I stagger back from the door and wait for a moment. It's as if the entire house has fallen quiet, and I can't help wondering whether the old man has abandoned me. What if he's wandered off and left the house, or what if he's died in the night? Either way, I'm trapped down here in this basement. The place is almost completely bare, and there's nothing that I can use. It's almost as if the old man has completely stripped the basement of anything that could possibly be useful, and I can't shake the feeling that in some strange way he was actually prepared for my arrival. Either that, or he just happened to have a high-security basement beneath his house, in case anyone dropped by to visit. Has this mad old man been out here all along, grabbing anyone who comes too close?

Despite the fact that the house looks like it's on the verge of falling down, there are definitely signs that someone took extra care to secure this particular space. The door is made of metal, and it definitely seems to be stronger and more secure than your average basement door. In fact, it's kind of suspicious to note how secure the basement appears to be, compared to the rest of this rundown house. The whole place seems to have been left totally untended, but the basement door is more like something you'd find at a bank. I have no idea what that mad old man could possibly want, and I feel as if I've wandered into the middle of someone else's private insanity.

Hurrying over to the small window at the far end, I climb up on a chair and stare out at the forest. Slowly, the first light of dawn is starting to spread the faintest light across the scene, and I can make out the truck parked nearby. The damn thing's only about ten meters away, and if I could get through this glass, I'd be able to drive off before the mad old man could catch me. Unfortunately, the glass is reinforced, and although I've tried during the night to smash my way out, I've had no luck. Again, it's clear that no expense has been spared in order to ensure that this basement is completely sealed.

Sighing, I take a step back and look across the dark basement. There's not much light, but my eyes have adjusted to the gloom and I can just about make out the shape of the room. This whole house is like something that has been left abandoned, and it's hard to believe that someone could actually live here. I have no idea who the old man is - I don't even know his name - but he seems to live completely cut off from the rest of the world. Climbing down from the chair, I wander through the darkness, trying to understand how anyone could exist in such a rundown kind of way. Back at home, our house was always kept neat and tidy, and even though I didn't appreciate my mother's efforts at the time, I'm starting to realize that she was fighting a never-ending battle against decay. As soon as life stops battling, things start to die and fall apart.

Finally, as I'm about to give up and try to get some sleep, I spot a pile of rags in the corner of the room. Wandering over, I see that there's a bunch of what appears to be old cloth sacks. Seeing as there's no bed down here, I figure I might as well use these to get some sleep. I reach down and pull them up, in order to make sure that they're fairly clean, but after a moment I realize that there's something beneath all the rags. There's still not much light coming through the window, so I crouch down and take a closer look, and that's when I realize what I've found. Under all the old sacks, there's the dry, almost mummified body of a dead girl.

ELIZABETH

Pennsylvania

"STOP HERE," TOAD SAYS abruptly, after we've walked in silence for almost an hour.

I watch as he drops his backpack to the ground and crouches next to it. Unzipping the top, he pulls out a handgun, which he sets down on the grass before removing a second gun.

"You ever used one of these?" he asks, shielding his eyes from the sun as he looks up at me.

"I don't like guns," I reply, instantly tensing at the thought of even being near one of those things.

"You don't have to like them," he replies. "Have you ever *used* one?"

"Not..." I pause. "Not really." As I stare at the gun in his hand, I can't help thinking back to the moment when Bob pulled the trigger and shot my brother. It's an image that has been haunting me for the past few days, filling my mind not only when I'm awake but also when I'm dreaming. There's a part of me that wants to turn and run, but I'm determined not to let Toad think that I'm weak.

"You're going to need to carry this," he says, holding the gun out to me.

I shake my head.

"It's not negotiable," he continues. "We're in a hostile environment. The odds of us running into something are low, but we still have to be ready." He waits for me to take the gun, and then he sighs. Getting to his feet, he steps over to me and takes my right hand, spreading the fingers out before closing them around the handle of the gun. "Feel that?" he asks. "That's the weight of the gun. You need to get used to it, and you need to start feeling natural around this thing. It's good to be nervous. Guns can kill -"

"I know," I say firmly, feeling tears in my eyes.

"I know you were grazed by a bullet the other day -"

"I wasn't *grazed*," I say firmly. "She shot me."

"It wasn't a real gun," he says, as if he thinks

my concerns are completely useless. "Believe me, if you'd been shot properly, you wouldn't be up and about so soon."

"I'm not touching that thing," I say, staring at the gun.

"You need to -" He pauses, and it's clear that he wasn't expecting me to react like this. "Elizabeth," he continues after a moment, "is there something I should know?" He waits for me to reply. "Is there a specific reason why you don't like guns?" he asks. "It's okay, but I need to know your situation. When two people are out in the wilderness together, they need to know if they can rely on each other." He pauses again. "Can I rely on you, Elizabeth?"

"My brother was shot," I say, turning the gun around and holding it back out for him.

"When?"

"Three days ago."

He stares at me for a moment. "Where is he now?"

"I buried him," I reply, feeling the first tear starting to trickle down my cheek. "I dug a grave in Central Park, and I buried him there. I tried to save him when it happened, but there was nothing I could do. It was a rifle. There was too much damage, and he bled to death." In some weird way, it actually feels good to be explaining what happened. I've run over and over the whole thing a million times in my mind, but it's different now that I'm actually saying things out loud. I'm pretty sure I'm still in shock.

"Who shot him?" Toad asks.

"A man," I say, shivering as I think back to Bob's evil, grinning face. "There was this guy, back in Manhattan. He had all these guns, and he tried to turn my brother into this little soldier. He told him that he had to grow up and be a man, and that the only way to be strong was to have a gun in his hand all the time. He got into his head and made him believe all this crap." I take a deep breath, trying to control my emotions. "He was going to shoot me, too, but I..." Pausing again, I think back to the moment when I plunged the knife into Bob's chest. "I killed him eventually," I say, my voice trembling, "but only after he'd shot my brother."

"You shot him?"

"I stabbed him," I reply, and I can immediately see the look of surprise in Toad's eyes. "He was going to kill me," I continue. "He chased me, and I had nowhere else to go. It was kind of a blur, but..." I pause. "I don't regret it. I hated doing it, but I didn't have a choice. He killed Henry and he was coming for me next."

"Sometimes we have to do what we have to do," Toad replies.

"Have you ever killed anyone?" I ask.

"No," he says. "I would, if I had to, but so

far it's never been necessary. I guess that's one area where you've got more experience than me."

"I wish I didn't," I tell him. It's crazy to think about how much stuff has happened recently. Life seems to be hurtling forward so fast, I can barely stop to think. This time two weeks ago, I was a normal girl living a boring life in Manhattan; this time one week ago, I was with Henry in our apartment and we were waiting for our parents to come home and for the world to get back to normal; now I'm standing in a forest with a man I only met yesterday, and he's trying to get me to carry a gun so that I can defend myself.

"You still need to have a gun out here," Toad says after a moment. "It's just a fact. I'm sorry about what happened to your brother, and I'm sorry you ran into some kind of maniac who thought guns were toys, but there's no reason to be scared. A gun is a tool, just like any other tool. As long as you respect it, and you don't start waving the damn thing around, there's no reason to be scared." He pauses, and for a few seconds I feel as if he's peering directly into my soul. "I wouldn't have invited you out here today," he says eventually, "and I wouldn't be forcing you to carry a gun, if I didn't already know that you're reliable."

"How do you know that?" I ask.

"I can see it in your eyes," he says with a smile. "I don't know if anyone's told you, but I'm a brilliant judge of character. Really, it's almost like a super-power. Guys like Thor and Erikson, I can see through their bullshit. I let them stay for now, but I'm onto them. I know they won't last. The only people around here that I trust are Bridger and Connors." He pauses. "And now you."

"I appreciate what you're saying," I reply, "but -"

"Don't over-think it," he says, taking a step back. "Respect the gun, respect human life, but be ready to defend yourself. Just because some guy misused a gun and killed your brother, don't assume that all guns are bad. Okay? Trust yourself. You can carry a gun, you can even use it if necessary, but it's clear that you're not the kind of person who'd be irresponsible. As I said, I'm good at reading people."

Looking down at the gun, I realize that he's right. Out here, in the middle of nowhere, we could be attacked by wild animals at any moment. "So what's out here?" I ask, looking back at him. "You said this is hostile territory. What does that mean? What are we supposed to be looking out for?"

"There have always been wolves around here," he says. "They don't normally attack, but given the circumstances, I have no intention of taking a risk. Then there are other things, things I don't really understand. I don't like when I meet something I don't understand, so maybe I'm a little over-cautious, but I figure that's better than running blindly into something that might be dangerous."

"You mean the creatures?" I ask.

"You've seen them too?"

"In Manhattan," I reply. "One of them talked to us. It didn't really make much sense, but it was definitely..." I think back for a moment to the creature trapped in the car. "Do you know what's happened?" I ask eventually. "I mean, the world's gone crazy, and I have no idea why. Do you know?"

He shakes his head.

"Do you think it'll ever go back to normal?" I continue.

"After all this?" He pauses. "I doubt it. I saw this coming, and I always knew it was going to be bad when it happened."

"How could you have seen all of *this* coming?" I ask.

"How could you *not*?" he replies.

"It came out of nowhere," I point out. "The power just went off without any warning. Planes fell from the sky. Everything just stopped."

"The world was getting crazier and crazier," he says. "Faster, dirtier, nastier. Civilization has been spinning out of control for too long. People were taking more and more shortcuts, more and more risks. Greed and anger were reaching unsustainable levels. Little accidents were happening everywhere, and I saw the writing on the wall. I had no idea *what* was going to happen, but I knew the shit was gonna hit the fan eventually. That's why I came out here and started to stockpile things. Food, gasoline, water, books. Everything I thought I might need in case the world came crashing down. I didn't make a big fuss about it, 'cause I didn't want people to tell me I was being paranoid, but I quietly got prepared. At times, I wondered if I'd lost my mind, but I kept at it. Looks like I made the right choice, huh? This time two weeks ago, I was a crazy guy living in the middle of nowhere. Now suddenly I look pretty smart."

I stare at him. In a way, he seems like the opposite of Bob. They were both prepared for the possibility of something like this happening, but while Bob became a megalomaniac, Toad seems more rational and calm. It's strange, but I feel safe out here, as if I know that this guy understands the natural world and recognizes the dangers.

"Come on," he says, hauling his backpack over his shoulder. "We've got a lot of ground to cover before the day's over, and I don't think the weather's going to hold forever. There's rain coming from the north, and when that happens, it usually sticks around. We'll just check the traps and get back to the farm."

As we start walking again, I try to stay calm. For the past few years, I've been getting on with my normal life, and it never even occurred to me that things might suddenly just stop. While people like Toad were able to see the way the world was headed, people like me were just running around, blindly assuming that nothing could go wrong. Now that the world has ended up in such a mess, I feel pretty dumb. It's a miracle that I'm one of the few people who managed to survive, but I don't have any skills for this new world. I'm helpless. If it hadn't been for Erikson and Shauna picking me up the other day, I'd probably have died on the journey. My luck can't hold forever, though. Sooner or later, I need to get better at looking after myself and making smart decisions. Still, I can't deny that the gun in my hand makes me feel a little safer. I just wish it didn't remind me of Henry's death.

THOMAS

Missouri

"GET ME OUT OF here!" I scream, banging on the door. "Get me the fuck out of here!"

I wait.

Silence.

"Help!" I scream, banging again. "Someone help me! Someone -" Before I can finish, I'm overcome by a wave of anger and I drop to my knees. I swear to God, if I ever get my hands on that old bastard, I'll kill him. I don't care if he's got a million excuses for doing this, I'll wring the life from his neck. With tears flowing down my cheeks, I try to stop panicking, but it's no use. I feel out of breath, as if there's not enough oxygen down here.

"Let me out!" I scream again. "You can't just

leave me down here!"

ELIZABETH

Pennsylvania

"BAD DAY TO BE a rabbit," Toad says as he reaches into one of the traps and pulls out his latest catch. Turning to me, he smiles. "What's wrong? Don't you eat rabbit in Manhattan?"

"Not really," I say, barely able to look at the poor dead creature. Toad has spent the past few hours checking a series of primitive traps, which are little more than small pits filled with sharp spikes, over which he's been setting thin layers of leaves. A set of small poles mark out the location of each trap, and Toad has been carefully guiding me through the undergrowth in order to ensure that I don't accidentally get my foot spiked.

"There's more meat on these things than

you'd realize," he continues. "I might not like the guy much, but Thor sure knows how to take your basic lump of rabbit meat and make it a little more appetizing. Trust me, we're going to eat well tonight. We've got plenty of vegetables around the back of the farmhouse, and even though a good old slice of rabbit might not seem like much right now, it's pretty damn good food." He pauses. "It's probably better than anything else you can find right now, unless we happen to luck into a deer."

I smile politely, even though the thought of eating rabbit is kind of disturbing. All in all, I feel totally out of place here, and it's as if Toad is going out of his way to remind me that I'm some kind of stuck-up, protected city girl. Sure, I've never caught and cooked a goddamn rabbit before, but that doesn't mean I'm an idiot. It's just that all my skills are linked to things that aren't any use out here. I can build websites and I can draw pretty well, and I'm pretty good at playing the clarinet. A few weeks ago, those things were kinda useful and I felt like I was really learning; now, it's as if I'm back to square one. I don't know how to catch or prepare my own food, so I guess I'm completely dependent upon other people.

"We don't exactly have a lot of choice around these parts," Toad continues, getting to his feet. He glances up at the darkening sky. "Believe it or not, I used to eat rabbit even before the world went to hell." He holds the rabbit up and admires its dead body. "You know how to skin a rabbit?" he asks eventually.

I shake my head.

"You want to learn?"

"Right now?" I ask skeptically.

"When we get back to the farm," he replies. "There's no point skinning it until we're ready to cook. We'll take it home, and then we'll get all the fur away, take out the parts we're not going to use, and season it up before we put it in the oven for a few hours." He smiles as he stares at me, and it's clear that he's enjoying every second of this. "Don't worry," he continues after a moment, as he places the rabbit in a plastic bag, "you don't have to do anything you don't want to do. I'm sure you've got other skills."

"Not particularly," I reply.

"Everyone's got skills," he replies. "I don't believe there's a person ever been born on this planet who can't do *something* better than average." He pauses, and moments later there's the sound of thunder in the distance. "We're due a storm," he says, sounding as if he's concerned. "It's coming in much faster than I expected. We should start heading back to the farm. This isn't the kind of place where you want to be caught out."

"But we don't have enough food," I reply, shocked that one rabbit could feed seven people.

"I brought some extra back over the past couple of days," he says, leading me away from the traps. "We'll be fine. I always like to have a few days' worth of supplies set up in advance, for precisely this kind of situation. Besides, you wouldn't believe how many tins of food I've got in the basement. Seriously, I've got enough food to last for a year, although it'd be a bit of a stretch with a full house."

"So why do you let people stay with you?" I

ask, as the first drops of rain start to fall. "Wouldn't it be better to just hold on to all your resources and wait as long as possible?"

"I'd go crazy," he replies. "Besides, it's a trade. It's useful to have Dr. Connors around in case anything goes wrong. Bridger's good with mechanics, and Thor kind of comes with Bridger. Erikson and his girlfriend aren't really much use, but they're not staying too long. People who stay are here because they've got something to offer, and I offer them shelter in return."

We walk on for a moment. "What about me?" I ask.

"What *about* you?"

"I don't have anything to offer," I point out. "I'm not good at anything."

"I thought you were just passing through," he replies. "Aren't you leaving with Erikson and Shauna in a couple of days?"

"I guess so," I reply. "To be honest, I don't really know where I'm going."

"Well," he says, "where did you come from? If you can work that out, maybe you can work out where you're going. Don't you have any momentum?"

"I have this friend who's heading up to Lake Ontario," I tell him. "I was kind of thinking of going to join her, but I don't know exactly where she'll be, and..." I pause, and finally I realize that even though

I keep telling myself that my destination is Lake Ontario, I have no idea whether that's actually where I'm going. "I guess I'll stick with Erikson and Shauna for a while," I continue. "If they'll let me."

As the rain intensifies, we pause to take shelter under a tree.

"You can stay," Toad says after a moment. "When Erikson and Shauna leave, I mean. I'll let you stay if that's what you want."

"I can't do anything," I remind him.

"You're smart," he says. "I can see that. Smart people are useful. I'm sure you'll demonstrate some kind of skill eventually."

"I've never really been good at anything," I reply.

"Then now's your chance to shine," he says, as the rainfall gets even stronger. "I think I've got us into a bit of a spot here," he continues. "I didn't know the weather was going to be so bad. We can't walk home in this, but it's okay, I know where we can go until it passes." There's a flash of lightning, and a couple of seconds later a rumble of thunder can be heard in the distance. "It's a proper storm," Toad says, leading me back out into the rain. "We can't hide under a tree while there's lightning."

"Where are we going?" I shout, barely able to hear my own voice over the sound of the rain.

"There are caves all around here!" he replies, heading to the left and starting to climb up a narrow bank of soil. "I know this place like the back of my hand, and there's nowhere else to go."

"Caves?" I ask, shocked at the idea. As I struggle to follow him, I slip and slide back down the bank; the second time, I manage to climb up and join him, just as another flash of lightning is accompanied by an almost simultaneous rumble of thunder. "That means it's right above us, doesn't it?" I ask, looking up. "When the thunder and the lightning come at the same time, that's a bad sign, right?"

"It's okay," he replies, grabbing my hand and leading me between the trees. "There's not much further to go."

"How long is this going to last?" I shout.

"The storms stick around sometimes," he replies, barely audible over the sound of rain falling all through the forest. "It's because of the mountains. Don't worry. I've seen worse. I just got caught out by how fast the storm reached us."

"Who's worried?" I reply under my breath, even though I'm already soaking wet and terrified.

A couple of minutes later, we reach the foot of a large stone cliff-face, and Toad leads me around to a gaping entrance. As soon as we're under cover, I pull free from his grip and turn to look out at the raging storm. Rain is still pouring down, and thunder continues to rumble up ahead. For a moment, I'm transfixed by the beauty of what I'm seeing. Having grown up in New York, I've never really been out in the wilderness, and although I'm very much aware that the natural world can be destructive, I can't help but stare in wonder as another arc of lightning lights up the darkening sky.

"It's like the end of the world," I mutter, and it's true. Whatever's happening, it's as if everything is getting worse and worse. I can't shake the feeling that the whole planet seems to be trying to scrub every last human away, and right now it wouldn't be too hard to believe that we're the last living things alive.

"Are you just gonna stand there," Toad asks after a moment, "or are you going to help?"

Turning, I see that he's already got his backpack open, and he's using a small shovel to dig into the ground. I stare for a moment, trying to work out why he'd bother trying to do something so pointless.

"So you just like to watch while other people work, do you?" he asks.

"I'm not like that," I reply, a little annoyed by his tone. "I'm not some kind of New York princess who can't do anything for herself."

"You're not."

"I'm not!"

"But you just said you've got no skills," he replies. "How the hell do you think you're gonna survive long-term if you can't do anything for yourself."

I pause for a moment. "Why are you digging a hole?" I ask eventually.

"I'm not," he says. "I'm creating a small trench so that when I start a fire, air'll be able to get underneath."

"So what do you want *me* to do?" I ask.

"Fetch some wood."

"From where?"

He glances at me, and for a moment he looks as if he thinks I'm an idiot. "Just grab whatever wood you can find close to the cave entrance."

"It'll all be wet," I point out.

"Don't worry," he says. "Just get whatever you can." Grabbing a small ax from his bag, he slides it toward me. "If necessary, hack some branches down, but hurry. We need to get dry."

Hurrying back out into the rain, I struggle to find anything that might be useful, and eventually I start using the ax to chop pieces off a nearby tree. It's hard work, especially since there's almost too much rain for me to be able to keep my eyes open. The whole thing feels totally hopeless, but after a while I manage to swing the ax a little better, and eventually I've got six fairly decent-sized pieces of wood, and I take them back into the cave. Still, they're soaking wet, and I don't see how they can ever be used to start a fire.

DAYS 9 TO 16

"Give me the ax," Toad says as I put the wood on the ground. For the next few minutes, he strips the wet bark from the edges. "The water hasn't gone too deep," he explains, before stripping the bark away and putting the rest of the wood over the pit. "It's not going to be the most spectacular fire in the world, but it'll keep us warm for a few hours and it might even help us to get dry. We don't want to get sick, not when we're so far from home." He pauses. "That's one of the most important things to remember. Things that might just be inconvenient and annoying most of the time, can be fatal right now."

I watch as he pulls some matches and a set of small white cubes from his backpack, and to my surprise he quickly gets a fire going. Immediately kneeling next to the flames and starting to get warm, I look over at Toad and see that he's still working to strip the branches I brought in from the rain. I can't help thinking that if he wasn't with me, I'd have had no idea how to get a fire started; then again, without him, I probably wouldn't have been out here in the first place.

"Oreo?" he says suddenly, reaching into his backpack and pulling out a packet of cookies.

"Seriously?" I reply, stunned that a guy like Toad would carry a packet of Oreos into the wilderness.

"Help yourself," he says with a smile. "I

think the storm has settled in for the day, so we might be stuck here for a few hours. If you don't like Oreos, I can always try to cook the rabbit, but to be honest, I'm hoping things don't get that desperate. It can taste kinda bland without herbs."

As I eat a cookie, I try to stop shivering, but the fire isn't managing to dry my clothes fast enough.

"Take them off," Toad says suddenly, grabbing two of the longer branches and propping them over the fire. "Lay your clothes out on there and they should be dry in an hour or so." Still cutting away at the wood, he smiles as he turns his back to me. "Don't worry," he continues, "I won't look. You can trust me. I'm worried you'll get sick."

"I'm not taking my clothes off!" I say firmly.

"I won't look," he says again. "You're going to get ill if you just sit there like that."

I stare at the back of his head, and finally I start slipping out of my wet clothes. I'm convinced that he's going to 'accidentally' turn around at any moment, but all I can think about is that I desperately need to get dry. Once I'm naked, I sit as close as possible to the fire, and the warmth feels good on my bare skin. At first, I try to crouch into a ball, to keep myself covered up in case he breaks his word and turns around, but eventually I become a little less defensive and I start to sit normally.

"How old are you, anyway?" Toad asks, still

with his back to me.

"Twenty-one," I reply.

"Huh," he says, still working on the branches.

"How old are *you*?" I ask eventually.

"A couple of years older," he replies. "Twenty-eight, to be specific." Without turning to look at me, he reaches back and tosses some more pieces of wood onto the fire, which seems to be burning pretty well. "How's it looking?"

"It's still burning," I tell him.

He doesn't reply. Instead, he continues to cut pieces of wet bark off the rest of the wood I brought from outside.

"It's okay," I say, placing an arm over my chest. "I can cover myself up. You don't have to keep your back to me like that."

"It's not a problem," he replies, still not looking.

"Aren't you wet too?" I ask.

"I'm used to it," he says. "You're not. Besides, I'm wearing waterproofs under my clothes. I'm mostly dry."

I sit in silence for a moment, listening to the sound of the rain. Every few minutes, there's a flash of lightning, accompanied by a rumble of thunder, and right now it's hard to believe that this bad weather is ever going to end. The storm is almost biblical in its intensity, and although I guess there's no reason to be scared, I can't help thinking that this much rain could surely cause some real damage.

"Do you think the world's going to end?" I ask.

"Do you think it hasn't already?" he replies.

I pause.

"It's just different," he continues after a moment. "*Very* different. It's not as easy to survive, but there's no reason why we can't keep going. I don't know why a random bunch of us made it out of whatever happened, but once things have settled down I think we should be able to restore a little order. I doubt it'll ever go back to how things were, though, and I can't say I'm particularly sorry about that. The modern world was getting too dangerous."

"I want it to go back exactly to how it was," I reply. "I want this whole mess to be temporary."

"Here," Toad says after a moment, reaching into his backpack and passing some kind of cloth bundle to me. "I forgot I had this. It's waterproof. At least it'll keep you covered up until your clothes are dry."

Unfolding the bundle, I find that it's a kind of dark blue raincoat. It takes me a moment to get it on, but finally I'm comfortable, albeit a little cold. At least, however, I'm totally dry. "It's okay," I say. "You can look now."

"You sure?"

"I'm sure," I reply with a smile, finding it

kind of cute to see how carefully he's making sure he doesn't see me naked.

He glances over at me.

"See?" I say with a faint smile. "Nothing to be embarrassed about."

"I'm sorry I brought you out here," he replies. "I knew there was rain coming, but I thought it'd take longer to arrive and I had no idea it was going to be so bad. If I'd known, I'd have made you stay behind at the farm. I don't know what's wrong with me. I never make stupid mistakes like this. In all the time I've been out here, I've never let a storm creep up on me."

"It doesn't matter," I point out.

"Of course it matters," he says, seemingly a little annoyed. "Mistakes like this can be fatal. One wrong move, and we could both end up dead. I put us in a huge amount of unnecessary danger." He pauses. "I was careless. I normally double-check these things and make sure I don't take stupid risks. I guess I was just focused on other things today, but I can't let anything like this happen again. This level of rain could cause mud-slides, floods... I can't remember the last time I got things so badly wrong.

"Don't worry about it," I say, finally feeling warm for the first time since we got out of the rain. I reach up and check my clothes, but they're still soaking wet. "It's not your fault that the weather's so bad." I pause for a moment. "So do you mind if I ask you a question? It's kind of personal."

"Is there any way I can stop you?" he replies with a half-smile.

"It's just... Why do people call you Toad?"

He laughs. "It was so long ago," he says. "I was just a kid, and -"

Before he can finish, we're both stunned by the sound of a long, agonized scream, coming from somewhere out in the rain-lashed forest. Lasting for several seconds, the scream is followed by cries of pain and anger.

"What the hell's that?" I ask.

Hurrying to the entrance, Toad stares out into the rain. Whoever's out there, they're still screaming, as if the pain is getting worse.

"Who else is in these woods?" I ask.

"No-one," Toad says, turning back to face me with fear in his eyes. "There's not supposed to be anyone for miles."

"Someone's out there," I say, joining him at the entrance and staring out at the storm-lashed forest. The screams are continuing. In fact, if anything, they're getting worse. Someone's out there, close by, and they're in agony.

THOMAS

Missouri

SLAMMING MY SHOULDER INTO the door with as much force as I can manage, I feel a sharp pain bursting through my body. I quickly drop to the floor, and it's clear that the door is undamaged.

Slowly, I get to my feet. My shoulder feels damaged, but I have to keep trying. I can't stay down here. Even if I have to smash my entire body apart, I'm going to find a way to break through that goddamn door.

"Please," I whisper, "you have to help me. Just give me the strength to do this."

For a moment, I feel as if all my energy is ebbing away. I stare at the metal door and realize that there's no way I can ever force it down.

"Please," I whisper again.

Limping over to the far end of the basement, I turn and stare at the door. Maybe this time I can break it down; maybe this time, God is going to help me. Taking a deep breath, I try to summon every ounce of energy that I've got left, and finally I run screaming across the room, once again throwing myself against the door. All that happens, however, is that I feel my entire body shake, and I drop to the floor in an agonized heap. Finally, I let out a cry of frustration.

I wait.

Right now, I feel as if I can't ever get to my feet. It's over. I'm done.

Eventually, however, I decide that I have to try again. If I'm going to die, it might as well happen while I'm still fighting. Despite the pain in my shoulder and arm, I haul myself to my feet and stagger painfully back over to the far side of the basement. I glance down at the spot where the dead girl's body is covered by sacks, and then I turn to once again face the door.

"Please," I say under my breath, "help me. Just give me the strength I need to get this door open."

I take a deep breath.

"Please."

With that, I run toward the door. I feel as if this time, maybe, I'm going a little faster before. Is it possible that this is going to be my lucky moment? As I slam at full speed into the door, however, I realize that it hasn't worked. Time seems to stand still as my crumpled, fractured body drops to the floor, landing in a heap. It's over. I can't do it again. I'm going to be stuck down here forever.

ELIZABETH

Pennsylvania

"STAY IN THE CAVE!" Toad shouts as he hurries through the rain.

"No way!" I shout back at him as I struggle to keep up. The rain is making it hard to walk, but at least I've got the waterproof coat to keep me somewhat dry. I feel as if I have to stay with Toad, because whatever's happening out here, he might need my help. I've only known the guy for twenty-four hours, but I figure we make a pretty good team, and there's no way I'm letting him run out alone toward a distant scream. I don't know how to survive out here, and I don't know how to get back to the farm, so if Toad dies, I'll be dead too.

"Have you got your gun?" he asks.

"Of course!" I shout, relieved that just as we were leaving the cave I remembered to grab the gun that he gave me earlier.

We make our way between the trees, and although there's still lightning flashing in the sky, it seems as if the storm is no longer directly above us. Still, the rain is lashing down and the sound of the screams is barely audible. We're definitely getting closer, though, and it sounds as if we're only a few meters away from whatever is making that terrible noise. With the sound of the rain all around, however, it's almost impossible to know for sure exactly what's causing the screams, but it definitely seems to be human. It's as if someone somewhere is in great pain, calling out for help and trying desperately to survive. The scream is almost primal.

"Careful!" Toad shouts, grabbing my arm. "I left some traps around here!"

"Maybe someone fell into one," I reply.

"There's not supposed to be anyone out here!" he shouts. "This is private property! There are signs! No-one's allowed on my land!"

"Maybe signs worked before," I point out, "but things have changed."

"We're miles from the nearest town," he continues. "There can't be anyone here! People know better than to come onto my land!"

"Over there!" I shout, spotting a bare patch where the forest floor seems to have collapsed, leaving a small pit. It looks like one of Toad's traps, and while it's not very big, I guess a human could fall down out of sight if he was unlucky. In that case, the spikes at the bottom of the pit are almost certainly the reason for such agonized screams. I don't care what Toad says: someone has come out here and ended up in one of his traps.

"Stay behind me," Toad says, taking his gun from its holster. "Let me handle this. Whatever's happening out here, you need to let me take the lead? Do you understand?"

I nod.

"Do you *promise*, Elizabeth?" he continues. "If you make one wrong move, you could put us both in danger. I need to know that I can trust you, and that you'll do what I say."

"I promise," I say.

With his gun still drawn, Toad starts to approach the pit. Thanks to all the rain that has come down over the past few hours, the ground is extremely slippery, so we both move carefully until finally we're able to look down into the pit and see that there's a figure down there, partially impaled on one of the wooden spikes that Toad has been using to catch animals. The figure's struggling, trying desperately to get free, but the spike is passing straight through his torso.

"What is it?" I ask, stunned by the sight of the struggling, screaming figure.

"It's one of them," Toad replies.

As I look closer, I realize that he's right. It's one of the creatures that I saw back in New York, and although its body is showing signs of decomposition, it seems to be holding together a little better than the creature that Henry and I met in the car. After struggling for a moment, the creature turns and looks up at us. His face is a kind of yellow-blue color, and one of his eyes is missing, but there's a smile on his lips and it's clear that he's capable of recognizing that he's being watched.

"Clever!" the creature shouts. "What can I say? I was careless, and you got me!"

"It's like he's partially decomposing," Toad says, shocked by what he's seeing. "I've only seen them properly from a distance before. I always destroy them before they can get anywhere near me."

"I've seen one close up," I reply. "It looked the same."

"Aren't you going to help?" the creature shouts. "I'm still learning to ignore the pain from each individual body that I'm controlling. It's not easy."

"Ask him what's happening," I whisper.

"Quiet!" he hisses.

"There are more of me," the creature continues. "You know that, don't you? I can't even begin to tell you how many bodies I can control right now. Billions. It's not easy, learning how to make them all do what I want, dividing my mind into so many different perspectives, but I'm slowly making improvements." He stares directly at me. "I recognize you," he says after a moment. "Manhattan. I saw you. You and some kid shot me. That was at the start, but I'm much better now." As if to prove his point, he starts easing his rotten body off the spike. "There aren't many survivors left," he continues, grimacing as he continues with his attempt to get free. Slowly, he starts sliding the wood out from his chest.

"Shoot him!" I shout at Toad.

"You can't shoot all of us," the creature says. "There aren't enough bullets in the world. Shoot me, and I'll be back sooner rather than later. I know where you are, and I'm already making my way toward this place in other bodies. Why bother fighting? There's no way you can get away from me. I'm everywhere, like God."

"Shoot him!" I say again, desperate to make sure that there's no way this creature can get to us.

"I want to know what he wants," Toad replies.

"I'll do it," I say, pulling the gun from my pocket.

"No!" Toad says firmly, grabbing my arm. "I told you to let me take the lead!"

"You have to kill this thing!" I reply.

"I will," he says, "but I want to learn why it's here first."

"Don't you want to know where this all came from?" the creature asks, still sliding off the spike, which has made a large hole in his chest. "Don't you want to know how I could be in all these bodies at once? One mind, controlling so many physical forms. It's a work of genius, really. I haven't managed to really explain it to anyone yet, and I'd like to hear someone else's view of my brilliance before I finish off the last of the survivors. Would the pair of you be willing to act as my audience? It's such a tragedy to pull off such a wonderful scheme without having anyone to see what I'm doing. It never occurred to me that I'd want an audience. I guess I'm a little more proud than I'd like to admit."

"What are you waiting for?" I ask, turning to Toad. "Kill it!"

"So much blood-lust in such a pretty young woman," the creature says with a smile. "I like it. You're a lot better than the ones who just scream."

"I want to know everything," Toad says, with his gun still aimed at the creature. "I want to know what caused all this."

"Of *course* you want to know," the creature replies. "You want to convince yourself that there's still a chance you might stop it. Do you really see yourselves as heroes? Billions of people around the planet are infected with a virus that, as far as I know, can't possibly be defeated. It's only a matter of time before the rest of you pathetic creatures can be picked off, and then this planet will have reached its evolutionary zenith. Billions of organisms, all of them with one unified soul. Isn't that better than having loads of pesky individuals, butting heads with one another? At least this way, we can cooperate. Everyone will be the same. Once I've picked off the last few survivors, anyway."

"What are you?" Toad asks, keeping his gun aimed down into the pit.

"How about you help me up from here?" the creature replies. "I'll be happy to explain everything before I kill you. You'll be the lucky ones. You'll get to know what's happening before you die. Then again, maybe that makes you the unlucky ones instead."

"You're not making any sense," Toad replies. "How about you tell us, nice and simply, what the hell you are. Stop talking in riddles, stop dancing around the subject, and just tell us the truth."

"As far as I can tell," the creature continues, "this body used to be a mountain ranger of some kind. Definitely something linked to law enforcement. He died in a cabin, a few miles away, just on the edge of your property. He was a very fit young man, which is useful, but he had another use.

Would you care to guess what it is? Do you have any idea why I was so pleased to get control of this particular body?"

"No-one's doing any guessing," Toad says firmly.

"Fine," the creature continues. "I'll show you." With that, he switches his position a little, and I realize that he's got a gun in his left hand; before I can react, a shot rings out.

Instinctively ducking out of the way, I land hard on the forest floor. As Toad lands next to me, I turn and see that there's a huge red wound in his left shoulder, and his eyes look empty and glassy. For a fraction of a second, I'm convinced that he's dead, but then he lets out a gasp and a pained groan, and I realize that there's still just about some hope.

"The fucker had a gun!" the creature shouts from the bottom of the pit, firing several more times into the air. "Can you believe my luck? There was a gun in his hand when he died! I didn't even have to pick it up! I just took over his body and there it was, already clutched in his delicate little hand!"

"Are you okay?" I ask, watching as Toad blinks a couple of times. With the rain continuing to fall, much of the blood from his shoulder wound is already starting to flood down onto the forest floor. He opens his mouth, as if he's trying to say something, but the effort is too much. He might be alive now, but he won't be for much longer unless I can find a way to staunch the flow of blood and patch him up properly. For a fraction of a second, I can't help thinking back to the moment a few days ago when I watched Henry die. Is the same thing about to happen again?

Panicking, I reach into the pocket of the waterproof coat and take out my gun. I check that the safety catch is off, and then I decide that I've only got one chance here. Filled with anger, I listen for a moment to the sound of the creature laughing in the pit, and then I step forward and fire straight into its face. The first shot blows one side of its head clean away, and as it slumps back down against the spike I fire again and again, and finally three more times until the gun clicks and I realize that I'm out of bullets. I stand and stare for a moment, convinced that the damn thing is going to still be alive, but finally I realize that I've blown its head apart. There's no hint of life, and no more movement other than a trickle of blood flowing from the neck. Still feeling breathless, I look down at the gun and realize that my hands are shaking.

With rain still falling all around me, I put the gun back into my pocket and hurry over to Toad. As soon as I kneel next to him and check his pulse, I realize that he's still alive, but he's bleeding heavily. For a moment, all I can do is stare at him, as if my mind has completely frozen. Finally, however, I realize that I have to do something. If I just sit here and wait, he's going to die, the same way that Henry died. I might not have much of a chance, but at least I have to *try* to save him. There's got to be a way.

"Can you hear me?" I ask, trying not to panic.

He opens his mouth, but no words come out.

"What do I do?" I continue. "You've been shot in the shoulder. What am I supposed to do? How do I fix it?"

For a moment, he seems to be trying to say something, but the effort is clearly too much.

"I'm taking you back to the cave," I say, struggling to pick him up. At first, I figure that there's no way I'm strong enough to carry him, but finally, somehow, I'm able to get to my feet while holding him in my arms. The effort require to carry him is immense, and I feel as if I'm going to collapse at any moment, but finally I start staggering across the forest floor, heading back the way we came. I don't know what the hell I'm going to do, but I have to try to do *something*. Three days ago, I lost my brother to a gunshot wound, and there's no way I'm going to let someone else die. If it's the last thing I ever do, I'm going to find a way to save Toad and get us back to the farm.

By the time we reach the cave, however, I'm almost ready to collapse. I place Toad on the ground, out of the rain, as I realize that the fire has already burned out. There's a rumble of thunder high above, and I look down at Toad's face, hoping for a sign of life.

"Wake up!" I shout, with tears running down my face. "You have to wake up!"

No response.

Reaching down, I check his pulse. To my surprise, I realize that he's not dead yet, even though he's lost a lot of blood. Still, he's unconscious, and he clearly doesn't have much time left. I know I should do *something*, but I'm scared that I'll just make everything worse. Blood is still flowing from his wound, and he's starting to look pale. If the situation was reversed, he'd know what to do; he'd fix me up and get us back to the farm. I'm useless, though. I don't know the sfirst thing about saving someone from a gunshot wound.

Outside, the rain seems to be falling more heavily than ever, and lightning is still arcing across the sky in the distance. I have to do something. I have to save Toad, and then I have to make sure that we get back to the farm. Right now, however, I feel as if I'm frozen in place. This is what happened when Henry died. I failed him, and I'm going to fail Toad. I'm no use in a crisis, and I can't even begin to save the life of someone who's been shot. He's going to die right here in front of me, and then I'll be trapped alone here, lost in the wilderness. It's over. I'm going to die out here.

THOMAS

Missouri

SITTING IN THE CORNER of the basement, with my back to the wall, I stare across at the dead body by the far wall. I've been over here in this corner for hours now, too scared to move, but I can't take my eyes of the horrific sight that I uncovered when I pulled the sacks away. I swear to God, this whole house is the creepiest, weirdest place in the world.

"Please," I whisper for the thousandth time, "get me out of here." I've spent the past few hours praying, desperately hoping that God might take pity on me and find a way to get the door open. Then again, God hasn't been much in evidence lately. Why would He allow the world to go to hell like this? Why would he let my parents die, and my brother, and all those other people whose bodies I've seen? Why would he let that Lydia woman die in such a painful and horrible way? I want to believe that there's some kind of plan here, that the world hasn't just fallen into chaos, but right now it's as if everything is falling apart.

Finally, after hours and hours of doing nothing, I get to my feet and start walking toward the far corner, where the dead body is partially uncovered. I've been putting this moment off for as long as possible, I figure I need to take a look and try to work out what happened. I've seen a hell of a lot of dead bodies over the past week, but I'm still not used to the damn things. Then again, as I get closer, I realize that this body is different to the others. She's not bloated or decomposed, and she doesn't seem fresh. In fact, if I had to guess, I'd say she's been dead for a hell of a long time. Years, maybe even decades.

Although my gut instinct is to turn and run, I crouch next to the body and stare at her face. Her mouth is open in a kind of twisted scream, and although her eyes have long since shriveled up, I'm pretty sure she was staring up at something. Her skin is totally dry and gnarled, and her limbs are almost like the roots of a tree. There's some long black hair still attached to the top of her head, and I can't help noticing that part of her neck looks to have been damaged, as if it's been eaten away. She's too far gone for me to be able to tell what killed her, or even how old she was when she died, but as I stare at her face, I'm overwhelmed for a moment by a feeling of pity.

Reaching down to the cloth sacks, I pull them away from her feet and see that there's a pair of iron chains still attached to her ankles. Did she also happen to stumble upon this house, many years ago? Did the old man capture her, the same way he captured me, and keep her down in this basement until she died? I've been assuming until this moment that the old man's madness has to be connected with everything else that's going on in the world, but what if it's completely separate? What if this girl was captured back when the world was normal? What if he just likes to leave people to die in his basement? Turning to look over at the door, I suddenly realize that maybe he isn't ever coming back.

DAY 12

ELIZABETH

Pennsylvania

FRANTICALLY TIPPING THE CONTENTS of Toad's bag onto the ground, I immediately see that as well as some food, he was also carrying what appears to be a set of bandages. Sure enough, I quickly find not only the bandages, but also a pair of scissors, some cotton swabs, and a small bottle that I'm hoping contains something I can use to clean the wound. He definitely came prepared.

"What do I do?" I ask, desperately hoping that toad might wake up and give me some advice. He seems like the kind of guy who'd have no problem performing a spot of battlefield surgery. If this was the other way around and I was the one who'd been shot, he'd have patched me up by now;

unfortunately, *his* life is in *my* hands and I'm the worst person in the world to have to do something like this.

He's going to die. Just like Henry.

I look over at him and see that he's still breathing, but only just. It's dark, but I've managed to get the fire going again. Having realized that we were both in danger of dying of exposure, I copied everything that Toad did earlier: I whittled away the wet bark from some pieces of wood, and I used some of his matches to get the fire restarted. I swear to God, it's the first really practical thing I've ever done, and I cried with joy when I realized that the fire was going to last. Sure, it might not last all night, but I've got more wood and I'm hoping I can manage to keep us warm.

"Okay," I mutter, carrying the medical supplies past the fire and kneeling next to Toad. "Now what?" I wait in vain for a reply. "If you can just wake up for a moment," I continue, "I can follow any instructions you give me. Please..." Reaching out, I gently tap his chest, hoping against hope that he might be strong enough to talk.

Silence.

The wound on his left shoulder appears to have stopped bleeding, but as I carefully peel his shirt away, I realize that there's more damage than I'd expected. It almost looks as if someone punched a fist-sized hole in the top of his arm, and for a moment I feel as if there's absolutely no way I can ever do anything to help. I hate the sight of blood, and as I peer closer at the wound, illuminated only a little by the light of the fire, I can't help thinking back to the injury that killed Henry. It's all happening again, except this time I'm going to try to do something.

"I'll take the bullet out," I say, looking at Toad's unconscious face. "I don't know if you can hear me, but I think I can see it, so I'm going to try to pull it out."

No reply.

"It's going to hurt," I add. "I don't know if you can feel pain right now, but I doubt I can do this cleanly, okay? It's going to..." I pause as I stare at the fleshy mess caused by the bullet, with blood glistening in the firelight and pieces of torn skin and meat around the edges. "It's *really* going to hurt," I continue. "Like, more than anything in the world. But I haven't got a choice."

Taking a deep breath, I grab the small bottle and open the lid, before splashing some of the liquid onto the wound. It smells strong and medical, so I'm going to assume that the wound is not sterile. I take the scissors and hold the blade in the flames for a moment, figuring that this should help to avoid any kind of infection, and then I take a closer look at the wound. I'm not certain, but I think I can see something dark and metallic deep in the flesh, and I can only assume that I'm looking directly at the bullet. In a way, the whole thing is strangely, beguilingly simple.

"Fuck," I mutter, realizing that there's no point hesitating.

I pause.

Why haven't I started yet?

I guess it's because I think he's going to die. While I'm preparing to do this, I can fool myself into thinking that there's a chance I might save him; somehow, I might turn out to have amazing, hidden surgical skills. The truth, though, is that there's very little hope. The most likely outcome is that I'll poke around in the wound a little, and then he'll die, and then I'll be left all alone out here.

"You can do this," I say out loud, hoping to build up my confidence even though my hands are shaking. Focusing for a moment, I manage to steady myself, and finally I realize that I have to get started.

Slowly, I open the scissors and slip the tips into the wound. Once I close them again, I realize that the black object is definitely made of metal. I make sure to get a good grip, and then I carefully try to pull the bullet out. To my surprise, it comes out fairly easily, although once I get a good look at it, I realize that the tip appears to have shattered, which means there are probably fragments deeper in the wound. I stare at the bullet stub for a moment, and it's as if my brain has frozen. There has to be a way to fix this, but at the same time, there's no way I can start digging deeper into Toad's shoulder.

Dropping the damaged piece of metal onto the ground, I peer more closely at the wound. I can just about spot what appears to be a bullet fragment, so I press the scissors into the wound, but Toad immediately lets out a faint groan and I sit back.

"Can you hear me?" I ask.

No reply.

"Please," I continue, close to tears. "You have to wake up. You have to tell me what I'm doing wrong."

I wait, but he doesn't reply.

Reaching the scissors into the wound again, I manage to get hold of the fragment and pull it out, and this time Toad doesn't respond. As I drop the second fragment, I look into the wound and see several more small pieces, but it's clear that the tip of the bullet was completely shattered, which means there's no way I'll ever be able to get every piece out.

"I can't do this," I say, my voice trembling. "If you can hear me, I swear to God, I did my best, but I can't do everything. You need a proper doctor."

Finally, I decide that all I can do is try to patch him up and then hope that he can survive until we get back to the farm. After all, Patricia's a doctor, so she should be able to help. Grabbing the bandages, I find that they each come with a small roll of adhesive tape. They seem woefully inadequate for covering such a major injury, but I don't have anything else, so I pour a little more of the sterilizing liquid onto the wound before finally placing the first bandage directly over the gaping hole in Toad's shoulder. I struggle for a while, trying to get the pad to stay on firmly, but eventually I manage to get it properly sited and I sit back.

I did it.

Sure, it's not perfect, and he's not out of danger, but I managed to remove the bullet, sterilize the wound and fix a bandage to hopefully prevent any further damage. I have no way of knowing for sure whether what I've done is actually going to save Toad, but I figure it can't hurt. I did my best, and at least he's still breathing. I have no doubt that he'd have died if I'd just left him alone, so all I can do is pray that somehow he's able to pull through. I guess there's a chance. At the very least, I've minimized the risk of infection. I just have to hope that I've done enough.

Looking down at my hands, I see that there's blood all over my fingers. I glance over at the fire and realize that it's still burning fairly well. I have no idea what time it is, but the rain is still falling outside and the sun has been down for a few hours.

Hopefully the rain will stop soon and sunrise will help me to work out which way we need to go in order to reach the farm. It's not exactly going to be an easy journey, but at least I'm starting to feel that there's a chance for us to survive. I remember where the sun rose this morning in relation to the farm, so I figure I might be able to work out roughly which way we need to go in the next few hours.

Walking over to the cave entrance, I stare out at the darkness. I have no way of knowing if another of those creatures is in the area, and even if we're alone, I doubt things will stay that way for long. I keep thinking back to the way the creature talked about coming after us, and it's hard not to imagine more of them - maybe hundreds, maybe even thousands - making their way toward us right now. Maybe we can ignore the danger for now, but sooner or later we're going to have to fight. Up until this moment, I've been allowing myself to dream that somehow the world is going to get put back to normal eventually. Finally, however, I'm starting to realize that things might never be the same again.

THOMAS

Missouri

ONCE I'VE PLACED THE cloth sacks back over the dead girl's body, I sit for a moment and try to work out what to do next. It's been more than twenty-four hours since I last heard from the old man, and I've managed to survive a whole night down here with the girl's body. Maybe I'm going crazy down here, but I feel as if she and I are somehow connected. After all, we've both ended up down here, and even though the rest of the world seems to have forgotten about her entirely, I figure that if I'm the one who happens to have stumbled onto her dead body, then it must be my responsibility to try to show her some respect.

Reaching into my pocket, I try to find

something I can use as a cross, but there's nothing. This whole damn situation is so far beyond normality, there's no way to mark the girl's resting place. Then again, I figure maybe I can move her. If I ever manage to get out of this basement, I'm going to dig a proper grave and put the girl's body where it belongs, and then I'm going to make a cross and mark her final resting place. It's not much, and she deserves much more, but it's all I can do right now.

At least she's not like those creatures I saw the other day. They were bloated and decomposing, but they were alive. I'm no expert, but I'm pretty sure that this mummified girl is just a corpse. There's no way she's going to come back to life, although maybe in some strange way I wouldn't mind if I could talk to her. I could ask her how she ended up down here, and what the old man did to her, and why she was never able to escape. I guess I'm finally losing my mind.

"Dear Lord," I mutter, putting my hands together in prayer, "I'm not gonna ask you why you did this, but I want to ask you to look after this girl's soul. Make sure she's right, and don't make her suffer. It's not her fault that she wasn't buried properly, so I don't think it's right that she should go to Hell or anything like that. If you can just wait a bit, I promise I'll put her in the ground properly. It's just gonna take a bit of time, that's all."

Silence.

"Amen," I add, before opening my eyes.

Damn it, have I lost my mind? I feel as if I don't know how to react to anything right now. I should be terrified of the girl's body, but somehow I'm not; instead, I feel drawn to her, as if she's my only friend in the world. I want to talk to her, to ask her about her life, to tell her that everything's going to be okay. I guess I'm going crazy, but for some strange reason, I feel as if I owe this girl a proper burial. Even if I can't get myself to safety, I'm damn well gonna get out of this basement and dig a grave for her somewhere. I swear to God, if that old man *ever* opens that door again, I'll get him. I don't know how I'll do it yet, but I'll kill him.

Just as I'm about to go back over to the other side of the basement, I realize that I haven't actually touched the girl's body yet. Normally, that would be a good thing, but I feel as if I should at least touch her once, just so that she knows she's not alone. Taking a deep breath, I lift up one of the sacks and see her mummified hand. Slowly, I reach down and brush one of my fingers against her dry, wrinkled skin. It's not much, but I figure she probably spent her last days in pain and misery, desperately hoping that someone would come and save her. No-one came, but at least I arrived eventually.

I try to work out what Joe would do in a situation like this. He'd probably have spent the whole night screaming and banging on the door, which is kind of what I did, but I can't help thinking that eventually he'd have come up with a plan. He'd have stayed angry and he'd have damn near ripped that door away. Then again, Joe was pretty strong, whereas I've always been kinda weedy. Joe would never even have got us into this mess in the first place. He'd have kept his guard up more, and he'd have made sure that no old man could ever get the jump on us. At least when Joe was around, I felt that we could manage, but now I feel as if it's only a matter of time before I die.

Once I'm back in the far corner, I can't help wondering if I'm going to end up like that girl. One day, will someone else be trapped down here, and will they find both of our bodies? For the first time, I feel as if I've got no hope at all.

ELIZABETH

Pennsylvania

AS SOON AS THE sun rises, I start getting ready for the journey back to the farm. The fire lasted most of the night, and my clothes - although a little smoky - are now dry. I get changed quickly, refill Toad's backpack as best I can, and then finally I kneel next to him and check his pulse. He's still alive, and there's no sign of a fever. With the rain having passed, I figure I just have to get him home as fast as possible. It's not going to be easy.

Based on the position of the sun, I figure the farm is somewhere beyond the line of trees directly facing the cave. It takes me a couple of minutes to gather Toad up in my arms. He's not particularly heavy, but I'm the kind of person who's never really had to carry anything heavier than a fully-loaded shopping bag, and even then I complained all the way home. I can feel my body struggling to hold Toad's weight, but I can't leave him in the cave, so I start to slowly stagger out into the forest.

Within a couple of meters, my feet slip on the wet leaves and I crash to the ground, with Toad landing on top of me. My first thought is that I might have made his injury worse, but he seems to be okay. I crawl out from under him and get ready to pick him up again, but at the last moment I'm struck by the realization that I can't do this. Sure, it'd be great if I had the strength to carry the guy for hours and hours, all the way back to the farm, but I physically can't, and there's no point getting us both killed just because I want to prove a point. I can move faster if I'm alone, and I figure I can get Patricia and bring her back here.

After I've placed Toad back in the cave, I work on getting the fire restarted. I use his technique to strip wet bark from the wood, and finally - after not too much effort - I get the fire going. I arrange him as close as I dare, and then I turn and hurry out of the cave. I don't have long, and I need to get back here with help well before nightfall.

The journey back to the farm is long and slow, and at times I'm not certain that I know the right way. At the same time, I'm careful to make sure that I know how to find the cave again. After all, there's no point making my way back and finding Patricia and the others, only to discover that I've no idea how to get us back to Toad. Hurrying through the forest, I force myself to cling to the hope that somehow, through some kind of miracle, I might actually manage to save Toad and prove that I can survive in hard times. The odds are low, but I can't give up just yet. I have to keep trying.

After several hours, I emerge from the trees and finally spot the farm in the valley below. For a few seconds, I stand and stare at the miraculous sight, barely able to believe that it's real. Hurrying down the side of the hill, I finally reach the front door and race inside to find Bridger standing in the kitchen, rolling dough.

"Where the hell have you two been?" he asks, before I see a hint of realization in his eyes. "Where's Toad?"

"He's hurt," I say breathlessly. "I need Patricia."

"In the store-room," he replies.

Racing past him, I run along the corridor and into the store-room. I pull up short as I see that Patricia is over in the corner with Thor, who's got his hand under her shirt, fondling her breasts.

"Elizabeth!" Patricia shouts, pushing Thor away and hurrying over to me, while also re-buttoning her shirt. "What's wrong? What happened out there?"

"It's Toad," I say, trying to stay calm. "He's hurt. I tried to help him, but you've got to come!"

"I'll grab my bag," she replies, hurrying out into the corridor.

"What did you do to him?" Thor asks, clearly annoyed at having his little session interrupted.

"One of the creatures shot him," I say, turning to follow Patricia before Thor grabs my shoulder and pulls me back toward him. "Get the hell off me!" I shout.

"I'm not gonna hurt you," he says quietly, refusing to loosen his grip. "I just want to make sure you realize that you owe me. Dr. Connors was gonna give me something nice just now. It's only fair that you compensate me for the loss. How about tonight?"

"Go fuck yourself," I say, pulling away and running out into the corridor.

"Maybe tomorrow, then!" Thor shouts after me. "But soon, okay?"

As soon as Patricia has got her medical kit together, she and I head back out to the forest. I explain everything as we go, filling her in on the encounter with the creature. She seems to find it a little hard to believe at first, and it's almost as if she doesn't quite trust me, but eventually she starts to accept that the story, however improbable, is exactly what happened. She's also worried that I don't know the way to the caves, and she keeps trying to lead me to some other set of caves that she thinks must be the ones we're looking for, but I'm adamant that I know the way and, sure enough, after a couple of hours we reach the small clearing next to the cave where I left Toad. The fire is still just about burning, and there's no sign that the scene has been disturbed while I was away.

"He's alive," Patricia says as she kneels next to him. Opening her medical bag, she immediately gets to work checking the wound on Toad's shoulder. Whereas I worked slowly and tentatively, she clearly knows what she's doing, and there's something reassuring about watching her deal with the problem.

"I did the best I could," I tell her, terrified that I might have made things worse. "I took the bullet out, but I think there are still pieces in there."

"You did good," she replies, grabbing a pair of tweezers from her bag. She dips the tip into a small bottle of sanitizer, before pouring the rest onto the wound. Finally, she starts extracting the last of the bullet fragments. "We have to get them all out," she tells me as she works. "Even the slightest piece could kill him later." Working in silence for a few minutes, she eventually sets the tweezers aside and grabs some tapes and gauze from her bag.

"What are you going to do?" I ask.

"We need to close the wound for the journey back," she explains. "Then it's just a matter of keeping it sterile and letting it heal."

I watch as she finishes her work. Within a few minutes, she's managed to get the wound dressed, and it looks a thousand times more secure and effective than the patchwork effort that I put together.

"Is he going to be okay?" I ask.

"He's going to be fine," she replies, before turning to me. "Show me the creature."

"Why?" I ask.

"I want to see it."

"Shouldn't we get going?"

"Show me the creature," she says again. "Or do I have to go wandering around out there until I find it?"

"There are traps," I reply. "I'll show you the way."

It takes a few minutes for us to reach the clearing where the creature fell into the trap. Sure enough, when we look down into the pit, the creature's body is still down there, although its carcass has been almost completely covered by rainwater.

"You destroyed its head?" Patricia asks after a moment.

I nod.

"That always seems to stop them," she replies, clearly lost in thought. "I guess the key is to separate the brain from the rest of the body. They're actually not that difficult to bring down, and most of them aren't even that fast." Kneeling next to the edge of the pit, she leans a little closer.

"Be careful," I say. "Can't we just leave it alone?"

"Toad never lets me go near them after we've killed them," she replies. "While he's incapacitated, I figure I might as well get a better look." Suddenly, with no warning, she starts climbing down into the pit, and soon she's examining the creature's corpse directly. She picks up a piece of its skull that has been floating in the rainwater, and carefully she scrapes a piece of brain matter away from the bone.

"What are you doing?" I hiss. "You have to get out of there!"

"It's dead," she replies firmly. "There's no risk of infection, either. I've seen people touch these things and avoid getting sick. As far as I can tell, those of us who've survived are simply immune to whatever virus is causing this to happen." She examines the stump where the creature's head used to be. "The decomposition process didn't stop," she says after a moment. "Eventually, this thing would have just rotted away. Unless the creatures can reproduce, which I highly doubt is possible, there's no way they can last more than a few weeks."

"So they'll just die off?" I ask.

She pauses. "I'd like to think so, but I also know that wherever there's a problem, life always finds a way. These things are intelligent, and I wouldn't be surprised if they've got some kind of plan. New lifeforms don't just spring up and then die away. There has to be a mechanism for them to keep going. Then again, maybe that's not what's happening here. These things didn't evolve. They were just suddenly here, which means someone created them."

"You shouldn't be down there," I continue. "You might get it."

"Get what?" She smiles. "You think the nasty monster is gonna convert me, huh?"

"What if it's like a virus?" I ask.

"I'm a doctor," she replies. "Do you seriously think I'm dumb enough to take a risk like that?" She pauses. "I've touched one of these things before, Elizabeth. Before I reached the farm, one of the creatures attacked me. Hell, it even scratched my arm and drew blood. I was terrified. I thought I'd turn into one of them, but eventually I realized that's not how it works."

"It's still dangerous," I tell her.

"What do you think's gonna happen?" she asks. "You think it's gonna infect me by magic? Don't be superstitious, Elizabeth. I'm starting to get a good idea of how these things work. If we're going to stop them permanently, we need to address the situation rationally. I'm not squeamish." She starts examining the creature again, using a small scalpel to cut away a section of skin and meat from its shoulder, before placing the specimen in a small plastic pouch that she slips into her pocket.

"You're taking part of it back to the farm?" I ask.

"Gotta have a souvenir," she replies with a smile.

"I think they've all got the same mind," I tell her.

She looks up at me. "That's impossible," she says after a moment.

"This creature remembered seeing me in New York," I reply. "It remembered everything that had happened to the other creature. It even talked about having to control so many different bodies. It's as if there's one mind, and it's in every one of these things. The other one, the one I heard talking in New York, mentioned something about being able to see people in Tokyo."

"I don't get it," Patricia replies. "How does that even work?"

"It's like there's one mind that's looking out at the world through hundreds or millions of pairs of eyes," I explain. "I know that sounds crazy, but all these creatures seem to have the same mind. I can't even begin to explain it, but I've heard two of them talking now, and they've both admitted it."

"We'll need a live specimen if we're going to work out what the hell's going on," she says, climbing out of the pit. "Toad thinks it's too dangerous, but it's *more* dangerous to be ignorant. It's a pity you killed this one, Elizabeth. It looks as if it was trapped already."

"He shot Toad!" I point out, annoyed that she thinks I did something wrong. "The damn thing had a gun!"

"Still," she replies, "it would have been useful to have studied it first." She pauses. "You did the right thing, though. You did really well here, Elizabeth. Toad almost certainly would have died if you hadn't been here to help him. You saved his life." She puts a hand on my shoulder. "So, are you up for the journey back. If you take Toad's feet, I'll take his shoulders. It's not going to be easy, but we can reach the farm before sundown."

"Sure," I say, and we start walking back toward the cave. I can't help wondering if Patricia's right. Did I really save Toad's life?

"You okay?" she asks.

"I'm fine," I reply, even though it's not really true. I feel as if my mind is blocking out as many of my thoughts and emotions as possible, leaving me with nothing but a kind of blank, empty fog in my mind; at the same time, all those emotions are still inside me somewhere, and I'm scared that eventually they'll burst loose and I'll be overwhelmed.

THOMAS

Missouri

"PLEASE," I WHISPER, SITTING by the door, hoping against hope that maybe the old man is on the other side, listening to me. "Let me out. I just want to get out of here. I'll do anything you want, but you have to let me out."

Silence.

"Please," I say again, with tears in my eyes. "You can't leave me down here. You can't just leave me to die. Why would you do that? I can help you. I can do things. Anything you need, just tell me and I'll get it done. All you have to do is feed me and give me water."

I wait.

"Just let me know that you're alive," I

continue, trying to keep my voice from trembling. It's crazy, but as much as I hate the old man, I desperately need him to come back for me. "You don't have to tell me about the girl down here. I really don't care, and it's not like I'm gonna tell anyone. Just let me out of here, and I won't give you any trouble. I promise."

No reply.

"What did I do?" I ask, hoping against hope that God might be able to hear me. "I tried to do everything right. I tried to make Joe do the right thing. It's not my fault that everyone died, so why are you punishing me?" Pausing fora moment, I realize that although I keep waiting for an answer, there might be another explanation. Maybe God doesn't exist after all. Why would he punish so many innocent people? Why would he leave this man alive, and let him lock me down in his basement? I want to keep believing, but at the moment it's too hard. The whole world just seems cruel and empty.

As tears pour down my face, I try to keep from sobbing. The truth is, I'm starting to think that there's no way I'll ever get out of this basement. Either by accident or on purpose, the old man has left me to die down here, just like he left that girl to die, and no-one's ever going to come and find me. I'm going to starve, or I'll die from lack of water. It's going to be slow, and it's going to be painful, and eventually all that'll be left of me will be a withered corpse, just like the girl.

ELIZABETH

Pennsylvania

"HEY," TOAD SAYS LATER that day, as I enter his room back at the farm. He's laid out on his bed, and although he seems weak, at least he's conscious. "I guess I owe you."

"How are you feeling?" I ask, wandering over and looking down at the blood-stained bandages on his shoulder.

"I've been better," he replies. "Never actually been shot before, so that's a first. I always wondered what it'd feel like, and now I know. It feels like crap."

Smiling, I sit on the old wooden chair next to his bed.

"It's definitely a story to tell people," he

continues. "The day I was shot by a zombie. I don't suppose you saved the bullet, did you?"

"Sorry," I reply. "I left it in the cave."

"Damn," he says, "that would have been a hell of a trophy." He pauses. "So Dr. Connors tells me that you basically performed some minor surgery on my shoulder. Without that, I probably would have died out there."

"You'd have been fine," I tell him.

"I don't think so. I'd probably have bled to death, and even if I hadn't, I'd have ended up with an infection." Sitting up, he grimaces with pain for a moment. "We've got painkillers," he continues, "but I don't want to use them up. I can handle this."

I smile politely, but I'm not really sure what to say. The whole experience out there in the forest has left me feeling kind of stunned, and even though I haven't slept for the best part of a couple of days, I'm totally wired and wide awake.

"So what's wrong?" Toad asks eventually. "You just spent two days in the wilderness, you faced down a goddamn zombie, and you saved a guy's life, but you look like something's bothering you."

"It's just..." I pause, wondering whether or not I should really say this to him. "I keep thinking about how I saved you," I continue after a moment, "and I can't stop thinking about my brother. If I'd done the same thing back then, maybe he'd still be alive. Maybe I'd have been able to save his life."

"You can't think like that," Toad replies.

"But it's true! What if he didn't need to die! What if someone smarter, someone better at this kind of thing, could have kept him alive?" I wait for him to say something, but I can see in his eyes that he knows I'm right. "Ever since Henry's death," I continue, "I've been telling myself that there's nothing I could have done to help him, but now I've realized that I *could* have done something. Do you think that's what he was thinking when he died? Was he wondering why I didn't help?"

Toad sighs. "I don't know what kind of injury your brother had. I don't know where he was shot, or what kind of gun was used. You said it was a rifle, so I figure there was more damage than I ended up with. Either way, you can't go back over every little detail and look for things you might have done differently. The past is the past, and I'm sure you would have saved your brother if there was any chance." He pauses. "I was right about you, though. I could tell you were smart, and you definitely proved it."

"I don't feel smart," I reply, unable to stop thinking about Henry. After a moment, I realize that there are tears in my eyes, and although I want to keep talking to Toad, I can feel my bottom lip starting to tremble. Putting my hands over my face, I try to hold back from crying, but it's no use. I just keep thinking, over and over, of his face as he died. He must have been waiting for me to do something. After all, I was his big sister, so he relied on me to keep him safe. He was probably hoping that I'd find some way to save him. Hell, I *should* have found a way. Why was I able to keep my head clear and look after Toad, but not my own brother?

"You did a good job," Toad says, reaching out and putting a hand on my knee. "What I told you out in the forest still stands. If you want to stick around after Erikson and Shauna leave, you're more than welcome."

I try to reply, but instead I just get to my feet and hurry out of the room. As soon as I'm in the corridor, I stop and take a moment to regather my composure, but instead I just end up sobbing more than ever. I know it's not my fault that Henry was killed, but I still feel as if there might have been some way that I could have saved him. I'll never forgive myself for not doing more. If I'd maybe tried to pull the bullet out, the same way I did with Toad, and then I could have disinfected the wound and tried to seal it up. In some parallel universe, maybe I'm still in our apartment in Manhattan, looking after him while he recovers. It's not fair that I survived and he died. I was supposed to protect him, and I didn't. I failed.

It takes me a while to calm down, but eventually I head through to Patricia's room, and I find her sitting at her desk, using a microscope to examine the slice of tissue she took from the creature's dead body.

"How's the patient?" she asks after a moment.

"He's fine," I reply. "He's talking." I stand in the doorway for a moment, watching as she works. "So if someone was shot in the chest," I continue eventually, "like, right in the middle of the chest, just below the collarbone, would there be any way they could survive?"

She turns to me. "Where exactly was this person shot?"

I touch my chest to show her where Henry was hit.

"What kind of weapon?" she asks.

"A rifle."

She sighs. "That kind of injury would almost certainly be fatal. Even in the unlikely event that the heart wasn't damaged, you've got the windpipe, the lungs... With proper facilities, there might be a chance, but it'd be touch and go. Why do you ask?"

"No reason," I reply. "But technically, it might have been possible?"

"Possible," she says, "but highly improbable." She pauses. "I don't have a problem with guns, but I've had to clean up two bullet wounds in the past couple of days. I don't like it."

"*You're* the one who shot *me*," I point out.

"Exactly," she replies, "and I don't like it."

Walking across the room, I look down at the sliver of discolored skin on the microscope plate.

"If you're wondering what I've found so far," she continues, "I'm afraid I don't really have anything to tell you. There's no real difference between this specimen and the kind of skin you'd find on a dead body after a few days' worth of decomposition. Basically, these creatures are just dead people who have somehow been reanimated." She smiles. "Fuck, can you believe what I'm saying? Dead people walking about. It's fucking insane, and yet..." Reaching into her pocket, she takes out her last cigarette and sniffs the end.

"You going to smoke that?" I ask.

"Not yet," she replies. "Still saving it." After taking another sniff, she puts it back in her pocket. "So Erikson and his girlfriend are talking about getting out of here in a couple of days," she continues. "Are you going to go with them?"

I pause for a moment. "I guess so," I say eventually.

"Really?"

"I came with them," I reply, "so it makes sense if I leave with them. I don't know where they're going, but, I mean, maybe..." My voice trails off as I realize that I don't really have much of a plan. Sure, I keep saying that I'm going to Lake Ontario, but I feel as if that's just some kind of pipedream that's never going to happen.

"What's the point of traveling," Patricia says after a moment, "if you're not trying to get anywhere? Especially when things are so bad."

"What's the point of staying anywhere?" I reply.

"Because it's marginally easier to stay alive," she points out. "Only marginally, but still..." She waits for me to say something. "We could use you around here. You're smart. You learn fast, and you've got initiative. I'm not saying you should settle here forever, but would it be so bad? What can Erikson and Shauna offer that you can't get here?"

"I don't want to stay still," I tell her. "I want to keep moving."

"Take a look," she replies, standing up and indicating the microscope. "Tell me what you see."

I lean closer and look into the eyepiece. Magnified several hundred times, the creature's skin is beautiful, and for a moment I just stare mindlessly at the folds of yellow and purple. It's as if there's a whole different world down at that level, and it's hard to believe that something could be so hideous when seen with the naked eye, but so gorgeous when examined more closely.

"Those things are out there," Patricia says after a moment. "Lots of them. More than we can imagine. If they're still decomposing, they should pretty much fall apart within the next couple of weeks, but until then, we need to stay safe. Toad has ammunition here. Not a limitless supply, but hopefully enough to keep this place defended if we get attacked. I don't really know much about Erikson and Shauna, but they don't seem particularly smart. If I had to choose between going with them or staying here, I know what I'd do."

"It's not that easy," I reply, stepping back from the microscope.

"You're scared to stand still?" she asks.

I nod.

"Toad wants you to stay."

"That's nice," I reply, even though I can't deny that I'm pleased to hear that he likes me. Still, it's not enough of a reason for me to stick around.

"I can even make sure that Thor backs off," she continues. "The guy's an oaf."

"I feel as if I have to get somewhere," I reply. "I don't even know where, but staying here at the farm would just be wrong."

"Don't make the mistake of assuming that you have a better chance of staying alive if you're on the move," she says. "Sooner or later, you'll run into more and more of the creatures, and as far as I can tell, you don't really have any supplies. I mean, what have Erikson and Shauna got in their van? Enough to keep the three of you going for the next few weeks? Have they got weapons? If you ask me, they're woefully under-prepared for any kind of journey, especially since she's almost full-term."

I pause for a moment. I know she's right, and I know that staying here at the farm would be the smartest move. At the same time, I have this insatiable urge to keep moving, as if I'm scared that I'll die if I stay still. Maybe I'm being irrational, but I feel physically sick every time I think about sticking around. I guess I'm secretly hoping that if I keep moving, eventually I'll find a place where things have started to get back to normal.

"I'm going with them," I say eventually. "I've made my decision."

"I guess so," she replies, sitting back down and turning her attention to the microscope.

As I leave the room, I can't shake the feeling that I'm making a mistake. Then again, I guess any choice right now is a mistake. Whether I stay here or leave, those creatures are coming, and I don't see that the world is going to set itself right any time soon. There's nothing I can do to fix things, but staying at the farm would feel like accepting the inevitable. I can't face the idea of staring at the horizon every day, waiting for those things to appear. I'd rather keep moving, and hoping that maybe around the next corner, there might be something that makes everything okay again.

THOMAS

Missouri

"LET ME OUT OF here!" I scream, staring up at the ceiling.

No reply.

"I'll do anything you want!" I shout. "I'll be your slave for life, but you have to let me out of here!"

Silence.

"Please!" I scream, before dropping to my knees. I can't take this any longer. My body feels weak, and I think I've seriously damaged my shoulder after all those attempts to break the door down. After a moment, I roll onto my side and stare at the nearby wall. I have to work out how to get out of here. I can't die in this hellhole. Not now. Not like this.

"Fuck you!" I scream, filled with anger. "What's wrong with you, you fucking pervert? Why did you leave her down here to die? Why are you doing this to me?" I wait. "Why won't you fucking answer me!"

No reply.

"Fuck you!" I scream again, and even though I'm starting to taste blood in the back of my mouth, I can't stop. "Fuck you!"

Eventually, I go back to the corner and wait. I don't even know what I'm waiting for, but I figure that I've got no other option. Time passes, and finally I notice that it's getting dark again. As I stare at the window, I see that the light is getting low, which means the sun is starting to set. I've spent another day down in this basement, and for most of that time I've simply been watching the window, trying to watch as the light's subtle changes become evident.

Damn it, I think I'm losing my mind.

No, I'm *definitely* losing my mind.

My throat hurts. I've spent the best part of the past two days screaming for help, and eventually I started to taste blood. When I try to speak now, my voice sounds harsh and gravelly. There's no way that old bastard didn't hear me, and I doubt there's anyone else around for miles. Barring some kind of miracle, I'm not getting out of here.

There's certainly nothing more I can do to save myself.

There's been no movement upstairs. No sound of the old man doing anything. As far as I can tell, he hasn't done anything at all, and I can't help wondering if maybe he died in his sleep. After all, he explicitly told me that he was going to put me to work, but now he seems to have forgotten about me. He seems so excited at the prospect of having a little slave to push around, and it's hard to believe that he would have changed his mind. I guess there's still a chance that he might suddenly open the door and start giving me orders, I'm becoming more and more certain that he's dead.

And if he's dead, then I guess I'm as good as dead too.

After all, there's no way out of this place. The door is way to strong, and the glass in the window is unbreakable. The walls of the basement are made of concrete, as is the floor, and there's no way to break through the ceiling. I'm starving, and I desperately need water, and as a result I'm starting to feel weaker and weaker. It's as if my body has already started to accept the inevitable. I barely have the energy to move, so all I can do is stay right where I am and stare at the window. As the sun continues to dip, I realize that I might not make it through the night. This might be the last light I ever see.

I can't help thinking about Joe. Given everything that has been happening over the past couple of days, I haven't really had time to process the fact that I killed and then buried my own brother. In the space of a week, I've lost my mother, my father and finally my brother. The only remaining member of my immediate family is my sister Martha, but she lives in California and even in the unlikely event that she's still alive, I don't think I'll ever be able to find her. I just hope that while he's determined to make me die in pain, God can find it in his heart to help Martha. The only hope I have left is that somehow she's still alive out there.

Time passes. How much time, I don't know, but enough for the last of the sunlight to disappear. There's nothing but darkness now, all around me, and while there was moonlight last night, this time I guess there are too many clouds. I'm starting to feel cold, too, and for the first time I feel as if death might actually not be such a bad thing. If it meant that this pain and misery would be over, maybe I'd welcome the end. Anyway, it seems totally inevitable, so why delay things any longer? Death always used to scare me, but now it feels like an all-encompassing nothingness that would soothe away all my fears.

But there's one thing I've got to do first.

Getting to my feet, I stagger unsteadily across the dark basement. I can't see where I'm going, but it's not as if I can get lost. My mind feels weak and vague, as if I can't quite put my thoughts together properly, so this is probably going to be the last thing I do before I drift away. Maybe I'm insane, but I don't care. All that matters, now, is that I'm not alone with I die. I need someone, anyone, to be close to me. If that means I have to lose my mind a little, I don't care.

Slowly, still fumbling in the dark, I manage to find the pile of cloth sacks in the corner of the basement. I lift them aside, and seconds later my hand brushes against the dead girl's withered corpse. Instead of withdrawing, I lie down next to her. I can't see her, of course, but I can feel my feet touching hers, and when I put a hand out into the darkness, I feel one of the cloth sacks that has been left over her torso. Right now, she just feels like another person, albeit one who isn't breathing. It's enough. I guess one day, if someone finds our bodies like this, they might think we were friends. That's fine by me. Closing my eyes, I wait for the inevitable. I just hope that death comes quickly.

DAY 13

ELIZABETH

Pennsylvania

"DO YOU KNOW HOW to use this thing?" Bridger shouts, holding a rifle out toward me.

I nod.

"Then take it," he spits, thrusting it into my hands. "And for God's sake, don't blow any of our heads off."

All around me, people are running and shouting. A couple of minutes ago, just after sunrise, Bridger raised the alarm. He'd been on sentry duty all night and he swears that as the sun came up, he spotted a distinctive, lurching figure on the horizon, stumbling toward us. In other words: one of the creatures.

"Are they smart enough to go around and try to come in through the back?" Thor asks.

"It's possible," Patricia replies, loading two cartridges into her shotgun. "We need to form a defensive perimeter. I'll take the north, Bridger takes the south, you take the east and..." She pauses, before glancing over to me. "You take the west, Elizabeth."

"Where are the others?" Bridger asks.

"Toad's too badly hurt to get up," she continues, "and Shauna's a liability in her current state."

"Eriksen was wasted last night," Thor points out. "The guy's probably still sleeping it off. There's no way in hell I'm giving that dick a rifle."

"We don't have time to stand around talking," Patricia says, heading out the door. "Everyone get ready."

We all follow, making our way onto the wooden porch that runs along one edge of the farmhouse. The whole world seems to be bathed in a warm orange glow, but there are plenty of shadows in which a creature could be lurking. As the four of us fan out and take our positions on different sides of the building, I can't help wondering whether I was right to say that I know how to use the rifle. I mean, I've used one before, but I'm no expert. I have no idea, for example, whether there's any kind of safety catch on the damn thing, although I can't find one. Taking up my position on the west side of the farmhouse, I stare at the nearby trees and look for any sign of movement.

"Anyone see anything?" Bridger shouts.

"Shoot on sight," Patricia replies. "Don't let the damn thing get close to you. As soon as you see it, blow its fucking brains out. Aim for the head or the chest. Remember, we don't have a whole lot of spare ammunition, and it's totally possible to finish one of these bastards with a single bullet. Aim for precision and efficiency."

My heart racing, I keep my eyes glued on the trees. I keep expecting one of those creatures to come stumbling toward me at any moment. Since I doubt I'm a very good shot, I figure my best option would be to let it get a little closer before firing straight at its face, although I'm worried that maybe the creature might be able to move faster than I'm anticipating. Every time I even look at a gun, I still think about Henry, but at least I'm no longer scared of the damn things. The rifle feels heavy and substantial in my hands; I respect and I know it's powerful, but I'm not terrified. It wasn't a gun that killed Henry. Not really. It was Bob.

"They can't run, can they?" I shout.

"What do you mean?" Patricia calls back to me.

"They're slow-moving," I continue. "Aren't they?"

"We don't know enough about them to be sure," she replies after a moment. "Don't make any assumptions."

"Are you sure you saw something?" Thor calls out.

"I'm not an idiot!" Bridger replies. "I looked toward the northern perimeter and I saw the damn thing lumbering along, headed this way. It was just like the other times we've seen them. It's definitely out here somewhere."

"Calm down!" Patricia continues. "Everyone just keep your head straight, okay? If Bridger says he saw something, that's good enough for me!"

"It should be here by now," Thor replies. "They just come straight for us. Why wouldn't it be here yet?"

"Maybe it's watching us," Bridger suggests. "Maybe it's planning something."

"Simmer down!" Patricia says. "Just stay calm, cut the chat, and focus on the task at hand! We'll have time to talk about the possibilities later."

Taking a deep breath, I adjust my grip on the gun. So far, I haven't seen a damn thing to suggest that one of the creatures is anywhere nearby, although I don't doubt Bridger for a second. He seems like a very down-to-earth, very sober kind of guy, and I'm sure that when he says he saw one of the creatures in the distance, he's telling the truth. The problem is, based on my limited encounters with the damn things, I'm convinced that they're pretty smart. The others seem to be expecting it to come lumbering mindlessly toward the farmhouse like some kind of zombie, but I'm worried that it might be out there, planning something.

Several minutes pass, and there's still no sign of the intruder. I want to believe that the panic is over, that maybe it just kept on going and didn't bother to come toward us, but deep down I know that's unlikely. Still, how long are we going to stand like this, waiting for it to make an appearance? If we keep this up for much longer, I swear to God, my heart's going to leap out of my chest. Besides, I can't shake the fear that there might be more and more of these things on their way.

"We should check the traps," Bridger calls out eventually.

"You think that's what happened to it?" Thor asks.

"Not yet," Patricia says firmly. "It might still be coming."

"It'd be here by now," Thor replies.

"Just wait a little longer!" Patricia insists. "We can't risk that thing coming up from behind and surprising us."

For a few more minutes, we maintain our positions. I've got my rifle aimed at the trees, with my finger on the trigger in case I spot anything. By this point, my mind is starting to play tricks on me and I keep thinking the shadows are twitching; telling myself to stay calm and not act like a panicky little idiot, I move my finger away from the trigger. The others seem so calm and controlled, and I know I haven't won their respect yet.

"Elizabeth!" Patricia calls out. "Anything?"

"Nothing on this side," I reply.

"Fuck," she mutters. "Where the hell is it?"

"It's out there somewhere," Bridger says firmly. "I know what I saw. It was as clear as hell. You know the way they walk, like they've got a slight limp? I saw the damn thing. I should've just gone after it myself instead of coming to get the rest of you. I should've maintained a visual fucking lock on it."

"You did the right thing," Patricia tells him.

"You think? Now we don't know where the damn thing is, but do you really think it just glanced in this direction, saw us, and decided not to pop in and say hi?" He pauses. "It's watching us. It must be planning something. Jesus Christ, maybe these things are smarter than we realized."

"I'm going to check the traps," Patricia calls out. "Everyone stay in position. I'll see if it maybe stumbled into one of the pits that Toad dug."

For the next few minutes, we remain in position while Patricia goes into the forest, looking for any sign that the creature might have been disabled. Every second seems to last for an eternity while we wait for her to come back, and I'm convinced that at any moment we might hear a gunshot or, worse, a scream. I want to call out to her, to ask if she's found anything yet, but again, I don't want to seem like the scared, naive member of the group. Forcing myself to stay calm, I keep my eyes focused on the forest. I've met these creatures before, and I know they're smart. If this thing hasn't shown itself yet, it's because it knows there's no point getting itself blown to pieces. I think Bridger's right: I think it's smart enough to be planning something, and it -

Suddenly there's a gunshot in the distance, ringing out through the forest.

"What the hell happened?" Bridger calls out.

"Patricia?" Thor shouts.

Silence.

"Stay where you are!" Bridger shouts. "Nobody move! We have to -"

"Stand down!" Patricia calls out suddenly. "It's over!"

"What do you mean?" Bridger asks as we all make our way around to the front of the farmhouse, just in time to see her walking out of the forest with her rifle slung over her shoulder.

"I found it," she says as she reaches us. "It was hiding behind a tree, watching me. When I saw it, it turned to run and I blew its goddamn head off. I tossed the corpse into one of the traps and left it to rot."

"Jesus," Bridger says, turning to Thor. "I told you."

"Are we sure there was only one?" Thor replies.

"Only one that I saw," Bridger continues, "but I've got a couple of hours left on duty. The rest of you can get back to sleep. I want to have a planning meeting later. Toad's defenses are good, but I'm not sure they're still adequate."

"I agree," Patricia says. "The sentry system's too unreliable. No-one can be expected to keep a proper eye on the whole place. We need something better."

"You think His Lordship's gonna listen to reason?" Thor asks. "Toad's not exactly the cooperative type. It's *his* farm, remember."

"He'll listen to reason," Patricia says.

"It's not like he can stop us," Bridger adds. "The guy can't even get out of bed right now. We're effectively a man down."

"I think I'll stay up with you," Patricia replies. "Just in case. We might need to start doubling up on the sentry duty from now on. There's no reason to assume that they can't show up in pairs, or from different directions. We need to assume that they're smart. They're definitely not dumb animals blundering toward us. They're capable of planning, and they can be stealthy. It's more than possible that one of them could come up with a plan and try to sneak through the door. I'd rather be over-prepared than get caught out."

Turning and heading to the house, Thor mutters something that the rest of us don't hear. Bridger walks back up onto the porch and rests his rifle against the wall, while Patricia stays next to me, clearly on the alert.

"You okay?" I ask.

"Of course," she replies, a little defensively. "Why wouldn't I be?"

"That was quick out there," I continue, starting to wonder if she's being entirely honest. "You were only gone a couple of minutes, but you managed to find the creature, kill it and get rid of its body."

"I was lucky," she replies. "Even in this crapped-up world, we get a little luck now and again."

I smile politely, even though I'm not entirely sure that I can believe her.

"Get some rest," she continues. "You're on sentry duty later. Believe me, most of the time it's dull, soul-sapping work."

"I'm hungry," I reply. "You want me to make something for you while I'm getting breakfast?"

"I'll eat later," she says. "Right now, I think I might go and double-check that all the traps are still in place. We're going to need to set some more soon. We need a whole perimeter warning system in place." With that, she turns and wanders around to the other side of the house.

Although there's a part of me that wants to go with her, I figure I need to forget about my suspicions and focus on getting something to eat. The important thing is that the creature didn't get to the house, and although Patricia's encounter seems to have been conveniently clinical and neat, I guess I just have to accept that she was lucky. After all, she's got no reason to lie.

ELIZABETH

Pennsylvania

"WHAT THE HELL WAS that racket?" Eriksen asks as he stumbles into the kitchen. "Was someone firing a fucking gun or something?"

"There was a creature," I reply, cutting a slice from the loaf that Bridger made last night. "We had to deal with it."

"What kind of creature?" he asks.

Sighing, I realize that the guy is completely clueless.

"Oh, right," he mutters. "Fuck, why do I always miss the fun stuff?"

"It wasn't exactly fun," I reply. "Patricia found it and killed it."

"My fucking head is ringing," he mutters,

grabbing the rest of the loaf and taking a big bite. "Isn't there any fucking jam?" he asks as he chews, dropping chunks of bread onto the floor.

"Careful!" I say, taking the loaf away from him. "You're wasting half of it!"

"Who made you mother?" he asks with a smile, before smiling. "Fuck it, look at us, arguing over jam. It's pathetic, isn't it?"

Ignoring him, I put the loaf back on the counter. It's crazy, but two weeks ago I was exactly like him: I just assumed that all the food and water was gonna keep on coming, and I never worried about wasting stuff. Now, I'm the complete opposite, and I've come to realize that if we don't keep an eye on our supplies, we could end up starving to death.

"Sure," he mutters, scratching the back of his neck. "Gotta preserve food and all that." He wanders over to the pitcher of water and takes a swig, although I can't help but notice that crumbs of bread from his mouth end up floating in the water. Eriksen clearly isn't very good at sharing. "I need a favor," he says after a moment. "I drank a little too much of Toad's home-brew last night, so if anyone asks, can you say you had some too? Just so I don't look like a fucking alcoholic."

"You're getting bread in the water," I say, watching as he takes another swig.

"Huh?" He looks into the pitcher for a

moment. "Shit. Sorry. Don't tell anyone."

"How's Shauna?" I ask, even though I'm pretty sure he's too drunk to give a damn about his heavily pregnant girlfriend.

"She's cool," he replies. "Probably. I mean, all she has to do is stay in bed and wait. It's not like she's got the hardest fucking job in the world. A little waiting, a little pushing, and then pop! Out comes a whole new generation of the Eriksen family." He laughs. "Nah, I'm sure there's a bit more to it. But still, she's cool."

I take a bite of the thin slice of bread I cut off a moment ago. I feel as if, while everyone else is being careful with food and water, Eriksen takes what he wants and expects the rest of us to work around him. I hate feeling like some kind of sanctimonious know-it-all, but Eriksen's really starting to bug me. He's usually too drunk to help out around the place, and he doesn't seem to respect anyone. If I was Shauna, I'm not sure I'd want such a complete asshole to be the father of my child.

"So you're good on the whole beer thing, right?" he continues. "I don't want to get a bad reputation, and Toad can be a little highly-strung from time to time."

"I don't want to get a bad reputation either," I tell him. "Anyway, I think you might have missed that boat."

"But we've gotta work together," he adds. "I

mean, these people, they're pretty tight. You came with us, so you're not really one of them, are you? We've gotta think as a team. You, me and Shauna. I told you we weren't gonna stay here forever, and I meant it. Onwards and upwards, so to speak."

I smile politely, even though I'm starting to reconsider my decision to leave with them.

"So we're thinking of moving out tomorrow," he says after a moment. "Me and Shauna, anyway. Or the day after. Not sure, really, but soon. Gotta keep thinking and moving, yeah? Ducking and diving and all that jazz. Like a shark. If a shark stops swimming, it dies. It's the same with us. I mean, this place is cool, but it's just fucking stasis, isn't it? Toad did a good job, but as preppers go, I don't think he's quite up there with the best."

"Where are you going to go?" I ask cautiously.

"West," he continues with a sniff. "Just west. Gotta be something out there, right? Sure beats sitting around here, waiting for a bunch of fucking zombies to come and pick us off." He pauses. "It's an American tradition, isn't it? When the shit hits the fan, you head west and keep going until you find a patch of dirt you can call your own. I've always fancied the cowboy lifestyle. Just a man out there in the wilderness with his wife and kids, living off the land. I think I'd be good at that kinda thing. I could even put up a little fence to keep the land neat."

"Sounds like a fantasy," I reply, convinced that this Eriksen guy wouldn't last five minutes in the wild. Seriously, the guy might fancy himself as a cowboy, but there's no way he'd make it. He'd probably end up starving to death, his bones picked clean by vultures and left to get bleached by the sun.

"The thing is..." He pauses, and it's clear that he's eying me up with suspicion. "The thing is," he continues after a moment, "I've gotta wonder how much I can trust you, and how much you wanna come with us. 'Cause we're not into dead weight, if you know what I mean. If you wanna come in our van, you need to be able to offer something. Like, everyone's got a unique selling point about themselves, right? One person's good at gathering food, another person's good at building, someone else is good at popping out babies." He pauses, and it's clear that he's got something in mind. "What about you, Miss Elizabeth? You must have a unique selling point. Something you're really, *really* good at."

"Like what?" I ask, starting to worry about his intentions.

"Maybe you should try to think of something," he continues. "You know, Shauna's due soon. She'll be popping that kid in a month or so, but until then, she's not much good for anything. It might be that you could take her place, in a way, and do the things she did before she got too fat. In fact..." He pauses again. "The van can take three people. It really can. Two would be ideal, though. Well, two and a baby. Gotta have a baby. That's the future, isn't it?" He grins nervously. "What I'm saying is that, when I drive outta this place in a few days' time, the person sitting next to me in the van... It doesn't *have* to be Shauna."

I stare at him for a moment, barely able to believe what he's saying. "She's carrying your child," I point out.

"You think that child's got much of a chance?"

"You have to try."

"And put it through misery before it inevitably dies? What kind of life could a kid have, anyway? Maybe it'd be fairer, and kinder, to not drag a new person into the world. I mean, what am I gonna say to the damn kid, even if it gets older? I can't tell it that the world's a decent place. It's just gonna be zombie-fodder. That's no life. I mean, it's just torture."

"Things are going to get better," I tell him. "By the time your child grows up -"

"What?" he asks, interrupting me. "You think the old world is gonna rise again, like some kind of phoenix? You think someone's gonna fix it? There's no-one who can fix this mess. It's gone way beyond fixing." He pauses. "We've gotta make do. All of us. We've gotta accept the situation and focus on ourselves. It's every man for himself right now. Things have fallen apart, and the best thing to do is to just grab a scrap and hope it's enough. The most any of us can hope for, and I really mean the absolute *most*, is that we can fucking struggle through until we reach the natural end of our lifespan. That's it. There's nothing better on the horizon. The future's just been taken away from us."

"One day, things will start going back to normal," I reply, even though I'm not sure I believe the words as they leave my mouth. "Everything has to get better eventually."

"No," he says calmly, "it doesn't. It really doesn't. What are you, a fucking Christian?"

"You can't give up hope," I reply, "and you can't abandon your child. You have to keep going and you have to assume that some day, something's going to start putting things right."

"Were you always so moral?" he asks. "Or did you become so fucking upright and responsible in the past few days? What were you like before disaster hit, huh? Just another fucking stupid New York brat?"

"I guess things have changed," I reply, not wanting to admit that he's right. It's hard to believe how much I've changed in just a few days. I barely even recognize myself.

"You seem like you're better cut out for that kind of life," he continues. "Shauna, she's not really very adaptable. I think she'd be miserable out there. Of course, the poor bitch loves me. I mean, she really loves me, and I love her too, but sometimes when you love someone, you have to set them free. So I was thinking of maybe making the decision for her and leaving her here. She'd have a better life anyway, and you and I could head out west and find somewhere to start afresh." He steps closer, and it's clear that he thinks he's offering a pretty good deal. "What do you say, Miss Elizabeth?" he continues, lowering his voice. "You look like you've got good hips for birthing, after all."

"You want to abandon your girlfriend and child?" I ask. "Seriously?"

"I don't *want* to," he says quietly. "I just think it'd be better for them, that's all. It makes sense. Something that was convenient and right in the old world suddenly doesn't make much sense anymore, does it?"

I open my mouth to reply to him, but the truth is, I'm disgusted.

"We have to adapt to the ever-changing world around us," he continues. "We have to recognize that all the stuff we used to do in the old days isn't necessarily relevant anymore."

"It's not like that," I say, even though I know that he might be right.

"Come on," he says, putting his hands on my waist.

"Get the fuck off me," I reply, pushing him away. Damn it, first Thor, now Eriksen. Are the men in this place completely sex-obsessed?

"Think about it," he continues with a leery grin. "Just take some time and think about it. Don't take too long, though. We haven't exactly got the luxury of time, not with a load of fucking zombies heading this way."

"I don't need to think about it," I say, trying to stay calm. "I'm not going anywhere with you. Forget it. Go fuck yourself. Even better, why don't you go and see if Shauna needs you?"

"Is that any way to talk to a guy who saved your life?" he asks, raising an eyebrow.

"When the hell did you save my life?" I ask.

"Back on the road," he continues. "When you were wandering along with that brain-dead little bitch." He pauses. "What, do you think you'd have managed to walk to wherever you were going? If we hadn't picked you up, you'd be dead by now. Look at you. You ain't got the means to take care of yourself. Let me tell you what would've happened. After a few days, you'd have run out of food and water, and your shoes'd be wearing thin. Pretty soon, you'd have been walking on bloody stumps, and you'd be wasting away. Right now, without me, you'd be rotting on some highway." He steps closer.

"That's a fact, Miss Elizabeth, and I think you should consider the debt you owe to me. You'd be being picked apart by rats right now if we hadn't given you a ride."

Staring back at him, I realize that he might be right about one thing: I probably would be dead if he and Shauna hadn't picked me up. I was hopelessly naive when I set out from New York. It's crazy to think that in just a few days, I've learned so much about the world. I honestly don't think that I'm the same person. The old Elizabeth Marter, the girl who spent her days hanging out with friends and chatting to people online, is dead and buried. Just like Henry.

"So what do you say?" Eriksen continues. "Do you wanna ditch this place and head out west with me? We could be good for each other. Shauna's not the right person for me. I need someone to whip me into shape. I can be a real man, just like you want me to be, if you know how to handle me right. We can even have some fun along the way. After all, you're still an innocent little city girl. I can teach you a hell of a lot."

"You've already taught me one very important thing," I reply.

"What's that?"

"You've taught me to stay away from people like you."

"Fine," he says with a smile, "I guess I'll

pick up girls here and there when I find 'em. I'm sure there'll be plenty who recognize the value of a decent man. You're nothing special. I doubt you'd be much good on the new frontier anyway. But when you're rotting in this place, or when one of those creatures is tearing your face off, I hope you remember that I gave you a chance. Sure, I might not be perfect, but we're not living in that kind of world anymore. The only thing that matters is survival, and that's what I was gonna give you." He turns and heads to the door, before glancing back at me. "You're gonna regret your decision," he adds. "You're gonna regret it real fucking bad."

Once he's gone, I take a deep breath. There's something about that guy that really creeps me out, and there's no way I could ever go with him. I guess that means I'll be sticking around the farm for a while. But for how long? Suddenly, I'm struck by the thought that even though Eriksen's a despicable asshole, he might be right when he says that there's no future for us at the farm. Am I just delaying the inevitable?

ELIZABETH

Pennsylvania

"IT ENDED UP IN a trap?" Toad asks with a furrowed brow. "Are you sure?"

I've been sitting next to his bed for the past half hour, filling him in on the details of this morning's excitement. He heard us shouting, and he heard the gunshot, but he's still recovering from his injuries and he wasn't able to come out and help us. To be honest, I was a little shocked when I came to see him today; he seems weaker than before, and I'm worried that he's developing a fever.

"Patricia said she -"

"Patricia said?" he continues, interrupting me. "Did you see it for yourself?"

"No," I reply. "I mean, Bridger saw it, from a distance, and then Patricia went out to look, and she shot it and dumped it in one of the traps. Now she and Bridger think that we should build more traps. I think they want to surround the whole farm with a kind of defensive perimeter, because they think that sooner or later, there are just going to be more and more of the creatures coming to attack us."

"Make sense," he replies. "It's something I was already planning to do. I've got some ideas already."

"I think they want to get started this afternoon," I tell him.

"No," he says, shaking his head. "It's my farm and I'm the one who decides what gets done and where. I don't want other people running around fixing stuff."

"But until you're up and about -"

"Tell them it's none of their goddamn business," he continues. "Tell them that, Elizabeth! Tell them I'll be back on my feet tomorrow and *I'll* be the one who fixes the new traps. I'm not having random people digging holes on my property." He pauses for a moment. "I need to know where the traps are, because otherwise I might walk straight into one."

"They'll mark it on a map."

"I don't trust them," he replies. "I don't trust

anyone. I'm sorry, but the only person I trust is myself. Tell those assholes that if they dig traps while I'm up here, they'll end up down there on the spikes themselves. Tell them I'll kick them out. They can go and fend for themselves if they don't like the way I run my farm."

"You don't mean that."

"Don't I?" He fixes me with a determined stare, and it's clear that he's getting pretty angry right now. "I should've kicked Eriksen out by now," he mutters. "I should've reminded everyone of my authority. I just didn't want to put Shauna in a bad situation. She'd just end up being dragged along with him. The guy's an asshole. They're all assholes. Don't tell me Patricia doesn't want to take over. She's got her eye on the whole place."

"You're sounding kind of paranoid," I reply.

"No," he says, shaking his head. "I'm not paranoid. I'm alert. People said I was paranoid when I moved out here and starting prepping for disaster. They laughed at me. Hell, they probably thought I was losing my mind. Look at me now, though. I'm the one who's sitting pretty with a well-stocked farm. Everyone here, everyone else, owes their life to me. I saved their asses."

Sighing, I realize that he seems absolutely determined to put his foot down. "Fine," I say after a moment. "I'll tell them to stop, but I don't know if they'll listen to me. They're scared." I pause. "To be honest, I'm scared too. This sentry system you're using doesn't seem like it works too well, and sooner or later there are gonna be too many of those things to handle. You remember what the creature said the other day, don't you?"

"I'll handle it," he says firmly. "It's my farm, and my responsibility."

Realizing that he's clearly not going to budge, I decide to stop pushing. "Patricia did a good job," I say, figuring I should try to change the subject. "She's the one who found the creature today."

"I agree," he replies, "but I still don't quite understand what happened this morning. It sounds too easy."

"Patricia said she got lucky."

"I don't believe in luck," he replies. "I believe in careful planning." He pauses, and it's clear that he's not convinced. Something seems to be bugging him today. I guess he's not very good at being a patient. He seems like the kind of guy who wants to be up and about, taking charge of everything, and all this bed-rest seems to be driving him to distraction. I can't help wondering if, deep down, he knows that he's starting to develop a fever, and maybe he's trying to prove that he's fit.

"What about the supplies?" he asks. "There should be enough for a few more weeks -"

"Bridger and Thor say it's under control," I

reply. "You're not the only person who can go out and find food, you know." Immediately realizing that I might have said the wrong thing, I try to backtrack. "I mean, we can take care of ourselves while you're getting better. You just have to focus on getting some rest. Are you sure you're not running a fever?"

He shakes his head.

"Let me check," I say, reaching across to him.

"No!" he says firmly, pushing my hand away. "You're not a doctor, Elizabeth. For God's sake, stop fussing over me."

Smiling politely, I realize I should probably leave him alone for a while, but something's making me stay. I guess I'm worried about him, and I want to make sure he's okay.

"I hate this," he says after a moment, trying to sit up in bed. "I've never been sick for a day in my life, and now look at me. I'm a goddamn cripple."

"You'll be back on your feet soon," I tell him, slipping another pillow behind his back. "You got shot, and you almost died. Patricia says you just need to rest for a few more days and then you'll be fine."

"Patricia says a lot of things, doesn't she?" he replies.

I stare at him for a moment. "She's not

trying to take over," I say eventually, starting to realize that he's pissed off about the possibility of anyone else managing to keep this place ticking over while he's in bed. He doesn't want to hear about the others managing to get things done; he wants to believe that they can't manage without him. "She's just... Someone has to make decisions, and the others are getting edgy. You don't have to worry about her, though. She wants what's best for the whole farm. It's better like this. At least someone's taking charge while you're up here, and Patricia's better suited than any of the others."

"Sure," he mutters.

"And when you're back on your feet," I continue, "believe me, everyone's gonna be glad to have you back in charge."

"They'd better be," he replies. "It's my farm. If anyone doesn't like the way I run things, they're free to leave. They can take what they brought with them, but nothing more. This isn't a charity."

"No-one wants to leave," I say, hoping to reassure him. "They trust you."

"And what about you?" he asks. "Have you thought about my offer?"

"I want to stay," I tell him, immediately feeling better now that my decision is out in the open. "I talked to Eriksen this morning, and there's no way I can go with him. The guy's a complete asshole. The sooner he leaves, the better. He's..." I pause as I try to decide how much to tell him. "I've seen a new side to him," I continue eventually. "The guy clearly only cares about himself. I don't think he even gives a damn about his child."

"Shauna's no angel," he replies, "but Eriksen's bad news."

"Tell me about it," I mutter, thinking to the asshole's clumsy attempt to pick me up in the kitchen earlier.

"I've known him for a long time," Toad continues. "He always had a bit of an edge, but these past few days I've seen something new in him. I guess recent events have changed us all to some extent, but Eriksen..." He pauses. "Don't trust him, Elizabeth. Don't turn your back on him, not even for a second. He only cares about himself and I think he could turn violent in the right circumstances."

"I've already worked that out," I reply. "Don't worry. He says he's leaving in a day or two."

"He told you that?"

I nod.

"Let's hope he sticks to that plan," he mutters. "If he doesn't, I'm gonna have to ask him to leave. He takes too much food and he doesn't contribute a damn thing. The guy's wasted half the time and sleeping it off the rest. It might sound harsh, but we can't afford to have people around who don't contribute to the group."

"He was talking about going out west," I

reply. "He wants me to go with him."

"What about Shauna?" he asks.

"I think he's considering leaving her here."

He sighs. "That's about typical for Carl Eriksen."

"He seemed nervous," I continue. "I can't quite put my finger on it, but something didn't seem quite right."

"Then *definitely* don't trust him. He's undoubtedly been going through the last of my beer, and I wouldn't put it past him to load up his van with as much of our food as he can take." He pauses for a moment, before shifting around and trying to get out of bed. "I have to make sure everything's secure," he says with a gasp. "I can't stay up here like this. The whole goddamn place is gonna fall apart."

"You're not well," I say, trying to push him back down onto the bed.

"I'll manage," he replies, getting to his feet and stumbling a couple of paces toward the door before, finally, he drops down to his knees.

"You can't go downstairs," I tell him, hoping against hope that he'll listen to reason.

"Help me," he says after a moment. "I need someone to support me."

"I'm not helping you leave this room," I reply.

"Help me downstairs," he says firmly.

"That's an order!"

"An order?" I pause. "Where do you think this is, boot camp?"

He turns to me, and I can see that there's real anger in his eyes. "This is my farm," he says after a moment, "and while you're my guest, you'll obey my instructions. Now help me up or..." He pauses, and for a moment his eyes seem to lose focus, as if he's finding it harder and harder to remain conscious. He's struggling to stay awake, but his body seems to be dragging him down.

"Toad?" I say after a moment. "Are you okay?"

"I..." His voice trails off, and he seems a little confused.

"You have to listen to me," I say, kneeling next to him and placing a hand on his forehead. "You've got a fever. I'm going to ask Patricia if she's got something I can give you, because right now, you're burning up. Your wound must be infected."

"I'm fine," he whispers, but he seems to be losing consciousness. "I have to get back down there. I have to make sure they're not taking everything. Those fucking thieves are gonna clean the place out..."

"No-one's taking things from you," I reply firmly. "They're just working on the same stuff as always. They're getting ready for lunch and drawing up plans for the new traps."

"They'll leave me with nothing," he says, before his voice trails off. He seems to be becoming increasingly delusional and paranoid, and the sweat is starting to drip from his forehead as he leans forward and tries to crawl toward the door.

"You have to rest," I say, hurrying after him. "Toad, please, you're going to hurt yourself!"

"I can't..." he starts to say, before stopping as if suddenly his whole body has seized up. "I can't move," he whispers, his voice sounding strained and tired. "I need... Elizabeth, I need... You have to help me. You have to... make them... stop."

Moving around behind him, I reach under his arms and start dragging him back toward the bed. It's not easy, and I almost drop him a couple of times, but I finally manage to get him back up onto the mattress. As I do so, however, his bandage falls away and I'm shocked to see a layer of pus oozing from the wound on his shoulder. It's clear that he's got a serious infection, and whatever Patricia's been doing to help him, it's not working. I pull the stained bandage away and toss it on the floor before rearranging Toad on the bed. I have no idea what I should do next, but that wound looks much worse than the other day.

"Can you hear me?" I ask. "Toad?"

His lips move slightly, but his eyes are closed and he barely seems to be aware that I'm here.

"I'm going to get Patricia," I continue, trying not to panic. "She'll know what to do. I'll get her to come and take a look. You've got an infection, but you're going to be okay."

ELIZABETH

Pennsylvania

"PATRICIA!" I SHOUT, HURRYING away from the farmhouse and making my way between the trees. "Something's wrong with Toad! You have to hurry!"

Having left Toad in his bed, I've come to get Patricia so she can fix his bandage and give him something to deal with the fever. The others claim that she headed out into the forest to check the traps, but so far I'm not having any luck finding her. I've got a rifle over my shoulder, just in case I run into any more of those creatures, and I'm starting to wonder whether Patricia was telling the truth when she said she was going to check the traps; after all, there's no sign of her so far, and it's as if she's simply vanished from the face of the planet.

As I trudge across the leafy forest floor, I start to feel more and more nervous. Glancing over my shoulder to check that nothing's following me, I can't stop thinking about the creatures and imagining them swarming toward the farmhouse. Eriksen might be an asshole, but he's got a point when he says that we can't just sit around here forever and hope we can pick the creatures off one by one. Sooner or later, they're going to arrive in greater numbers, and we need something that's more effective than a bunch of rifles and a dwindling supply of bullets.

Just as I'm about to call Patricia's name again, I suddenly realize I can hear a voice in the distance. I immediately take the rifle from over my shoulder, before cautiously making my way between the trees. It sounds as if Patricia's out here talking to someone, but as far as I know everyone's back at the house. Finally, I spot her up ahead, standing in a small clearing and staring down into what appears to be one of the traps.

"If you think that," she's saying, unaware of my presence, "you're insane. I've got no reason to do that. You're lucky I've kept you alive this long. The others would've put a bullet through your head as soon as they saw you."

"I don't feel lucky," says a voice, apparently coming from down in the trap. "You might as well kill me. This body is becoming an inconvenience. I have so many more, and most of them are in much better condition. Please, do me a favor and finish this one off so that I no longer have to pay it any attention."

"Not until you've given me some answers," she replies. "I want to know exactly what the hell you're doing here and what's going to happen next."

"You think I'm going to open up to you?"

"I think you're going to talk eventually," she says firmly. "I think you're smart enough to understand that your current approach is failing."

Taking a step forward, I accidentally tread on a sharp twig; it snaps, and Patricia turns to face me.

"What are you doing out here?" she asks, looking shocked.

"Do we have company?" asks the voice in the pit. "Good. You were beginning to bore me."

"I was looking for you," I say, getting closer to her. As I reach the edge of the pit, I look down and see to my shock that one of the creatures is down there, with a wooden pole running through its chest and pinning it down. It's a remarkably similar sight to the creature that Toad and I encountered the other day in the forest.

"It's okay," Patricia says, her voice filled with tension. "He's not armed. He can't hurt us."

"You again," the creature says with a smile.

He looks to have been a middle-aged guy, at least when he was alive; now that he's dead, his skin is gray and yellow, and he's clearly started to rot. "Why do I keep running into you, girl? Do you think it's destiny? You might as well tell me your name, at least. Maybe you did already, but I have so many things to keep track of."

"What the hell's happening out here?" I ask, turning to Patricia.

She pauses, as if she's not quite sure what to say.

"This is the creature from this morning, isn't it?" I continue, suddenly realizing that Toad was right when he said the whole thing seemed too easy. "You didn't kill it. You captured it."

"Scientific research," she replies. "I need to know what the hell these things want, and for that, I needed a live specimen."

"But -"

"There's no point just blowing their heads off every time they get close," she continues. "The others would be too scared to let one of them stay alive like this, so I figured I'd keep it to myself." She pauses. "You can't tell them. There's no way this thing can get loose, so it's not a threat. I just need to know what's happening, and the only way to do that is to perform first-hand scientific research on a representative sample."

"She's going to torture me," the creature

says, smiling as it stares at me. "Humans are always so quick to pull things apart when then don't understand them. She thinks she can cut me open and find out how I work. I hate to break it to you, doll, but that's not going to do you much good. I doubt you've got the intelligence or the equipment to understand a damn thing."

"Don't listen to it," Patricia says. "It's trying to play mind games. Believe it or not, the damn thing actually seems to have a sense of humor."

"You have to kill it," I say, turning and aiming my rifle at the creature. "You can't let one of these things near us!"

"Don't be stupid," she replies, pushing the barrel down toward the ground. "Elizabeth, you're smart enough to understand this from my point of view. If we keep killing them, we'll never understand what they are or where they came from or what they want. We have to take a scientific approach to the problem. We're not cavemen, and we're not so dumb that we have to run around in blind panic, shooting everything that scares us." She pauses for a moment. "We have to be brave. The others are too reactionary, but I'm convinced you can understand the value of this work."

Looking down at the creature, I realize that she's right: I *can* see why she's doing this. For the first time, instead of wanting to run and get away from one of these things, I find myself drawn to look closer. This thing is hideous, but we have to understand what it is and how it can be stopped. If we just keep running and shooting, eventually we'll run out of bullets and they'll overwhelm us.

"Maybe we can find a cure," Patricia says after a moment. "Maybe we can reverse this, or at least find a way to stop them. I'm not promising anything, but it's a start. We have to assume that there are millions, maybe even billions of these things on the planet. We can't spend the rest of our lives in fear. Throughout history, humanity has made advances through scientific inquiry, and that's exactly what we're going to do now." She waits for me to say something. "Some people pray to God," she adds, "and some people pick up a scalpel and try to understand what's happening in the world around them. I want to do both."

"So what's the first step?" I ask hesitantly, aware that the creature seems to be listening intently to our conversation.

"I'm trying to engage it in conversation," she replies. "It thinks it's pretty smart, and it certainly doesn't seem to want to let anything slip so far. It keeps trying to play games with me, but I'm convinced I can learn something useful before I move on to stage two."

"And what's that?" I ask.

"Stress tests," she continues. "I want to know what this thing can withstand, and I want to know its abilities. For one thing, it looks as if it's rotting. If that's the case, it might just die naturally in a few days. And then..." She pauses. "And then there's stage three. Dissection."

"That sounds fun," the creature says with a grin.

"This isn't magic or fantasy," Patricia continues, walking around to the other side of the pit. "This is a real-life creature, and it's subject to the rules of biology, just the same as any other creature on the planet. It wasn't created with pixie dust or fairy magic. This is life, Elizabeth, and life always finds a way to move forward. Life can overcome any problem that's put in its way, and this creature is a perfect example of that quality."

"How romantic," the creature sneers. "Even when you're talking about science, you can't resist throwing in some bullshit to sweeten the deal."

"I can do this," Patricia says after a moment, fixing me with a determined stare. "I know I can. I can analyze this creature and I can work out what to do next, but only if I'm given the chance. If the others find out, they'll come out here, pour gasoline all over the damn thing and burn it until there's nothing left. Even Toad won't be able to understand why I need to keep it alive." She pauses again. "Elizabeth, I need to know that you can keep this project to yourself, and I need to know I can trust you."

I take a deep breath. "What if I say no?" I reply after a moment, unable to ignore the fact that she's got a pistol in one hand. "What will you do if I refuse?"

She pauses. "Is that your answer?" she asks eventually, and it's clear that her mind is spinning as she tries to make a decision. I can't help but feel that Patricia's the kind of person who'll do anything to get her way.

"No," I reply. "It's not." I look down at the creature and realize that I have to go along with her. We can't just keep shooting at these things as if we're never going to run out of ammunition; we have to understand them, and then we have to come up with a better way to stop them. "You're right," I continue eventually. "Cut it up. Slice it down the middle. Whatever. If it helps, you have to do it. I can even help, but first you have to come back to the farm. Toad's sick."

"What's wrong with him?" she asks, clearly concerned.

"He's got a fever," I reply, "and his wound looks as if it's infected."

"Infected?" the creature says with a grin. "Are you sure he's not becoming like me?"

"His *wound* is infected," I say firmly. "That's all. It's not the same kind of sickness that other people have been getting."

"We'll see," Patricia says, clearly

unconvinced. "Okay, I'll come and take a look, but after that I'm coming back out here. If anyone asks about me, just tell them I'm working on the traps. Whatever happens, don't let anyone come this way. I don't want them to find this creature. That's why I lied earlier and claimed I'd killed it. Bridger and Thor and the others, they wouldn't understand. You can't even tell Toad. You're the only one I trust, Elizabeth. Please, don't let me down."

"I won't tell anyone," I reply, "but we have to get back to the house. Toad might be dying. There's pus in his wound and he's delirious with fever."

As we hurry through the forest, I can't help noticing that Patricia seems unusually quiet.

"What are you thinking about?" I ask eventually.

"When you say that Toad seems sick," she replies, with a worried look in her eyes, "what *exactly* do you mean? What kind of sick?"

"Not like the creatures," I reply. "It's not that, it's just -"

"We have to be cautious," she says, interrupting me. "I know you and Toad seem to get along pretty well, but no-one's above suspicion. We can't risk infection spreading through the house. If he's sick, we need to quarantine him and make sure no-one else goes near him."

"He's not infected," I tell her. "Not like that.

It's just an infection from his wound."

"Let's hope you're right," she says as we reach the edge of the forest and start making our way over to the house, only to hear Bridger calling for Patricia from out front. He sounds panicked, as if something's wrong.

"It seems I'm popular," she says uneasily.

"Quick!" Bridger shouts, running over to us. "Where the hell have you been? We need you. It's Shauna. She's gone into labor!"

"She's not due for another month," I point out.

"Tell that to the baby," he replies, grabbing Patricia's arm and pulling her toward the house. "It's coming, and Shauna's panicking like hell. She's convinced the baby won't survive. There's a whole lot of blood, and no-one knows what the hell to do."

"Get some water and heat it over the fire," Patricia says, hurrying to the door. "Bring some towels and blankets, whatever you can find!" She turns to me. "I'll get to Toad, but this is an emergency, okay? You have to come up with me. I can teach you what to do, in case you're ever in this situation."

"I can't deliver a baby," I reply, stunned at the suggestion.

"You're not going to deliver it," she snaps back at me, "but you're going to help. You need to learn how to do things like this, Elizabeth. Maybe one day you'll save someone's life."

I watch as she turns and runs up the stairs.

"Where's Eriksen?" I ask, as Bridger opens a nearby cupboard and starts pulling out various blankets.

"Where do you think?" he asks. "Drunk, as usual."

"But -"

"We don't have time for a long conversation," he replies, shoving some blankets into my arms. "Take these up. Tell Patricia I'll bring the water."

From upstairs, there's a scream of pain, and it's clear that Shauna's not in a good way. I follow Bridger up to the room, but as soon as we go inside, I'm shocked by the amount of blood. Shauna's on the bed, with her legs spread wide, but blood is soaking the sheets and I can tell from the look in Patricia's eyes that something's wrong. It's a horrific scene, and it's hard to believe that somewhere in that bloody mess, the baby could still be alive.

"Elizabeth," Patricia says, turning to me. "I'm going to need your help with this."

"Is it still alive?" Shauna whimpers, her eyes filled with tears. "Please God, tell me it's still alive..."

DAY 14

AMY CROSS

THOMAS

Missouri

"GET UP!" HE SCREAMS. "Get the fuck up!"

As I open my eyes, I'm doused by a bucketful of freezing water, which immediately jolts my body into action. I scramble to get back on my feet, but my arms and legs feel tired and heavy; I end up slamming back down against the concrete floor, panting and shivering as the cold water soaks through my clothes and reaches my skin.

"Get up!" he shouts, kicking me hard in the belly.

Rolling onto my back, I stare up at the ceiling and watch as the old man leans over me.

"Fucking Christ," he mutters, with a shocked look on his face. "What's wrong with you?" He kicks me again, not quite as hard this time, and then he leans closer. "Are you in there, boy? Can you hear me?"

I try to open my mouth, to say something, but I can't really control my body properly. All I can do is wait as I hear the old man walking away, and moments later the door to the basement slams shut. Shivering violently, I try to work out what the hell is happening, but finally I realize the most shocking and surprising thing of all.

I'm alive.

Somehow, I'm alive.

THOMAS

Missouri

AFTER THREE DAYS WITHOUT food, the bread tastes good. I wolf it down, curled up in the corner of the basement like an animal. Hunger has become more than just a feeling in my body; it has become the only thought in my mind, pushing my normal thoughts to one side; even though I know I should probably slow down, I end up barely even chewing the bread, swallowing it in large, thick chunks instead, and then washing it down with big gulps of water.

    A few minutes later, the pain kicks in. My gut feels as if it's burning, and I roll onto my side, clutching my belly and letting out a gasp of agony. I guess I ate too much, too fast; my stomach has been empty for three days, probably consuming itself, and now I've over-filled it with bread and water. For a while, curled up in a ball and wracked with pain, I start to wonder if the whole stomach might just burst. Finally, however, with sweat pouring down my face, I realize that the pain is slowly starting to ease.

I wait.

The basement is cold, dark and quiet. It's been about half an hour since the old man came down here with a plate of bread and a cup of water. I've barely had time to think about what this all means, but I know one thing for sure: I thought I was going to die. I spent a few days down here, completely alone and with no indication that the old man was still alive, and I finally gave up. I don't think I woke once yesterday. Instead, I was just passed out here on the floor, wasting away. So why did the old man suddenly come and give me food? Was he just testing me and teasing me, or has something changed?

Once the pain has completely left my stomach, I sit up. I've removed my soaking wet clothes, and the old man left some kind of old, stained set of overalls for me to wear. They stink of oil and body odor, and they're too big for me, but they're warm and dry so I put them on. Something about this whole situation feels very wrong, and I can't work out why the old man would suddenly give a damn about me. I guess maybe he was trying to break me, in which case he did a pretty good job. I feel completely exhausted and strangely blank, as if the top layer of my mind has been permanently ripped away to expose a tender, raw new layer below. Looking down at my hands, I start to wonder if maybe I'm imagining the whole thing. Is it possible that somehow I actually died, and this is what comes next?

Getting to my feet, with the manacles still attached to my ankles, I limp over to the narrow window at the far end of the room. Rain is falling outside, spattering the glass and creating a faint, distant tapping sound. In a way, it's a comforting feeling to know that the weather, at least, is continuing as normal. This might be the first rain in two weeks, and I like the idea that it might be washing away all the bad things that have happened. Still, I know that's not what's really happening. It's just rain, and those creatures - whatever they are, and whether they're near or far - aren't going to be washed away in a flood. As I watch the rain hitting the truck, I can't help but think about Joe's grave in the forest. I guess the rain should help to flatten down the soil on top of him.

Above me, the floorboards creak.

The old man is moving about.

This is no dream. I must have been at the brink of death when he chose to revive me. I can't help but wonder what he wants.

Walking over to the steps, I glance back at the pile of cloth sacking and bones in one of the corners. It's weird to think that someone else was down here before me, and that whoever she was, she died in this room. The old Thomas would have been scared, and would probably have worried about ghosts, but the new Thomas is strangely comforted by the presence of those tattered, broken old bones. Whoever that girl was, she probably went through the same things that I've been through, except she didn't make it; at least I know that I'm not the only person who ended up down here, although I'm damn sure I'm going to be the last. I don't know how I'll do it yet, but I'll get the hell out of here and I'll break the old man's skull. Maybe I'll have to wait and be patient, but I'll make him suffer. Not for me, but for the girl who died down here. Whoever she is, or was, she deserves justice.

Limping up the steps, I reach the door and pause for a moment.

"Hello?" I call out, my voice sounding harsh and weathered.

I hear the sound of someone shuffling about upstairs, and finally footsteps come closer to the door. There's another sound, as if someone's jangling a set of keys, and finally I hear the door being unlocked. I take a step back, as the door finally swings open and I find myself face to face with the old man. He's holding a rifle in one hand, and as he steps aside, it's clear that he wants me to go upstairs.

"You try anything," he mutters, "and I'll blow your fucking brain clean out of your skull with one shot."

Figuring that I need to pick a moment when he's less cautious, I take a step past him and head up into the kitchen. The place is a mess, and with rain and dark clouds outside, there's not much light in here. Shivering a little at the cold, I walk over to the window and stare out at what appears to be a proper rainstorm. It's almost as if the heavens are trying to wash everything away, to scrub the planet clean and start again. To be honest, I can't say that it sounds like a bad idea.

"You've got a job to do," the old man says, walking over to the sideboard and grabbing a large knife, which he sets on the table between us.

Staring at the knife, I try to work out what he means.

"If you're thinking you can use that thing on me," he continues, "I should advise you of the following. I served five years in Korea. I fought bastards who were twice as tall and twice as wide as you, and I brought 'em down. Maybe you could get a lucky move in and stab me. Maybe. Probably not, but I guess it's a possibility. Still, I'd take you with me, boy, and I know just where to stick the blade and how to twist it, you understand? You're not getting out of here alive until I tell you it's time to go. You got that?"

I stare at him.

"You got that?"

I nod.

He sighs, before grabbing one end of a long chain and tossing it across toward me.

"Attach that to the chain between your legs," he says, "and close the lock. Don't worry, I've got a key. I'm not risking you running off."

Realizing that I don't have any option other than to obey for now, I crouch down and do as I'm told: the end of the chain is easily looped through the linking chain between my ankles, and I close the lock with a firm snap. I've spent so many days chained up now, I can barely even remember what it's like to be free.

"Now I don't know what you brought here with you," he continues, keeping the rifle pointed at me, "and I don't particularly *want* to know, but it's time to get rid of it. You understand? It ain't staying. I want it gone. I'd shoot it myself, but..." He pauses. "Well, never you mind why I figure this is a better way. I'm sick of people asking dumb questions and expecting me to explain myself, you hear? I won't have it, so what you need to do, and I'm only gonna explain this once, is you need to go out there and slice its fucking head off."

I stare at him for a moment. "What?" I ask eventually. "I don't know what you're talking about."

"That thing," he continues, adjusting his grip on the rifle before raising it and aiming straight at my head. "I swear to God, boy, you're gonna go out there and kill it."

"What is it?" I ask, even though I'm fairly sure it must be one of those creatures.

"You know," he sneers.

I stare at him.

"I don't give a damn what it is, okay?" he continues. "All I care about is that it's gone. I don't like the thought of it lurking out there, like it's hungry."

Turning and looking out the window, I see nothing out there but trees and rain.

"This isn't a debate," the old man continues. "I've got the other end of this chain, so don't think you're gonna just run off. I've also got this rifle trained on your, so again, don't go getting any ideas. Just get out there and do a nice, clean job. Finish that fucking thing, you understand?"

"I don't -"

"Don't bullshit me!" he shouts, stepping closer. "Don't you fucking bullshit me, you little ass-wipe! Get out there and cut its goddamn throat!"

"I don't -"

Before I can finish, he swings the butt of the

rifle at me, catching me on the side of the face and sending me slamming into the fridge. I take a moment to steady myself before reaching up and feeling blood on my cheek.

"How many times am I gonna have to do that," he says after a moment, "before you get out there and do what I'm telling you to do." He turns the barrel of the rifle back toward me. "Or should I just end your miserable fucking existence right now?"

Figuring that he seems pretty trigger-happy, I look down at the knife for a moment before realizing that I probably don't have much of a choice here. I'm determined to get the jump on this guy, but I need to choose the right moment. One bad move and I could end up with a bullet in the brain. Slowly, and hesitantly, I pick up the knife and start walking toward the door. I'm not certain, but I think my cheekbone might be fractured after that impact with the rifle butt; there's a kind of dull pain radiating up toward my eye, and part of my face is starting to feel numb.

"This ain't no gab-fest," he continues, turning the rifle so that it remains trained on my head. "I don't want you going out there and trying to sweet-talk that thing into leaving. Just get out there, get close to it and fucking kill it. You understand? No fucking about. Just kill it dead."

"Yes."

"What was that?"

"Yes, Sir," I say firmly.

"Go on, then. If you get this right, I'll let you go straight after. You can just in your truck and fuck right off."

"Sure you will," I mutter under my breath, before opening the door and staring out at the pouring rain. The forest looks so cold and uninviting, it's hard to believe that there could be any kind of creature out there, but I guess it's impossible to second-guess these things. To be honest, between this trigger-happy old psycho and one of those creatures, I'm not sure which would be the worst option right now.

"What are you waiting for?" the old man asks.

"How long's the chain?" I ask.

"About ten meters," he replies. "Now move!"

Taking a deep breath, I step out into the rain. Shuffling forward, my feet already soaking wet from the deep puddles of mud, I stare at the forest, waiting for any sign of life. The knife in my hand feels woefully useless, but at the same time I figure I can take down one of these things, so long as it's not armed with a gun. Dragging the chain through the mud, I get close the truck before crouching down and checking underneath, to make sure that there's nothing hiding on the other side. Deciding to steer clear anyway, I shuffle away from the vehicle, constantly turning to check if anything might be coming up behind me.

"There's nothing here!" I shout back at the old man.

"It'll come!" he shouts back. "Don't you worry about that, boy!"

Sighing, with rain already soaking through my overalls, I decide that I need a better strategy. The most important thing is to keep away from anything that might provide cover for an attack. From that point of view, I need to be out in the open and I need to be constantly vigilant in case the creature tries to ambush me. Then again, I guess there's a chance that it'll see the knife and decide to hold back. I don't know how intelligent these things are, but based on everything that happened a few days ago with Clyde, I'm not convinced they're as dumb as they look.

Suddenly I spot movement nearby. Turning, I realize that there's a dark figure lurking about ten meters away, partially hidden by a tree. I immediately feel a shiver pass through my body as I realize that it's watching me. Every other time I've seen one of these things, they've seemed frantic, so it's a surprise to find that this one is apparently biding its time. I can't help wondering if maybe they're getting smarter.

"Come on, then," I whisper, daring the

creature to come closer. "Try it."

"You see anything?" the old man shouts.

I pause for a moment. "Yeah!" I shout back eventually. "I see it!"

The creature seems to take a step back for a moment, as if it's not sure what to do next. It seems hesitant, and I'm fairly sure that the chain attached to my legs isn't long enough for me to chase after it.

"Come on," I call out to it. "What are you waiting for?"

"I can't reach it!" I shout back to him.

"What the fuck are you moaning about now?"

"The chain!" I reply. "It's not long enough!"

"Then get it to come to you!"

Again, there's a moment of hesitation, before finally the creature stumbles out from behind the tree and takes a couple of lumbering steps toward me. It still seems nervous and awkward, as if it knows that the knife in my hand might be enough to kill it. There's none of the confidence that the other creatures had; this one seems determined to stay in the shadows, keeping its face hidden. Finally, however, it comes a little closer, and its features emerge from the gloom.

"What's the -" I start to say, before suddenly I realize that this isn't just any creature. My mind races as I try to convince myself that there's been a mistake, but finally I'm forced to admit the truth.

The creature in front of me, with its dead eyes staring straight at my face, is my brother. It's Joe. Or at least, it's his body.

THOMAS

Missouri

"WHAT ARE YOU WAITING for?" he asks as he gets a little closer, his voice almost impossible to hear over the pouring rain. "You've got a knife. Use it."

I take a step back, stunned by the sight of Joe as he stares at me. His head is badly damaged, with one side looking as if it's been completely smashed away, while there's also a huge gash on his shoulder that had left his left arm hanging by the bone. Whatever's happened to him, it's clear that he can't have survived my attempt to kill him the other day, which means that there's only one possible explanation: he must have been infected by the same virus that infected all those other people back in town.

"It's me," he continues, still staring at me. "I know that's probably difficult to believe, but it *is* me, Thomas. Look at me. That... *thing* got into my head, but I managed to fight it off. I forced my way out of the grave and then finally I just... I made him leave me alone."

I take another step back.

"What are you waiting for?" the old man shouts from the house. "Finish him off!"

"I can feel him in my head," Joe continues, taking another tentative step toward me. "It's like this second voice, constantly trying to drown me out and take control. Sometimes, just for a few seconds at a time, he's successful, but I always manage to push him back. I always told you I was stubborn, huh? Turns out I'm a regular fucking genius, Tommy boy."

"Keep back," I say, holding the knife out toward him. He might look like Joe, and he might sound like Joe, but there's no way I can trust him. For all I know, this creature has the same mind as all the others, and he's just pretending to be my brother.

"Good," he replies. "That's good, Thomas. You're finally growing up. At least you're not a naive little shit anymore." He glances over at the house. "Who's your friend, though? He let off a couple of rounds at me earlier. Poor old bastard was spitting and cursing, I thought he was gonna drop dead of a heart attack." He pauses. "I don't blame him, though. I caught sight of my reflection in the truck window. I look pretty fucking bad, right? I don't really wanna look too closely, but I'm thinking that, like, one side of my face is all fucked up."

"I'm sorry," I whisper.

"What for?"

I open my mouth to reply, but no words come out. There are tears in my eyes, though, and although I'm holding the knife out toward him, I don't think I could use it. I can't kill my brother. Not again.

"You did the right thing," he continues after a moment. "When I was under the tarpaulin, I was in so much pain, I was begging you to finish me off. You might not have been able to hear me, but I swear to God, I was pleading for death. When it finally happened..." He pauses again. "I only felt it for, like, a fraction of a second. I remember the first strike, smashing the front of my face in, and then another strike, and then it all went black. After that, there was nothing until I was almost out of the grave. This thing is inside me, Tommy. It's swarming through my brain and it's trying to -"

Before he can finish, he drops to his knees, and it's as if he's in pain.

"Your brother's pretty strong," he says suddenly, his voice sounding much calmer as the other part of his mind asserts its dominance. "They don't normally fight back quite so hard. They usually fade away and become nothing more than an annoying scream. This one, though... he's angry about something. So much rage and fury. It's not my fault, either. His anger is old and it has become the foundation of his soul. I almost admire him. Almost."

"Leave him alone!" I shout.

"Or what?" he asks with a smile. "You gonna use that little blade on me? I promise you, if you do, I'll make sure your brother feels every second of it. As soon as the pain hits, I'll abandon his body and let him enjoy those final moments."

"What do you want?" I ask.

"What do you think I want?"

"To kill me."

He shakes his head. "Don't take it so personally. I want to kill all the old humans. There must be nothing left but my kind, my mind. Then, perhaps, we can complete our search in peace."

"What are you searching for?" I ask.

"The progenitor," he replies. "That's all I care about, and I'm damn certain you don't have a clue where I can find him."

"The what?" I reply, poised to defend myself in case he attacks.

"The progenitor," he says again, slowly getting to his feet. "There are billions of us, boy. All over the planet, swarming like ants, and our minds are all linked, except..." He pauses. "There's one missing. The most important one. The progenitor isn't part of the network. We need to find him. You haven't seen a six-foot guy with a receding hairline and a dirty little beard, cowering in a corner anywhere, have you? It's almost as if he's hiding from us." With that, he lurches toward me, although he stops as soon as I hold the blade up toward his face. "I thought not," he says with a smile. "You know what? This body is a complete waste of time. I'll let your brother have it back until it falls apart. But if you happen to run into a guy named Joseph Aldred, tell him we're looking for him. Tell him we want our god back."

"You -" I start to say, but suddenly he drops to the ground again. I step back, my heart racing as I try to work out what to do next. Watching as he tries to crawl toward me, I realize that the two minds in Joe's body are pushing at one another, trying to gain permanent control.

"Kill the fucker!" the old man shouts. "Jesus Christ, kid, what's wrong with you? I'll let you go, but first you have to kill that bastard!"

I watch as Joe slowly raises his head and stares at me.

"Joe?" I say, hoping against hope that it might be him again.

He opens his mouth, but all that comes out is

a faint groan.

"Tell me it's you!" I say, holding the knife out toward him. "Joe!"

"I'm not strong enough," he says after a moment. "I thought I could keep him back, but he keeps overpowering me. It's like he's playing with my body, using it when he wants but..." He pauses. "I feel like my head is connected to something. My mind is part of... They're everywhere, Thomas. You can't run from them. Every few seconds, I get a glimpse through their eyes, and I see the whole world at once. There are other survivors, but they're being picked off one by one. You can't... I don't know how you can stop these things. Sometimes I... I get a glimpse into the rest. It's like seeing the world through billions of eyes all at once. It's madness."

"Kill him!" the old man shouts.

"Did he do this to you?" Joe asks, staring at the manacles around my ankles. After a moment, he spots the cut on my cheek. "Did he hurt you?"

"He's keeping me in his basement," I reply.

"He's out of ammunition, you know," he continues.

"No," I say, "he's *really* not."

"He is." He pauses. "He was firing at me, and then he stopped, and I saw him searching for more. I've been watching him for the last day or so. He's been desperately searching for some more ammunition, but he's got nothing left. Why do you think he hasn't come out here and shot me by now? He can wave that fucking rifle around all day, but he hasn't got a single bullet left to fire."

I turn and look over at the old man. It makes sense, in a way, that he's bluffing about the rifle; after all, why else would he have bothered to revive me? It's clear that he'd decided to let me die, but he obviously realized at the last moment that he could use me to kill Joe. I guess he's too scared and too old to come and do the job himself.

"I'll do it," Joe says, getting to his feet. "Watch. He won't shoot. He can't. He can't do anything, not before I get to him." Lumbering past me, he starts making his way slowly toward the house, limping through the mud. Even though he's my brother, he makes for a horrific sight, with torn and rotten skin hanging from his body.

"What are you waiting for?" the old man shouts, his voice filled with panic. "If you don't do it, I swear to God, I'll blow the rest of his head away and then I'll fucking turn this thing on you. Kill him! Right now!"

I open my mouth to shout back at him, but finally I realize that Joe's right: the old man *is* bluffing. He was happy to leave me down in the basement to rot, and he'd have used the rifle on Joe if he had any ammunition left at all. Instead, he looks absolutely terrified as he slowly steps back into the house.

"What are you gonna do?" I ask, hurrying over to Joe just as he reaches the door.

"I'm gonna kill the creep who hurt my little brother," he replies, stepping inside. "Family's family, Tommy boy. It's the last thing I can do for you. I haven't been the best brother, but I sure as hell can get rid of this asshole."

"I'm warning you!" the old man shouts, still aiming the rifle at us. "If you want to get out of here, boy, you'd better kill this fucking thing right now or I swear to God, I'll blow you both away."

"Go on, then," Joe says, making his way around the kitchen table. "Why don't you pull the trigger? That's a very big gun you've got there. You could blow my head across the kitchen, so why don't you? You're a coward, so do what cowards do best."

"Don't think that I won't," the old man sneers. "If you come one step closer..."

"I want you to," Joe continues, stepping toward him. "You think it's fun being like this? I *want* to die. Blow my head clean off. Make it so this body can't ever be used again. I dare you. Hell, I'm begging you! Do it!" He pauses, waiting for the old man to pull the trigger. "Do it!" he screams.

"Keep back!" the old man shouts, before turning the rifle around and swinging the butt straight at Joe. He narrowly misses, and the momentum is enough to send him tumbling back. He lands hard against the concrete floor as Joe steps closer. "Stop him!" the old man screams, obviously in pain. "For God's sake, kid, stop this thing! It'll kill you next! Don't think you'll be safe! You have to save us both!"

I want to say something, or to turn and run, but all I can do is watch as Joe steps closer to the old man. Finally, his eyes filled with terror, the old man turns and scrambles down the steps, making his way into the basement and pushing the door shut. It's as if, gripped by terror, all he can think to do is lock himself in the basement. Joe tries to break his way in, but the steel door is too strong.

"How do we open this thing?" he asks, clearly determined to get through and kill the old man. "Tommy boy, help me! I need to get in there!"

Spotting the keys on the counter, I pick them up and stare at them for a moment.

"No," I say eventually, putting them in my pocket. "Leave him in there. He doesn't deserve a quick death." After all, the old man was willing to leave me to rot down there, and I don't have any regrets about doing the same thing to him. He can go through exactly the same thing that I went through, except this time the door won't ever be opened again. For what he did to me, and what he did to that girl whose bones are down there, the old bastard deserves to rot in the basement forever.

THOMAS

Missouri

"WHAT'S HE DOING IN there?" I ask, with my ear pressed against the steel door.

"Dying, hopefully," Joe says, standing by the kitchen table. "Slowly and painfully."

The truth is, I'd been expecting the old man to start banging on the door, demanding to be released. I doubt he intended to lock himself in there forever, but he probably forgot that he didn't have the keys with him, and once the door swung shut and locked automatically, he was stuck. I'm pretty sure there's no back-door to that place and no other way out, but while I can hear him shuffling about down there, there's no sign so far that he wants to come out. Maybe I've become a little sick and twisted, but right now, I want him to scream and beg for his life; I want to know that he's terrified. Maybe I'd let him out, or maybe I wouldn't, but I want to hear the fear in his voice.

"You need to get out of here," Joe says after a moment. "Thomas, are you listening to me? You need to go. This place isn't good. Look at it. The whole fucking house is about to collapse at any moment."

"We can head to St. Louis," I tell him. "If there's no-one there, we'll go to Chicago."

"Are you kidding?" he replies. "You want to go to a fucking city? Do you have any idea how many of these creatures there must be?"

"But that's where the army's gonna start helping people first," I reply, turning to him. "They have to, Joe. They've probably got all these plans worked out already, but if we wait out here, in the middle of nowhere, it might be weeks or even months before they get to us. We have to go to where there are other people."

"That didn't work out too well the last time," he points out.

"This'll be different," I continue. "We'll -"

"I'm dead, Thomas," he says suddenly. "This voice that's in my body," he continues, "sometimes lets me see through other eyes. I've seen people all around the world, Tommy boy, running and screaming and dying. It's pretty fucked up, but do you want to know the one thing I *haven't* seen? Not once?" He pauses. "I haven't seen one soldier, or police officer, or anyone who looks like they're taking charge. It's just chaos all over the place. It's been two weeks now since all of this started, and the world isn't getting its shit together. Nothing's gonna change. This is how it is now."

I take a deep breath. There are tears in my eyes, but I'm damn well not going to let him see that I'm on the verge of crying.

"Look at me," he continues. "The only reason I'm standing here now is that this thing, whatever it is, dragged my body out of the grave, but..." He holds his hand out in front of his face, as if to remind me that the flesh is starting to rot and fall away. "I won't make it to St. Louis," he says eventually. "Look at me. I'm falling apart already. If my body was worth saving, that voice would have made more of an effort. He abandoned my body precisely because he knows that there'll be nothing left in a day or two. I'm just winding down while the maggots get ready to do their shit."

"We can find a way to save you," I tell him. "We can -"

"More miracles?" he asks with a faint smile. "Is that really your plan, Thomas? Go to a city, hook up with some miraculous bunch of people who're gonna save the world, and then find some fucking doctors who can perform another miracle by saving me?" He sighs. "Face it. This body is old and gone. I'm already dead. I just have to wait for my mind to catch up."

"I'm not leaving you," I say firmly.

"I don't want you to leave me," he replies. "I want you to finish me off."

I shake my head.

"Please."

"I can't," I reply, trying to stay calm. "I already did it once, Joe. I can't do it again."

He pauses. "I was in pain that time," he says eventually. "I'm not in pain now. It's just about waiting, but that seems kinda pointless, right? Just sitting around, waiting for the lights to go off?" He pauses. "Fuck that shit, man. Do you know how I always *wanted* to die? In a fucking blaze of glory! You know, like some kind of fucking hero, with machines guns in my hands and hookers everywhere." He smiles. "Real immature shit, yeah? The full Troma kind of thing. And obviously that's not gonna happen, but at least I don't have to sit around, dragging it out forever."

"You can't just sit around and wait to die," I tell him. "That's insane!"

"I'm not waiting to die," he replies, turning and heading over to the table. Carefully, he lowers himself into a chair. "I'm already dead, dip-shit. I'm just waiting to rot away to nothing." He pauses. "Do you remember how Mom died at the kitchen table?

It's hard to believe that was only about a week ago. I guess... I guess now it's my turn. I'm gonna die at a kitchen table too, just like her. Talk about a fucking comedown, huh?"

"No," I say firmly. "You can't just sit around like this."

"And how are you gonna stop me?" he asks. "If you try to drag me out of here, you'll probably end up pulling my goddamn head off anyway. I'm already falling apart." He pauses again. "You need to leave, Thomas. You need to get the hell out of here and just forget about me. I'm okay with it, really. It's too late for me, but you've still got a chance." He waits for me to say something. "Go on, Tommy. Get the fuck out of here. At least one of us should make it."

"I'm not leaving you."

"Then you can stick around and wait until my fucking head falls off," he replies. "Believe me, there are already maggots chewing through my flesh. It doesn't hurt, but I can feel them. They're hungry little bastards, burrowing their way through the meat. I can feel some of them wriggling in my brain, it's..." He pauses. "It's okay, Thomas. I'm not scared. Maybe I should be, but I just feel like I'm ready, you know? I've already died, really. Those few seconds when I knew you were killing me, I felt so free. I liked it, and I want it again. I'm at peace." He laughs. "Well, peace is the wrong word, but I'm pretty chill about it all."

"I'm not leaving you," I say again, sniffing back the tears.

"You wanna sit around and watch your older brother's head rot off?" he asks. "Seriously?"

"I'm not leaving you."

"Pervert."

I take a deep breath as I try to work out if there's any other way. Joe sure looks as if he's about to fall apart, and I guess I should accept his decision. Still, I know that when he's gone, I'll be alone. It's not as if I've got any chance of finding my sister Martha again, even if she's alive, so once Joe's gone, there'll be no-one left. Slowly, I walk over to the kitchen table and sit facing him. He's all I've got left, and once he's gone, I don't know where I'm supposed to go. Sure, I can get in the truck and drive away from this place, but what do I do after that? I know he's right about the cities, but at the same time it doesn't seem as if the countryside is much better. Every time I try to work out some kind of plan, to decide where to go, I come to the same conclusion: there's nowhere that's ever going to be safe.

"Come on," he says. "You've gotta be kidding. Get in the fucking truck and get the fuck out of here!"

"I want to be here with you," I tell him, sniffing back some more tears. "I don't care how long it takes, but I want to wait with you. It's my decision, Joe, and there's nothing you say that'll make me change my mind, so you'd better just get used to it, okay?" I take a deep breath. "I'll keep you company," I add, "and then I'll bury you, and then I'll get going."

"Don't bury me," he replies. "I'm claustrophobic."

I sigh.

"I mean it," he continues with a smile. "You can just leave me sitting here at this table. You never know, some kids might come by one time and get freaked out. I kinda wish I could stick around and see their faces, but I can already feel my body being destroyed. There's not much time left. Sooner or later, one of these maggots is gonna chew through an important part of my brain, and it'll be lights out."

"I'm going to wait with you," I say firmly.

"You're not making the right decision," he continues. "Don't be dense, Tommy."

"I don't care if it's the right decision or not," I reply. "It's what I'm doing."

"I'm not gonna be much company," he replies. "Jesus fucking Christ, I can feel a big fat maggot in my brain right now. It's trippy as shit."

"You swear too much," I point out. "Maybe we oughta pray or something."

He raises an eyebrow. "Pray?"

I nod.

"What the fuck for?"

I open my mouth to reply, but at first I'm not sure what to say. "I don't know," I continue eventually, "but it seems like it might be a good idea. You know..." I pause. "Something good might come out of it."

"You wanna sit here with your zombified, rotting brother, with some kind of fuckhead Nazi asshole locked in the basement, with the world falling apart all around us, and... you wanna put your hands together and pray?"

"I do."

"Fine," he says with a shrug. "What the hell? I've never tried it before, not since school anyway, so go ahead. Let's do this shit."

"Repeat after me," I say, closing my eyes. "Dear Lord."

"Dear fucking Lord."

"Joe!"

"Dear Lord," he says with a sigh.

I pause for a moment. "We ask you to look over this world and deliver us from whatever catastrophes you've seen fit to visit upon us. We ask you to keep us safe and to watch over us, and we ask you to watch over our sister Martha. Wherever she is, we ask that she's in good health and that she'll be okay."

"Yeah," Joe says, sounding a little more

subdued, "look after Martha. None of us deserves this shit, and she's not a bad person. Keep her out of too much trouble, okay?"

"Amen," I add.

"Amen."

We sit in silence for a moment, before I suddenly realize that I can hear a voice somewhere nearby. Looking over at the door to the basement, I realize that the old man is talking down there.

"What's old Adolf going on about?" Joe asks.

Getting to my feet, I walk over to the door and take a moment to listen.

"Please," the old man is saying, his voice filled with fear and pain, "I'm begging you, don't come any closer. Leave me alone, please. Dear God..."

"What's he saying?" Joe calls out to me.

"Hang on!" I hiss, keen to hear more.

"I'm sorry, Sara," the old man continues. "Maybe I didn't treat you right, but I'm your father, for God's sake. I command you to go back over there! Get back in that corner!" I can hear him scrabbling about for a moment. "Get back over there!" he shouts. "I didn't tell you to get up! Obey me! You're my daughter and I command you to stop this! Leave me alone!"

I reach into my pocket, ready to get the key out, but at the last moment I reconsider. The truth is, I like hearing the fear in the old bastard's voice. If that makes me a bad person, after everything that's happened to me over the past few days, then I guess I just have to accept that I've become a little meaner than before. The old Thomas probably wouldn't have made it this far anyway; the old, naive Thomas would have panicked and ended up dead.

"Sara, please," the old man whimpers, "for the love of God and all that's holy, stop! I'm begging you! See? I'm on my knees and I'm begging you. Don't do this. Go away! Leave me alone!" There's the sound of footsteps hurrying up the stairs, and suddenly he starts pounding on the door. "Let me out of here! Get me away from her!"

"Who's he talking to?" Joe asks.

"Help!" the old man screams, still banging on the door before, finally, he lets out a cry of pain and falls quiet.

"What the hell's happening in there?" Joe asks.

"I..." I start to say, before realizing that the old fool must be talking to the pile of bones in the corner of the basement. As he continues to whimper and moan, I put the key in the lock and struggle for a moment with the awkward, slightly warped door, before finally getting it unlocked and pulling it open. At the last moment, I hear a clattering sound, like bones being dropped onto the floor.

The first thing I see once the door is open is the set of bones, except now they're in the middle of the room, and the old man's body is next to them. I walk cautiously down the steps and head over, only to see that the old man's eyes are wide open, staring up at the ceiling with a horrified look on his face. I kick him gently in the side, but it's clear that he's dead. Turning and looking down at the bones, I can't help but stare at the skull.

"Sara?" I whisper after a moment. "Was that your name?" I pause. "What did he do to you?"

Silence.

"What's happening in there?" Joe shouts.

"Revenge," I whisper as I continue to stare at the skull for a moment. "I guess she waited."

Without saying anything else, I turn and hurry up the steps. At the last moment, I glance back down at the old man's body. I don't know what the hell happened down here, or what exactly he thought he saw as he was dying, but somehow it seems strangely fitting. Whoever that Sara girl was, I guess he treated her about as well as he treated me, in which case I don't feel any pity for the old bastard at all. Maybe I'm getting tougher or more mean-spirited, and maybe what I'm thinking isn't exactly very Christian, but he got what was coming to him.

DAY 15

ELIZABETH

Pennsylvania

"HOW'S SHE DOING?" PATRICIA asks as she walks quietly into the room.

I nod, not wanting to disturb the baby as she sleeps in my arms. It's about 6am and the sun's first rays are starting to lift bring light to the farmhouse. Having cried for most of the night, the baby has finally fallen asleep and seems to be absolutely content in my arms. I'm terrified to move, though, in case I wake her from her slumber; she looks so peaceful and happy, and there's a part of me that thinks she's better off sleeping. Every time she opens her eyes, she seems upset and troubled, almost as if she senses that there's something horribly wrong with the world.

"Did you change her?" Patricia asks, sitting next to me on the edge of the bed.

I nod again.

"And you used talcum powder?"

I nod again.

"And did she sleep okay?"

"It wasn't too bad," I reply. "She cried once, around two in the morning, but that was because there was another of those booms in the distance. Did you hear it?"

"The windows rattled," she replies, and it's clear that she's worried.

"It was the fourth one this week," I point out. "What do you think it is?"

"Probably nothing."

"It's *something*!" I reply. "It comes from different directions at different times. It's like..." My voice trails off for a moment as I realize that I don't quite want to say what's on my mind.

"Like the end of the world?" she asks with a smile.

"I just wish it'd stop," I continue, "or if something's going to happen, I wish it'd hurry up and just happen. I'd rather get it over with." As the baby starts to screw her face up, as if she's about to cry, I lean down and kiss her forehead; she seems to calm down, and she reaches up and touches my nose with her wrinkled little fingers.

Patricia smiles. "You're a natural." Looking

down at the baby for a moment, she pauses. "Some people have got what it takes to be a mother, and some haven't. It's genetic."

"I'm just doing what anyone would do," I reply uneasily.

"She bawled non-stop when I held her yesterday," she points out. "Face it, Elizabeth. You've got the gift."

I take a deep breath. I keep telling myself not to get too attached to the baby, but the truth is, I already feel as if she and I have some kind of bond. After all, no-one else has paid her nearly so much attention. Somehow, I seem to have fallen into the role of her carer, and although I'm wary of taking on too much responsibility, I can't deny that this role seems to be coming to me very easily and naturally.

"Do you think she knows?" I ask after a moment, keeping my voice down. "About her mother?"

"I have no idea," Patricia replies. "Not on a conscious level, obviously, but maybe..." She pauses. "No," she says eventually. "I guess that's a conversation she'll have to have later, when she's older."

"Was it hard?" I ask. "I mean, you had to make a decision right there and then, whether to save Shauna or the baby... Was it hard to choose?"

"Not at all," she replies. "The choice was between a fully-grown woman and a new-born child. I chose to prioritize the child, even though I knew it meant the mother would likely die. I think that's a perfectly rational decision. The child, theoretically, has more years ahead of her. It's simple math."

"But you can't look at it like that, can you?" I reply. "You can't reduce it to logic and numbers?"

She nods. "Yeah," she says after a moment. "I can, actually. It saves a whole lot of time. If I'd stopped to debate the ethics of it, they'd probably both be dead." She pauses for a moment, staring down at the baby's face. "So has anyone decided on a name for her yet?"

"I guess that's Eriksen's job," I point out.

"He doesn't give a crap," she replies. "Does he even bother to hold her?"

I shake my head.

"She needs a name," she continues. "Maybe you should choose?"

"Me?"

"Why not? If Eriksen isn't going to do it, you seem like the best-placed person to -"

"I'm not her parent," I say, holding the baby out and trying to get Patricia to take her. Suddenly filled with a kind of panic, I feel as if I'm in danger of being installed as a substitute mother, and that's not something I'm ready for. "Why don't you look after her? You're a doctor, aren't you?"

"She cries when I hold her," she replies,

pointedly refusing to take the child. "You're doing a good job with her, Elizabeth." She pauses, and it's clear from the look in her eyes that she's amused by my reaction. "What's so bad about choosing a name for her? Just pluck something out of thin air. It doesn't have to be anything special. Make something up. What was *your* mother's name?"

"I can't use that," I say quickly, feeling as if I'm about to hyperventilate.

"Why not?" She puts a hand on my arm. "Jesus, Elizabeth. It's just a baby. You're not tied to it for life."

"I know," I reply, "but..." I take a deep breath, trying to calm down.

"So isn't there a name you like?" she continues. "Don't think of it as some kind of chain, binding you to the baby forever. It's just a name. Don't you think she needs a name?"

I stare down at the baby. I know Patricia's right, but at the same time I also feel as if, by naming her, I'd be accepting even more responsibility. This isn't my child, and I don't feel as if I can handle the job of looking after her.

"How's Toad?" I ask, hoping to change the subject.

"He had a difficult night," she replies, with a hint of concern in her voice. "The infection isn't spreading, but it's pretty well rooted. I've tried everything in my kit, but it's not like we've got a plentiful supply cupboard. I have to balance his needs with the importance of keeping some stocks in reserve." She pauses. "He's feverish and he's not responding as well as I'd have liked. In normal circumstances, I'd have shot him off to hospital, he'd be pumped full of drugs, and he'd recover without a doubt. As it is, he's..." She pauses again, and it's as if she's debating whether or not to be completely honest with me. "It's fifty-fifty whether he'll get through the day without deteriorating further. If he gets much worse, I don't think I can continue to throw the last of our dwindling medical supplies at him."

I stare at her for a moment as I realize what she's saying. "So you'd rather let him die," I say eventually, "than keep trying to help him?"

"I can't throw good drugs after bad," she replies. "If I make a judgment call that he's unlikely to get better, I need to keep those drugs back in case someone else needs them some time."

"You have to save him," I continue, starting to panic once again. "We need him!"

"You seem very attached to Toad all of a sudden," she replies, with a hint of a smile. "Tell me something. If it was Bridger or Thor, or me, in the same situation, would you be quite so concerned?"

"Of course," I reply, even though there's a heavy sensation in my belly that makes me realize I might not be telling the whole truth. "Is it really so easy for you?" I continue. "First Shauna, now Toad. Can you just quantify human life like this and make calm, logical decisions about whether someone lives or dies?"

She nods.

"Really?"

"Really." She pauses. "I've always been able to take the emotion out of a situation. Even back at medical school, other people would get all tied up in knots, and I'd be able to just stand back and make a calm, calculated decision. Believe me, as a doctor, it helps to be able to take a step back. I don't know whether that makes me a good person or a really bad one, but it's just how things have been. Always."

"I wish I was like that," I reply after a moment.

"It might not be up to us anyway," she continues. "The others have got wind of Toad's condition, and they're starting to worry that..." She pauses. "There's been some talk about his condition, about what might really be causing it. Some of the others are starting to worry that maybe he's infected by the same thing that's causing those creatures to keep showing up."

"He's not," I say firmly. "It's the wound in his shoulder. *That's* what's making him sick."

"I know that," she replies, "and you know that, but... we're only two people. Bridger, Thor and

Eriksen are three people. If it came down to a vote -"

"No-one's voting," I reply, starting to feel as if things are spiraling out of control. In my arms, the baby wriggles a little and lets out a gurgle, as if she's picking up on my sense of panic. "This is about someone's life," I continue. "You're a doctor. Your decision should be the one that stands."

"We try to do things democratically around here," she replies. "One person, one vote. Sure, I'd expect the others to listen to me, but that doesn't mean they'll blindly do what I say. Anyway..." She pauses again. "There are other politics involved, Elizabeth. One less mouth to feed means more for the rest of us, and that's certainly one viable way of looking at things."

"This is Toad's farm!" I point out.

"So what?" she replies. "It's survival of the fittest, Elizabeth. The strong survive and the weak die. No pack prospers by spending precious resources on the needs of the weaker members. Sure, it'd be nice if we could look after Toad and do everything in our power to keep him alive, but in case you haven't noticed, we're hardly living in an ideal world. Toad was one of the strong ones, but he got unlucky and now he can't really look after himself. The weaker members of a pack always have to die, otherwise they slow the group down."

"But Toad's going to get better!"

"I'm just saying that people are worried," she continues. "There's a plan to discuss it later. You can say what you need to say, and I'll certainly give my opinion, but if the others insist on a vote, I can see things going against Toad. I'm not saying that's what I want, but..." She pauses, before getting to her feet and walking over to the door. "It's democracy," she says, glancing back at me. "The vote carries the day, Elizabeth, and if the others ask me whether Toad might be infected with something dangerous, I'm going to have to give them an honest answer."

"And what would that be?" I ask, even though I'm pretty sure I already know what she's going to say.

"That I don't know," she replies, before leaving the room.

In my arms, the baby starts to wriggle again. I look down and see that her eyes are open, and she's staring up at me with a look of wonder. I want to tell her that everything's okay, but I know that'd be a lie. Instead, I force a smile and wipe away a tear from the corner of my eye. This is no world for a child. I want to believe that things are going to get better, but the truth is, everything seems to be going to hell. I can't even begin to imagine the world that this child will inherit, even if she somehow manages to survive until adulthood.

"It's okay," I lie, leaning down and kissing her forehead. "Everything's okay." And that's when, for a fraction of a second, a name flickers into my mind. I force it out. I'm not naming this child. If I name her, that means I'm taking responsibility for her, and that's not what I want. Someone else can give her a name. Someone who's actually going to be around while she grows up.

DAYS 9 TO 16

THOMAS

Missouri

"THIS PLACE IS CREEPY," I say, standing in the hallway and staring up the stairs. "Seriously, Joe. It's like something out of a horror movie." I wait for a reply, but after a moment I turn and look back through to the kitchen, where Joe is still sitting at the table. "You okay?" I ask.

After a few seconds, he nods.

"What's wrong?" I ask. "Is it happening?"

"I'm..." He pauses. "I'm checking something," he continues after a moment. "It's okay, I'm just... Following him."

I wait for him to continue, but he seems lost in thought. "Following who?" I ask.

"The guy who's been inside my head," he

replies. "It's like, he can move from body to body, seeing out of different eyes all over the world, and I think I can..." His voice trails off again. "I think I can follow him," he adds. "He's searching for something. He's getting pretty frantic about it, too. Whatever it is, it's bugging the shit out of him. It's kind of a mind-fuck, but I can see people in all these different cities."

"What's it like out there?" I ask, even though I'm worried about the answer. "Is the rest of the world like this?"

He pauses. "Yeah," he says after a moment. "There's not many people. They're scared of the creatures, but the creatures are just focusing on..." He pauses again, as if his mind is far away. "They're definitely looking for something," he continues eventually. "It's not like they're rampaging through the streets or nothing like that. They're trying to find a..." He pauses yet again. "I think it's a person," he adds after a moment. "I think they're looking for a guy."

I open my mouth to ask another question, but finally I realize that there doesn't seem to be much point. It's hard to understand what Joe's going through; he seems to be in another world entirely, and every time I try to talk to him, the conversation is punctuated by these long periods where his mind wanders.

"I'm trying to find out what's causing those

booms," he says after a moment. "You know the ones in the distance? I can't work out what's happening."

"It's nuclear power stations," I reply. "Isn't it? Each boom is another one blowing up."

"You've been watching too many shitty films," he mutters. "It's not nuclear fucking power stations. Whatever it is, it's something bigger. Something deeper in the ground."

"I'll be upstairs," I say after a moment, turning and starting to make my way up the narrow, rickety wooden stairs that lead to the upper floor of the building. To be honest, exploring some kind of messed-up, remote old house isn't exactly my idea of fun, but I have to do something while I wait for Joe to... get to where he's going. I can't kill him, and I can't leave him, so I just have to stick around for a day or two longer, and try to distract myself from the inevitability of what's happening to him.

When I get to the next floor, I realize that there's a pretty foul stench in the air, like rotten eggs mixed with vinegar and ham. Seeing as that old guy was a goddamn psycho, I wouldn't be surprised by just about anything I might find in this place, and there's a part of me that just wants to turn around, go back downstairs and not go poking my nose around. Then again, I feel like I want to know more about what happened here. Hell, in all this time, I never even learned the guy's name. The sick asshole tortured me, almost killed me, and then tried to get me to kill my brother; I figure I should at least know his goddamn name.

Taking a step forward, I -

"Sara?"

I freeze.

From one of the nearby rooms, there's a creaking sound, as if something's pressing on the floorboards. I take a deep breath, but my heart is racing. It never occurred to me, after the old man died in the basement, that there might be anyone else here. I never heard him talking to another soul, but I swear to God, I just heard a woman's voice coming from one of the rooms. I wait, terrified in case she speaks again. I want to believe that I imagined it, that it was just some crazy sound that popped into my head for a moment; to be honest, I'd rather believe that I'm losing my mind than that there's someone else up here.

"Sara?" the voice says again, sounding old and frail. "Help me. I need something to eat. This food is moldy and your father won't bring me anything fresh."

I stare at the doorway, with the door hanging halfway open. Whoever's in there, it seems they're trapped somehow. Did the old guy keep someone else prisoner up here? I'm starting to think that he was more than just some old Nazi; it's as if he was a complete psychopath, and I just happened to stumble upon him at the worst possible moment.

"If your father around?" she asks suddenly. "Sara, answer me. I know you're out there, girl. I need food!"

Turning, I run down the stairs and head through to the kitchen, where I find Joe still sitting at the table. I open my mouth, trying to tell him what just happened, but no words come out; it's as if my brain has seized up and I can't even believe it myself. As I wait for him to acknowledge me, I hear another creaking sound from upstairs, almost as if something or someone is trying to move. Whatever this thing is, I don't think it's a ghost; I think it's a real, live human being.

"What's up with *you*?" Joe asks after a moment, turning to me. "Jesus fucking Christ, Tommy. You look pale as shit. You crapped yourself or something?"

ELIZABETH

Pennsylvania

"AREN'T YOU GOING TO ask how your daughter is doing?" Patricia asks, sitting at the kitchen table and watching as Eriksen takes a swig of water.

"She doing okay?" he asks, wiping his mouth.

"Why don't you hold her?" Patricia continues. "Find out for yourself."

He pauses, before letting out a burp. "Later," he mutters.

"What's wrong with now?" she asks.

"Later," he says again, more firmly this time.

Sitting over by the window, with the baby in my arms, I instinctively bristle at the mere suggestion that Eriksen might hold the child. For one thing, the guy's clearly either hungover or still drunk, probably a little of both, and he'd probably just drop her; for another, I can't deny that there's a part of me that just wants him to go away and never come back. I know I should probably be trying to get him to grow more attached to his daughter, but I'm convinced he'll be a terrible parent, so what I really want is for him to turn around, walk out of here and leave the farm forever.

"She'd just cry," he says after a moment. "No point setting her off again. If there's one thing I can't fucking stand, it's the sound of a baby screaming its lungs out."

"Have you come up with a name for her yet?" Patricia asks.

"I figured I'd let her grow up first," he replies with a grin, "and then she can pick her own. I want her to be free, not saddled with some random name I pick out of my ass for her."

"In other words," she replies, "you don't give a damn."

"If that's your interpretation of my response," he mutters, "go ahead. I really don't give a shit what you think."

Taking a deep breath, I force myself not to respond. It's hard to believe that Eriksen could be so uninterested in his own daughter, and there's a part of me that wonders whether he's scared of getting close to her. If that's the case, then it's fine by me, although I'm still worried that I've started to be seen by the others as the natural choice when it comes to caring for the baby.

"Hold her," Patricia says after a moment. "Elizabeth, come and -"

"No," I say quickly, although I immediately realize that I probably sound a little too defensive.

"Maybe if Eriksen holds his -"

"She's settled," I reply, hoping that she'll shut up and stop pushing. "She's asleep."

Patricia stares at me with a cautious, amused expression. It's as if she's started to suspect that I'm getting attached to the baby, which I guess might be true.

"See?" Eriksen says with a sniff. "She's fine." He pauses for a moment, before a leering smile crosses his lips. "So have you two ladies discussed which of you might try to breast-feed the kid?"

"She's making do with the last of our milk," Patricia replies, clearly not amused.

"Yeah, but -"

"Don't," she says firmly. "Carl, just... don't. Leave a little dignity to the whole thing, okay?"

"Stop giving me a hard time," he replies. "In case no-one's bothered to think about it, I lost the love of my life the other day. Fuck, Shauna might not have been perfect, but we were gonna head out west together and start a new life together. I had all my plans and dreams built up on her, and now everything's been rudely snatched away." He pauses. "It might do you good to remember that I'm in mourning. It's only natural that I should get a little funny. Since Toad's got his feet up, I'm commandeering his share of the beer supply. I need to think and mourn, and beer helps with both those things."

"You've been wasted since you got here," Patricia replies darkly. "How's the thinking been going so far? Come up with any great ideas yet?"

"How's the patient?" he snaps back at her. "Unless Toad comes wandering down the stairs in the next few hours, I think we've got a much bigger problem than whether or not I hold that fucking kid, okay?" He pauses for a moment, and it's clear that this is a subject that has been bothering him. "Toad's a fucking liability. Someone needs to just go up there and finish him off. Humanely, of course. I mean, I like the guy and I don't wanna torture him or nothing, but something's gotta be done. What if he's got it? What if he spreads it to the rest of us? We can't take that risk." He turns and looks at the baby. "My newborn daughter can't be exposed to no disease. She's the future of the human race. We've gotta prioritize her needs."

"Don't you think you're jumping the gun?" Patricia asks, as Bridger enters the room carrying a tray of what appears to be some kind of leafy crop from the garden.

"What do you think?" Eriksen asks, turning to me. "No, wait, you'd never agree to hurt your boyfriend, would you?"

"He's not my boyfriend," I say firmly.

"What about you?" he continues, turning to Bridger, and then to Thor as the latter comes through to the kitchen. "What do you two think? Come on, the pair of you usually keep your mouths shut, but there's gotta be some kind of activity in your brains. You've gotta have opinions, haven't you?" He waits for an answer. "Well? Don't wait for someone else to tell you what to think. Speak your fucking minds!"

"It's hard to say," Bridger mutters, although it sounds as if he's carefully trying to avoid giving an opinion.

"Hard to say?" Eriksen replies with a laugh. "Bullshit. Why don't you fucking say what you're thinking, man?" He waits for a reply, but Bridger seems to be completely focused on arranging the food on the tray. "I know why," Eriksen continues after a moment. "You don't want to rock the boat, do you?" He turns to Thor. "What about you, man? Come on, I know you're more of an individual. What do you think we should do about the weaker members of our little group? Should we continue to divert valuable resources to their possible survival, or should we just accept that there's nothing more that can be done?"

"It's not quite as bad as that," Patricia replies. "He's suffering complications from the wound, and there's an infection that -"

"Don't bullshit me," he snaps. "I overheard your little chat with Elizabeth. You can't guarantee that Toad isn't infected, and even if he wasn't, you still don't think you can do much to save him. You said it just an hour ago. You can't say one thing in private and then come in here and say something completely different. You have to be honest with us all."

"Is that true?" Thor asks.

Patricia opens her mouth to reply, but it's quickly clear from the look on her face that she can't lie. "If we had proper facilities," she starts to say, "we could focus on dealing with Toad's problems -"

"We don't have proper facilities," Eriksen says, interrupting her. "We've got, what, a little medical kit bag and a few old cloths?" He smiles. "That's fuck all, really, isn't it? Face it, if any one of us gets more than a scratch, it's curtains. We're not exactly living in an age of medical miracles. Not anymore."

"Can you keep your voice down?" I say

firmly, as the baby starts to grumble. She looks upset, as if she's about to cry, and although I'm trying to calm her down by rocking her gently, it's clear that she's picking up on the bad vibes in the room. It's been less than forty-eight hours since she was born, but I can't help worrying that she's already been exposed to enough shouting and arguing to last a lifetime.

"You don't agree with me, do you?" Eriksen asks, stepping over to me.

"I think -"

"It's fine," he continues, "I heard what you said earlier." Reaching down, he clumsily takes hold of the baby and pulls her from my arms. "It's nice of you to wanna look after her and all," he adds, "but if you're not on my side, then you're not on my side, and that's all there is to it." He rocks the baby back and forth for a moment. "She's fine with her Daddy, right?"

"Maybe you should let Elizabeth hold her," Patricia says calmly.

"Maybe we should take a vote on Toad," Eriksen replies. "We're all here, so let's get on with it. Who here thinks we should give Toad the benefit of the doubt and continue to let him fester in bed, potentially spreading his disease to the rest of us?"

There's silence in the room for a moment. It's clear that no-one wants to be the first to show their hand.

"Who thinks," Eriksen continues, picking his words carefully and with an amused expression, "that for the good of the group, and especially the children, who need to be protected the most, we should bite the bullet and find a way to humanely and quickly put poor old Toad out of his misery?" After a moment, he balances the baby in one arm while raising a hand in support of his own motion.

I look over at Bridger and Thor, and it's painfully obvious that they're on the verge of agree with Eriksen. If that happens, there'll be three of them, which makes a majority.

"Come on," Eriksen continues. "If everyone just votes the way they truly think, we've got a functioning democracy. I'll ask again. Who here thinks we should humanely put Toad out of his misery and protect the group from the possibility of an outbreak of whatever fucking disease is causing all of this bullshit?"

Slowly, Thor raises his hand.

"What about you?" Eriksen asks Bridger. "What do you think? Don't be scared. There'll be no recriminations. Just vote with your head and your heart."

Slowly, Bridger starts to lift his hand up.

"Twenty-four hours," Patricia says suddenly, turning to him. "A compromise. We'll wait twenty-four hours, and if there's no improvement in Toad's condition..." She pauses. "If there's no improvement, I'll vote for a humane end to his suffering. There are a few drugs in the cabinet, I can put something together that'll knock him out completely and then we can finish the job. He won't even have to know. As far as he knows, he'll just go to sleep."

"You can't do that!" I say, shocked that she'd even consider such a possibility.

"It makes sense," she says. "It's logical!"

"I don't care about logic!" I reply. "You can't kill someone just because -"

"Hush!" Eriksen says firmly, as the baby starts to cry. "Jesus Christ, Elizabeth. See what you've done? For God's sake, can't you keep your voice down?" He grins as he starts rocking the baby roughly in his arms. "Come on, little girl. Ignore the nasty shouting voices. Everything's okay. Daddy's here."

"Twenty-four hours," Bridger says. "That sounds reasonable."

"I agree," Thor adds.

"Fine," Eriksen mutters, "we'll give him twenty-four hours to get better. Not that it's gonna make much difference anyway." He glances over at me. "It doesn't matter what you vote, Elizabeth. There's four of us already in agreement, so democracy carries the day and we've made a group decision. If Toad isn't back up on his feet in twenty-four hours, we'll end his misery."

"And you're okay with this?" I ask, turning to Patricia.

"It makes sense," she replies calmly. "It's logical."

I want to argue with them all, but it's clear that I'm in the minority. Looking over at Eriksen, I watch for a moment as he tries to calm the baby's cries; the sight of him trying to be a good father is completely grotesque, and finally I realize that I can't be in the room any longer. Turning, I hurry to the door and out into the gloomy mid-morning yard, where a gray sky promises a hint of oncoming rain. The truth is, I know deep down that Toad's condition is unlikely to improve in twenty-four or even forty-eight hours, but that doesn't mean I think it's fair to kill him. This is his farm, and we've been using his resources and his supplies, and now the others are using the pretense of democracy to get rid of him. It's completely unfair, but at the same time, I can't see a way to help. He's doomed.

THOMAS

Missouri

"HOLY FUCK," JOE SAYS as we get to the top of the stairs. "It stinks up here."

"Who are you?" the woman's voice calls out, sounding terrified. "Where's my husband? Where's Sara?"

Joe turns to me, and I can see the look of amused shock in his yellowing eyes. "Who the fuck is that?" he whispers. "Have you had some woman stashed up here all this time, and you weren't gonna tell me?"

"I've got a gun!" the woman shouts. "I'm warning you right now! I've got a gun and I'm not afraid to use it! If you come into my room again, I'll blast your brain across the wallpaper!"

"Bullshit," Joe says quietly. "If she had a gun, her old Nazi husband would have come and taken it to use on me the other day. She's bluffing." He smiles. "She's probably just frigid. She probably think we're gonna go in there and have our way with her." Pausing, he glances over at the door. "Is she hot? I don't mind if she's a little on the mature side. I mean, any hole's a goal, right?"

"What if she's isn't bluffing?" I ask, my heart still racing as I try to ignore Joe's dumb comments. "We don't need to go in there, Joe. Let's just leave her!"

"Where's your Christian spirit?" he replies. "Anyway, I'm not scared no more. If she blows my fucking head off, it's a favor." With that, he limps over to the door and heads into the room.

"Oh my God," the woman says, her voice filled with fear. "Dear Lord, protect this house from -"

"Never mind any of that crap," Joe says with a grin, before turning to me. "Tommy boy, come and look at this. I've found the source of the stink up here! Forget what I said about giving her a whirl, though. Some holes just ain't a goal after all."

I shake my head.

"Come on," he continues. "It's like a fucking freak-show in here."

"Get out!" the woman yells, although she sounds too weak to put up much of a fight.

"Where's that gun you were yapping about?" Joe asks. "Come on, I dare you. Pop a cap right in my head, right between the eyes if you can manage it. I could really use the favor, actually, on account of my little brother not having the guts to finish me off twice."

"Beau!" the woman screams. "Sara! There's a strange man in the house!"

"Beau?" Joe replies with a smile. "Is that the old Nazi's name, huh? Beau. Well, at least now I know. It's always nice to be able to put a name to a grizzled old face." He turns to me. "Isn't that nice to know, Tommy? The old bastard who almost killed you was named Beau. Beau the fucking Nazi prick."

"When my husband gets here," the woman continues, "he'll wipe that smile off your face. As God is my witness, your trespass won't go unpunished. My husband isn't the kind of man you should ever dare to cross. He was in Korea. He's killed men with their bare hands. He'll put a bullet between your eyes and hang your corpse out for the jackals."

"Your husband's dead," Joe replies. "He's down in the basement, along with the bones of someone named Sara. Does that make any sense to you?"

"My Sara is not dead!" the woman shouts.
"She -"
"She's not dead!" she screams. "Don't you

dare speak such untruths! My Sara is a good girl and she's... she's... she's not dead! She'd never leave me!"

"She's dead as anything I've ever seen before," Joe continues. "There's nothing left of her but a few stained bones and a couple of scraps of skin and hair. She's down in the basement right now. Your husband, as it happens, was keeping my little brother locked up in that very same fucking basement. Damn near starved him to death, too. I mean, seriously, without being too harsh, that old guy was a complete fucker. A real old Adolf, if you know what I mean. The guy clearly had a few screws loose."

"Get out of my house!" the woman shouts.

"Why don't you climb out of bed and make me?" Joe replies.

"You unholy brute!" she yells.

"Tommy," Joe says, turning to me again, "you have to at least see this. It's fucking disgusting, but you've really gotta see it to believe it!" As he speaks, a book flies across the room and hits him in the chest. "You can throw your Bible at me all you want," Joe continues with a grin, "but it ain't gonna make any difference. You can't even get out of bed, can you? Jesus..." He turns to me again. "Tommy, are you gonna drag your ass in here and take a look at this? It's fucking unreal what we've got sitting here shouting her head off at us. She looks like that puppet off that fucking TV show about that haunted crypt and shit."

I want to tell him to go to hell, but something compels me to walk toward the door. I guess I feel that I can't afford to shy away from things anymore; with the world having completely collapsed, I need to grow up and be a man, especially now that Joe's not going to be around for much longer. Even though I want to turn and run, therefore, I step through the door and look over at the bed on the other side of the room.

"Fucking Christ..." Joe whispers with a smile.

At first, I don't see what I'm supposed to be looking at. There's a bed, sure, and it's messy, but apart from a bunch of crumpled, dirty sheets, all I can see is some kind of gray mass, thin and straggly as if...

And then I see the eyes.

"Take a closer look," Joe says enthusiastically, before catching me by surprise and pushing me across the room.

Stumbling, I land on the corner of the bed, and when I look over at the other end I see a horrific, shriveled gray face staring back at me, with skin so tight that its eyeballs are almost completely exposed in the sockets. It's just about possible to determine that the figure in the bed is a woman, thanks to the huge, frilly pink nightgown covering her gaunt, withered frame, and there's a thin straggle of white hair on her head, but she looks more dead than alive and it's hard to believe that her heart could possibly still be beating.

"Who are you?" I ask, unable to stop staring at her.

Slowly, she reaches out to me, and I see the skin clinging to her bones, with not an ounce of fat anywhere. Her bony hand pushes against me, and finally I realize that she's trying to get me off her bed. She obviously has very little energy left, but she's filled with panic and fear. It's hard to believe that she's alive, and she looks worse than some of the creatures we've encountered, but something about her seems different.

"Sorry," I mutter, getting to my feet. "I..." My voice trails off as I realize that I have no idea what to say to her.

"Look at the crazy old hag," Joe continues, still standing by the door. "Fuck, Tommy, did you ever see anything so fucking wretched in your entire life? Jesus Christ, that dried-out old prune looks like something you'd dug up in a pyramid in Egypt. I bet you any money in the world that a cloud of dust comes out her pussy every time she coughs."

"Don't talk like that," I reply, seeing the hurt, shocked look in the woman's eyes. "What happened to you?" I continue, kneeling by the bed. "How long have you been up here?"

"Sara stopped bringing me food," she says slowly. "After that, Beau stayed downstairs. I had to eat whatever I could find. I had..." She turns to look over at a pile of mold on the bedside table; as she moves her head, there's a faint creaking sound, as if her bones are grinding against one another. "I had one sandwich left, and a bowl of soup. Over the years, the mold kept growing, so I just ate the mold and left the sandwich and the soup."

"Fucking brilliant," Joe mutters from over by the door.

"Where's Sara?" the woman asks, with tears in her eyes. "Fetch Sara! I need Sara!"

"There's no-one called Sara here," I tell her. "Not anymore."

"Don't you lie to me!" she hisses, her eyes filled venom as she lashes out at me with a weak, bony hand. "Bring my Sara to me! You bring my Sara to me right now, do you hear? I won't have strange men in my room! You bring my daughter here and then you leave, do you understand?"

"What do you think?" Joe asks, clearly amused by the whole thing. "Should we do what she wants? Should we bring what's left of Sara up to see her? Hell, we could even drag the old man up too and orchestrate a good old-fashioned family reunion."

"Let's just leave her alone," I reply. "Joe, we should just get out of here."

"And miss the fun?" he asks with a grin. "Fucking hell, no way. If this old bitch has been bed-bound for most of her life, which seems to be the case judging by the fucking stink in this place, I don't see why we shouldn't have a little fun. What do you think? Should we bring the other two up here to join her, or should we carry her down to the basement?"

ELIZABETH

Pennsylvania

TRUDGING THROUGH THE FOREST, I stop for a moment and glance back at the farmhouse. I know it's dangerous to be out here, but at the same time I feel as if I'd rather take that risk rather than sit around in that place with a bunch of assholes who think they've got some kind of right to sit in judgment over other people. Besides, I can't bear to watch Eriksen holding his daughter; I know it's his right, but I still hate to see that poor child being rocked in his arms.

    The forest floor is a little damp as I make my way between the trees. There's a light mist in the air, and after a few more paces I stop and stare into the distance. For a moment, I allow myself to consider a truly horrific possibility. If Eriksen wasn't part of the group, I'm convinced that Bridger and Thor would be much more willing to listen to Patricia, and I could probably get them on my side. It's so tempting to imagine the ease with which Eriksen could be forced out of the way. After all, the guy's drunk half the time, and it's not as if anyone would really miss him. After thinking for a few seconds about how easy it'd be to kill him, I realize with a shiver that I'm contemplating cold-blooded murder. It's hard to believe that I could even entertain the possibility. What the hell is happening to me?

Taking a deep breath, I decide that it's time to go and talk to Patricia. There has to be a way for her to help Toad. She's a doctor, and it's not as if he's suffering from some kind of mystery illness. It's an infected wound; she *has* to be able to think of something.

"Who's there?" a voice calls out suddenly, as I'm turning to head back to the farmhouse.

Looking back over at the nearby clearing, I suddenly realize that I've come close to the pit in which Patricia has been keeping one of the creatures captive. For a moment, I consider turning and running, but I can hear the creature struggling down in the pit and I realize after a few seconds that there's no reason to be scared. It's not as if he can get up here and hurt me. In fact, given the intensity of events back in the farmhouse, I can't shake the feeling that the creature in the pit might actually be the sanest person I can talk to around here right now.

"It's you," he continues, his voice sounding gnarled and ravaged. "I recognize the sound of your footsteps. Elizabeth's your name, isn't it? I've seen you before, in New York and at least one other time."

I stand completely still, my heart racing.

"What are you doing out here alone?" he asks. "Do you know what that bitch is planning to do to me next? I can't feel pain, but I can feel boredom. I suppose I should abandon this body, but I'm still curious to see what that woman wants."

Taking a deep breath, I glance around to make sure that we're alone, before walking over to the edge of the pit and staring down at the creature. He looks a little worse than when I first saw him a couple of days ago, as if his body has continued to rot. That's one of the things I don't understand about these creatures; if their bodies are rotting away, aren't they going to just die off eventually? Pausing for a moment, I start to feel as if maybe I have the upper hand here.

"What's wrong?" he asks. "Something's bothering you, isn't it? You wouldn't be out here alone if everything was honey and roses." He pauses. "The look on your face is priceless. What's wrong? Are you starting to realize that other humans aren't necessarily all they're cracked up to be? Believe me, I can sympathize. Before all of this started, back when Joseph was just a laboratory technician, he hated humans too. That's why he created us, to wipe them all out and replace them with something better. Our progenitor had some good ideas."

"I don't hate humanity," I say firmly.

"Just the ones around you?"

"It doesn't matter," I mutter.

"Humans are scum," he continues. "They kill each other constantly. They hate and they spew venom and they don't care who they hurt. Sure, there might be a few exceptions, but the vast majority of humanity is a huge cesspool of evil and cruelty. This planet is going to be a thousand times better off once the last of them have been wiped away and replaced by..." He pauses. "You know what I am, don't you? You understand what's coming next? There's no way to stop it, no way to hold back the new order that's coming to take control. You might as well just go with it. Hell, maybe there's even a place for one of two of the old humans to still be around. Does that sound like something that might appeal to you?"

I shake my head.

"Think it over," he continues. "I heard a baby crying earlier. What if I offered you a deal? Take the baby and get out of this place. You know there'll be more of me soon, and we'll rip this goddamn farm apart until everyone's dead. Do you really want to spend the rest of your life running from me? I promise you, it'll be a short, painful and uncomfortable existence, not only for you but also for that baby. On the other hand, if you agree to become one of the select few who stay behind in the new world, I can promise you a long life, and the same goes for that baby."

"You're trying to make a deal with me?" I ask, stunned by what he's suggesting.

"Are you up for a deal?" he replies.

I shake my head.

"What do you say?" he continues. "Come on, I know it's probably a bit of a shock, but it makes sense. Those assholes in the house, arguing about democracy and voting rights... They're just the last dregs of a dying civilization. They're already turning on one another. Once they've picked off your friend, they'll turn on someone else, and then someone else again, and finally as the resources start to dwindle they'll just collapse completely. It's not exactly much of a survival strategy, is it? Don't you want that baby to have a better chance in life? Don't you want her to have a proper future?" He pauses. "You can give that to her, Elizabeth. You can give her a future. Just accept my offer, and all the pain and fear and doubt can go away."

"I'm not making a deal with you," I reply, my voice tense with fear.

"You think I'm a monster?"

"I think you're a..." I pause as I try to find the right word.

"A what?" he continues. "A zombie?" There's a pause, and a smile crosses his rotten, decaying face. "You've got things the wrong way round, girl. Humans were the real zombies. Mindless, groaning things, swarming all over the planet and causing endless harm and destruction. It's precisely that kind of behavior that I'm trying to get rid of. Sure, I've been learning how to control the bodies, and the rotten ones might look a little alarming, but I'll get there soon. Once I've got a handle on these things, and once I've found the progenitor, we'll start a whole new society, filled with harmony and peace."

"And they'll all have the same mind?" I reply.

"At first," he says, "although I've come to think that over time, some degree of variation might be permitted. Variations on a theme, in a way... Different versions, rooted in the same basic personality. Variety and similarity, all at the same time, and I'm offering you a chance to be part of that world. You'd be separate, in a way, because you'd still have your own mind. Does it really sound so bad?"

I stare at him. The truth is, part of his argument kind of makes sense to me. I can see how someone might want to change the way society works. What I *don't* see, however, is any reason to think that these creatures are the answer.

"Come on," he continues. "Carl Eriksen? Bridger? Patricia? All those people are just examples of the worst kind of humanity. They're scum. Eriksen doesn't even care about his own child. Out of him or me, which one do you think would be better off contributing to a new era of life on this planet?"

"He -" I start to say, before suddenly a moment of realization hits me. "What did you say?" I ask after a few seconds.

"Carl Eriksen is human garbage," he replies. "He's a repellant piece of trash. You know it, and I know it, so why not -"

"I know it because I was there with him," I say, interrupting him. "I talked to him and I listened to his bullshit. That's how *I* know it, but how do *you* know it?" I take a step back as my mind fills with different explanations, until I realize that there's only one that makes sense. "You were in there," I say. "You were in there with us."

"I'm staked to the ground in a pit," he replies. "How the hell could I have been in there? I just heard your voices arguing. I'm not deaf!"

"You're too far away to have heard everything," I reply.

He stares at me for a moment, and the smile has left his lips, replaced by a look of concern.

"You were in there with us," I continue, "because you're in the mind of one of the people in the farmhouse, aren't you? You've already infected someone, but you've managed to pass unnoticed."

"You're a smart girl," he replies after a moment. "Instead of running off in a panic, why don't you sit down and talk to me properly, like two intelligent individuals."

"Who is it?" I continue. "Bridger? Thor?

Patricia?" I take a deep breath, trying to think back to anything over the past few days that seems out of place. "It's Patricia, isn't it?" I say after a moment. "No, wait, she wouldn't have kept you down here. It must be Thor. He's quiet, doesn't say much, but sometimes..." I pause again as I realize that I have no idea which of the other people in the farmhouse might have been infected. Hell, for all I know it might be more than one of them. "Eriksen?" I ask.

The creature doesn't reply. He just stares at me, as if he finds me amusing.

"It's not Toad," I continue. "It can't be Toad..."

"How do you know it's not you?" he replies. "How do you know I haven't already infected you? Maybe I'm looking out through your eyes right now, and you don't even know I'm in your head?"

"I'd know," I say calmly.

"Would you?"

"I'd *know*," I say again, this time with more confidence. After all, if there was someone else in my head, I'd definitely be able to feel or hear them. "It's one of the others."

He smiles. "Good luck finding out. I could tell you, but then there wouldn't be any fun, would it? The best part is, while you rip one another apart and your little community collapses into fear and suspicion, I'll have a perfect, ringside seat for the whole thing."

I stare at him for a moment, before turning and starting to run back to the farmhouse. I can hear the creature calling after me, but all I can do is keep running. By the time I get back to the front door, I have to stop for a moment and work out what to do next. I can hear the others arguing inside, so I push the door open and slip into the kitchen. At first, no-one seems to even notice that I've arrived, but finally, one by one, they glance over at me. As the room falls silent, I realize that they've recognized the look of horror on my face. Patricia, Bridger, Toad and Eriksen are all waiting for me to tell them what's wrong, except one of them already knows.

One of them is already infected.

THOMAS

Missouri

"WHAT?" JOE ASKS, FOLLOWING me down the stairs. "Seriously, Tommy, what the hell's wrong with you now? You're acting all, like, fucking priggish and superior. You know who you remind me of sometimes? Mom. You remind me of Mom. How do you feel about that particular compliment, huh?"

Heading through to the kitchen, I stop for a moment, trying to work out what to do next. All I know is that that old woman can't just be left up there. She's clearly lost her mind, and it'd be inhuman and cruel to just head on out of here and leave her to rot in that bed. Still, as I hurry over to the drawer and pull it open to look at the knives, I realize that there's no way I can just go up there and kill her. I'm not that kind of person.

"You want me to do something about her?" Joe asks from the doorway.

"Like what?" I ask, trying not to let him hear that I'm scared.

"I know what you're like," he continues. "You're always banging on about doing the right thing, and I reckon this is right up your holier-than-thou creek, isn't it?" He pauses. "You want to put the old bitch out of her misery, but you don't know if you can actually do the deed. You talk the talk, but you can't actually do anything, can you?"

"We can't just leave her here," I reply, turning to him. "We have to do the right thing."

"Which is?"

"Ending her suffering."

"In other words, cutting her throat."

"No!"

"Then what?" He stares at me. "Come on, Bambi, enlighten me here. Tell me exactly how you reckon we can resolve this fucking situation in a way that doesn't hurt, upset or even mildly perturb anyone. I'm all fucking ears, kid, 'cause I don't reckon you've got any fucking clue!"

I take a deep breath. I know he's right, but I hate the fact that he seems to be so goddamn pleased with himself. I guess people never really changed: even after he's died and come back to life, my brother is still, deep down, an asshole. The biggest problem, however, is that even when he's at his most annoying, he has a habit of being right about things.

"Sometimes you have to do the wrong thing," he says eventually, "to do the right thing."

"That's bullshit," I reply.

"Killing's wrong," he continues. "I get that, I really do. Maybe God's up there in Heaven, watching down on us, and he's all, like, pissed off and angry that we'd even consider killing someone. Hell, maybe God's gonna turn green and start smashing stuff. Maybe all this crap that's happening, maybe it's God's way of saying everything's fucked up, and maybe by killing that old woman, we'd be making him even more mad." He pauses. "I figure it's worth the effort. If God's real and he's pissed off at me for saving some old hag from suffering any longer, well, I'm willing to take God's wrath. I'll sacrifice my good standing with the Lord in order to help another poor bastard out in her time of need."

I stare at him.

"Can you do that?" he asks. "Can you overlook your need to be a good boy, and do the right thing? Or are you gonna let that old bird suffer in pain, just so you can tell yourself you've still got a good relationship with the Lord? Are you that fucking selfish, Tommy?"

"You're good at killing people," I say after a moment. "It seems to come pretty easily to you. Remember that cop? Was that the right thing?"

"He had it coming to him."

"No-one deserves to die," I point out.

"Cops do."

"That's a bullshit answer and you know it," I reply. "You've always liked killing. Even when we were kids, you used to catch squirrels and mice in the barn and torture them. There's something wrong with you, Joe. There always has been, and there always will be."

"I'm dead," he replies. "It's a bit late for me to turn over a new leaf."

"The worst thing," I continue, "is that any time anyone actually points this stuff out to you, you just make some crumby joke and act like it doesn't matter."

We stand in silence for a moment.

"That cop was half-dead anyway," he replies eventually. "I mean, fuck, I basically just ended his suffering. My personal feelings don't come into it one way or another. Hell, the guy was probably grateful to me, just like..." He pauses. "Well, just like I was grateful to you when you bashed my head in. It's not your fault that things didn't quite work out as planned, but..." He takes a deep breath. "You know your problem, Tommy? You fucking think things through too much, and while you're doing that, you end up letting bad things happen. That old bitch should be dead by now, except she's gotta suffer a little longer while you go through some kind of fucking moral debate with yourself."

"I'm not a murderer!" I shout.

"You murdered me," he replies, fixing me with a determined stare. "I mean, how do you know I wouldn't have pulled through? How do you know that, in a couple of days, I wouldn't have sat up with a bit of an ache in my shoulder, and been absolutely fucking okay?"

"You *wanted* me to kill you," I reply, close to tears but determined not to let him see any emotion in my eyes. "You said it yourself! You were grateful!"

"Still," he replies coldly, "you were able to do it. So here's what I wanna know, Tommy. Help me out and tell me why I shouldn't be offended. After all, you were willing to bash my head in, but when it comes to some random old woman neither of us have met before, you're too timid and holy." He pauses. "I can't help thinking that maybe you wanted to do that to me," he adds. "Like, maybe you got a kick out of it. Maybe, after all these years, you wanted to do it."

"Don't be stupid," I reply.

"Huh." He pauses. "Fine. I'll sort the old dear out." Limping over to the drawer, he takes out a large steak knife. "That should do the trick. Don't worry, I'll make it quick and painless. Well, as quick and painless as possible, anyway." He pauses for a moment. "Or are you gonna try to stop me?" he asks. "After all, if you've got a moral objection, then you *should* try to stop me, shouldn't you? Or are you relieved that I'm gonna do it, so you don't have to?"

I stare at him, but I don't know what to say. He's right, even if I can't admit it.

"What the fuck are you gonna do when I'm not around?" he asks with a smile, before turning and limping toward the door. "Stay down here, Tommy boy. I'll be back in a few minutes. Just gotta go and do the right thing by a scared old woman whose entire family seem to have popped off prematurely."

I wait in the kitchen, listening as he slowly makes his way up the stairs. After a moment, I hear him walking into the old woman's bedroom, and seconds later she starts to call out for help, begging Sara to run up and save her. I take a deep breath as I hear a loud creaking sound, as if Joe is getting onto the bed, and finally the old woman lets out an agonized scream that cuts off abruptly. There a heavy thump, and then I hear the floorboards creak again as Joe leaves the room. By the time he's making his way back down the stairs, I feel as if my mind is completely blank and empty.

"There," he says as he reaches the doorway.

"There wasn't even much blood. The poor old hag was dried out like a fucking prune, but it's done." He pauses. "So out of the two of us, Tommy, which is the one who did the right thing today and which is the one who was weak and cruel?"

DAY 16

ELIZABETH

Pennsylvania

"THIS IS CRAZY," BRIDGER says, getting up from the table and walking over to the pitcher of water. "It's gone midnight. We're not going to get anywhere by sitting around here like this and staring at each other. No-one's infected."

"That's what an infected person would say, isn't it?" Eriksen replies, with his feet up on the table. Grinning, he looks over at Patricia, then at Thor, and finally at me. "Isn't it? Jesus Christ, you guys, have you all lost your sense of humor?"

In my arms, the baby lets out a faint gurgle.

"Maybe it's her," Eriksen continues. "Maybe the kid's infected."

"You're sick," I reply, unable to hide my disgust any longer. He's barely even held his own daughter, and now he's suggesting that she might have been infected.

"You think kids are immune?" he asks. "Seriously? If I was some fucking weird-ass sentient virus thing and I wanted to hide, I'd go for the newborn baby. Makes total sense, doesn't it?"

"No-one's excluded from suspicion," Patricia says firmly, clearly pissed off with Eriksen, "but at the same time, it's highly unlikely that the baby would be a carrier. She's had far less exposure than any of the rest of us. Granted, we don't know the mechanism of transmission, but let's not just to conclusions just yet, okay?"

"The voice of medical reason, huh?" Eriksen says with sarcasm dripping from his voice. "The world was full of fucking doctors and so-called experts, and now look at the fucking mess we're in."

"We all know who it is," Bridger says solemnly. "He's upstairs right now, and he's getting worse."

"It hasn't been twenty-four hours," I point out.

"So what?" He pauses, before turning to Patricia. "I went in to take a look at Toad earlier. The guy's sweating like a pig. He's getting worse and worse. There's no point waiting twenty-four hours, not when he could spread this thing to the rest of us. We need to take action. We need to put him out of his misery, and then..." He pauses.

"And then what?" Patricia asks uncomfortably.

"That *thing* you're keeping out in the forest," he continues. "We have to kill it."

"It's too valuable," she replies. "Our only hope for finding a cure is if -"

"There's no cure!" Bridger says firmly, exhibiting more passion than I've ever seen from him. "There's nothing! This whole world is just dying, and we're the unlucky ones who got to sit around a little longer than the rest and watch what happens! You have to kill that thing before we all get sick!"

"Try to be rational," Patricia replies. "You're acting on instinct. You're no better than a caveman. If we're going to get out of this situation, we need to be calm and logical and -"

"Screw that," Eriksen mutters with a laugh. "We've tried being calm and sensible, and now look at the fucking mess we're in." Reaching over to the table, he picks up pistol. "I can do it if the rest of you are all too fucking scared. I'll go up and put a bullet in his head while he's asleep. It's not like he'll even know that anything's fucking happened. He'll just never wake up. It's just like killing a chicken."

"We agreed to wait twenty-four hours," I say firmly.

"That was before the situation became so fucking urgent," Eriksen replies, getting to his feet. "I don't see why we should sit around and let that fucking disease get stronger and stronger." He pauses. "I'm going to put a vote to the group, and a simple majority carries the day. I propose that I go upstairs and deal with the Toad problem, and then I'll go outside and deal with that fucking creature, and then we'll decide where to go from there. Who agrees with me?" He raises his hand, and waits for the rest of us to do the same.

"No," I say, turning to Patricia.

"No," she says, staring down at the table, almost as if she's in a trance.

"I agree with Eriksen," Bridger says, raising his hand.

"You can't!" I say, shocked that he'd turn against Toad so easily.

"I'm just being logical about it," he replies. "We can't let one person put the whole group in danger!"

"What about you?" Eriksen asks, turning to Thor. "You've got the deciding vote, old pal. What do you reckon?"

Thor stares at him for a moment, before turning to the rest of us one by one until, finally, he looks down at the baby.

"I vote with Eriksen," he says eventually. "I don't like it, and I appreciate everything Toad's done for us, but if we're going to have even half a chance, we need to make tough decisions. This is the only way. All the evidence we have so far suggests that the most likely threat comes from Toad. We have to act."

"Then it's decided," Eriksen says with a faint smile, as he gets to his feet with the gun in his hand. "I guess I'll carry out the actions that have been chosen democratically by the group. I just want to say, first, that it gives me no pleasure at all to be doing these things. Toad was a good friend to me for many years, and although I hadn't seen him for a while before I rocked up here, I still hate to have to plug him. I'm sure he'd understand, though. This is the only right thing to do."

With that, he turns and heads over to the door.

"You can't!" I shout, standing up and hurrying over to him, with the baby still in my arms. Before I can reach Eriksen, however, Bridger grabs my arm and holds me back.

"Just let him do it," he says firmly.

"It's murder!" I shout, as the baby starts to cry.

"It's democracy," he replies uneasily.

"It's okay," Eriksen says. "Democracy ain't about pleasing all of the people. It's about pleasing the majority." He pauses for a moment, and a grin breaks across his face. "What matters is that the people of this place have spoken, and now we're going to -"

Suddenly there's a loud bang and Eriksen jerks back into the door-frame as one side of his head explodes, spraying blood and brain matter across the wall. As he slumps to the ground, I turn and see, to my horror, that Patricia is sitting at the table with a gun in her hand.

"Holy shit..." Thor mutters.

Calmly, Patricia stands up and fires at him, dropping Thor to the ground with a single hit to the chest. Without blinking, without even registering any kind of reaction at all, she turns and fires once again, hitting Bridger directly in the eye and sending him falling back against the wall. Turning to me, she pauses for a moment with the barrel aimed straight at me, and then slowly she lowers the gun.

"I'm sorry," she says after a moment. "I had no choice."

Looking down, I see the bodies of Eriksen, Bridger and Thor on the floor. I take a step back, unable to suppress the sense of panic that's flooding through my body.

"They were losing their heads," Patricia says calmly. "Eriksen was always a live-wire, and Bridger and Thor were starting to be too easily led. If I hadn't done something, they'd have messed everything up. They'd have killed Toad based on little more than superstition, and then they'd have killed the creature, and I couldn't allow that to happen. All three of them had crossed a line, and there was no way back for them."

"That doesn't give you a right to execute them," I reply, staring at the gun in her hand. "You can't just... You can't take matters into your own hand like that!"

"Why not?" she replies. "Because we had a vote?" She pauses, and there's a barely-suppressed smile on her lips. "People can have all the votes they want, but if they end up with the wrong decision, it's up to the smarter members of society to put them in their place. If I hadn't acted, they'd have formed this little three-person voting bloc and they'd have pushed on with a series of increasingly dumb decisions until this whole place came crashing down, and then it would've been every man for himself. They were out of control. All I did was hurry things along."

"But -"

"I'm sick of being held back by idiots," she continues. "Seriously, those men were dumb. They were useful, sure, but at the end of the day, they were starting to cause more problems than they could solve. What was I supposed to do? Let them fuck everything up, just because we all had a vote about it?"

"But the creature," I reply, trying to decide

whether or not I need to turn and run. "One of us is still infected!"

"Maybe," she says, clearly lost in thought, "or maybe not. I haven't seen any firm evidence that the infection has reached us. If it has, the most likely culprit is Toad, but I want to see some proof. Decisions have to be made based on science and fact." She looks down at the bodies. "We need to burn them," she says after a moment. "One of them might have been infected, and we still don't understand the mechanism of transmission, so -"

"How can you be so calm?" I ask, interrupting her. "You just shot three men in cold blood!"

"It was the right decision," she replies, as if it's the most natural thing in the world. "I let you live because I trust you, Elizabeth. I think you understand the importance of making decisions based on logic rather than emotion, and for that reason, I'm hoping you'll be useful." She pauses. "I'm not going to regret that decision, am I?"

I stare at her for a moment. "If I say the wrong thing," I reply eventually, "are you going to shoot me too?"

She smiles. "No. But I'd appreciate it if you could help me get these bodies out of the house. I'll go and build a bonfire, and then we can burn them. It's better to be safe than sorry."

As the baby starts to cry, I try gently rocking

her back to sleep. I want to turn and run, to get away from Patricia, but I feel as if I'm trapped here. Although I can just about see the logic in everything she says, I can't shake the feeling that she's *too* calm and *too* rational; she can't see the human side at all. She heads outside to get started on the bonfire, and as I carry the baby over to the window and watch Patricia's progress, I can't help thinking that I'm not safe here. When she decides I'm no longer useful, she'll kill me, just like she killed the others.

THOMAS

Missouri

AS SOON AS THE sun comes up, I start loading the truck. There's not exactly an abundance of supplies in the creepy old man's house, but I manage to salvage a few items that might be useful, and I still have a few days' worth of gasoline. I don't really know where I'm going to go, other than just to keep heading east. I figure that sooner or later, I have to bump into someone who can help. At the end of the day, I refuse to believe that there's no-one out there who can turn things around. Maybe it's taking longer than expected, but the army or the government or someone has to get their act in shape eventually.

Once the truck is loaded, I look back toward

the house. Joe has been much quieter over the past twelve hours, as if he's finally losing the ability to remain conscious in his decaying body. He manages a few words here and there, but it's clear that the end is coming. In fact, having spent a couple of hours putting supplies into the back of the truck and making sure that everything's ready, I'm starting to wonder if maybe I've missed the point of Joe's second death. Trudging toward the front door, I brace myself for the possibility that all I'll find will be his withered body, with his mind having long since drifted away.

"What took you so long?" he asks as soon as I enter the front room.

"I was sorting out the truck," I tell him.

"You should get going soon. There's no point leaving it 'til tonight."

"I'm not going yet," I reply. "I told you, not until..."

He smiles. "Not until what, Tommy boy? Not until I'm dead?" He pauses. "See, here's the thing. I've been thinking long and hard, and I've kinda made a decision." He takes a deep breath. "I don't want you to get all uppity about this or nothing, but I don't wanna die with an audience. I don't reckon it's right. I wanna die alone. Just sitting here will be good enough for me, but I don't want no-one seeing me or touching my body or anything like that. It's not natural to have someone around when you're about to fall off your perch. It's a private thing, and it should be done in private, with no-one watching."

"I'm not leaving you," I say firmly, even though I can feel my resistance starting to wear down.

"You've already done enough," he replies. "I *want* to be alone when it happens, Tommy. Maybe I'm being stubborn or vain or whatever, but I don't want you or anyone else here when I die. Anyway, I figure you should hit the road as soon as possible. You don't wanna be late."

"Late?" I reply with a faint smile. "For what? A long drive to nowhere?"

He pauses. "Remember how I told you that I could see through other eyes?" he says after a moment. "The psycho who's behind all this, he can occupy all these bodies at once, seeing out of their eyes all over the world, and when I forced him to leave me alone, I saw how he left. I followed, and I realized I can go wherever he goes, so..." He pauses again. "I've been looking for Martha," he continues eventually. "I've been looking through the eyes of all the creatures out in California, around San Francisco, and it took a while, but I found her."

I stare at him, unable to believe what he's saying.

"Martha's alive," he continues. "She's with some other people, and they'd been hiding out. But now..." He pauses, as if for a moment his mind isn't quite stable. "I spoke to her," he says finally. "I told her to meet you at that four state corner monument place. You know the one? Where, like, Arizona and New Mexico and a bunch of other states meet? You've gotta go there, Tommy. Martha's already on her way. I figured it'd be kinda roughly half-way between where she is and where you are, but you've gotta get a move on. If you hurry, you can be there tomorrow evening."

"Martha..." I pause. "You haven't found Martha," I say after a moment. "You *can't* have done."

"She's family," he replies. "Maybe that made it a bit easier. Fuck knows, but she's gonna go and meet you, so you'd better get your ass over there, you understand? Pedal to the metal, boy, and don't look back. I don't know where the pair of you are gonna go after you've found each other, but two heads are better than one, right? At least I was able to give you a hand before..."

I wait for him to finish. "Are you sure?" I ask eventually, with tears in my eyes at the thought that maybe I'm not going to be completely alone after all. I'd already forced myself not to hold out hope that our sister might ever turn up, and I'm still not quite ready to believe she might still be alive. I'd like to think that Joe would never joke about something so important, but I know him too well to let my guard down just yet. "Is it really Martha?" I ask. "Are you completely certain?"

He nods, but he's clearly in pain.

"And you swear you're not kidding me?" I ask, my voice starting to tremble. "I swear to God, Joe, if this is some kind of trick, I'll never forgive you!"

"Why would I..." He pauses again, and finally that old, well-worn smile crosses his lips one last time. "I tell you what, Tommy. I'm gonna prove it to you. Kinda, anyway. I'm gonna show you that I can do what I claim I can do. You know that old broad in the bed upstairs? She was infected with whatever this thing is, even though she wasn't dead. And that means I can... abandon this body and go into hers and..."

I wait for him to continue. "Joe?" I say after a moment. "You're not making sense!"

Silence.

Stepping closer, I reach out and touch the side of his neck, and I realize that he doesn't have a pulse. I guess his body has finally given out.

"Rest in peace," I whisper.

"Hey!" a voice calls out suddenly, from upstairs. "Up here!"

Looking up at the ceiling, I'm gripped by a sudden sense of fear.

"It's me!" the voice calls again. It sounds like the old woman, but at the same time, there's something very familiar about the way she's speaking... something that reminds me of someone else. "It's Joe!" she shouts. "I'm up here! Come on up and see!"

ELIZABETH

Pennsylvania

"PUT HIM WITH THE rest," Patricia says. "Let's get them on top of each other, so they burn faster."

As I pull Thor's dead body across the yard, I almost stumble in the mud. Managing to stay upright at the last moment, I finally get to the small bonfire that Patricia has built in the clearing, and with the last of my energy I manage to haul the corpse on top of the other two. Taking a step back, I try to get my head around the fact that an hour ago, these three men were still alive, and now they're piled up ready to be burned. I hated Eriksen, I disliked Thor and I never really got to know Bridger, but I never felt they deserved to die.

"You did a good job," Patricia continues, picking up a can of gasoline and starting to pour it over the bodies. "Were you careful? Until we know how this thing transmits from one person to the next, we need to be careful. You didn't take the gloves off, did you? Not even for a moment?"

"No," I reply, feeling as if my mind is completely blank. I guess I can't quite take in the enormity of what I'm seeing. It's just a few minutes since these people were talking and arguing, and now they're just corpses, lumps of meat and bone ready to be tossed onto a fire and burned. "Do I have to stay and watch?" I ask after a moment.

"You need to toughen up," she replies.

"But do I really have to watch?"

"Just hang on a few more minutes," she replies, splashing gasoline over Bridger's head. "We won't be much longer."

"I think he's still alive!" I say suddenly, as I spot a vague hint of movement in Bridger's hand.

"Not for much longer," Patricia replies matter-of-factly.

"You can't just burn him like this!" I shout.

"I'm not wasting a bullet," she says calmly.

"What the fuck's wrong with you?" I ask, taking a step back. "You didn't have to do any of this!"

"Any one of them could be infected," she replies. "Do you really want us to take the risk?"

"But you said it yourself," I continue, "you don't even know how the infection spreads. For all we know, the whole house could have it, and we could be infected as well!"

"I admit," she replies, "I've been considering that possibility. However, I've fairly confident that some of us seem to have a kind of genetic immunity. After all, we've both been in heavily urbanized areas where the disease was presumably running rampant. The fact that we didn't get sick means, in my opinion, that we're safe." She pauses. "Either that, or the disease is able to hide itself much more convincingly in our minds. I suppose that's a possibility that we should consider. If I'd known for sure that one of these three was infected, I'd have performed an autopsy. As it stands..." She pauses again. "Maybe I acted rashly. Maybe I should have simply incapacitated them by shooting their kneecaps, and then held them in a pit until I was able to work out how to deal with them more effectively and -"

"You're a monster," I say, interrupting her.

"Please," she replies with a faint smile, "let's not get melodramatic here. You're letting your emotions get the better of you, Elizabeth, and I think we've already seen today that such things can have very bad consequences."

"I mean it," I continue. "You don't even care about these people, do you?"

"I've tried caring about people in the past," she replies. "It... didn't end well. In my experience, the best approach is to focus on my own needs. If that makes me a bad person or a 'monster', then I guess I just have to accept whatever labels people throw at me. At the end of the day, I'm still alive and billions of other people aren't, so I guess I must have been doing something right all this time." She takes a deep breath. "I don't need you to agree with every decision I make," she continues eventually, "but I hope we can work together, Elizabeth. We have common interests."

"I don't know," I reply after a moment. "I mean, I can't..." Staring at the dead bodies on the bonfire, I try to see things from Patricia's point of view. After all, Eriksen *was* causing trouble, and he did seem to be persuading Bridger and Thor to see things from his perspective. At the same time, I don't see that Patricia had any justification for killing them. The world might have gone to hell, but we're still human beings and if we just start killing each other indiscriminately, we're no better than the creatures that are hunting us down. Then again, I can't help wondering if I'm just being hopelessly naive.

"Shit," she mutters. "You don't get it, do you?"

"Help me," Bridger moans suddenly, trying to move despite the fact that he's got both Eriksen and Thor on top of him. "Get me out of here!"

"Can you save him?" I ask, turning to Patricia.

"Maybe," she replies, putting the can of gasoline down before lighting a match. "I don't see the benefit, though. He's already cost me a bullet."

"But shouldn't we say something?" I ask, trying to delay the moment when she sets fire to the bodies. "I mean, shouldn't we..." I pause, trying to work out what, exactly, I mean. My mind is racing and I'm starting to panic, and all I know is that I can't let her burn Bridger alive. "Maybe we should say something," I continue, "to mark their passing."

"Go on, then," she replies, with a frown, "but this match is burning pretty fast."

I watch as Bridger reaches out, his hand searching for something, anything, that might save him.

"I just think," I say eventually, "that maybe we should be careful to -"

"Time's up," Patricia says.

"No, I -"

With that, she takes a step back before tossing the match onto the bodies, causing a huge fireball that immediately consumes all three corpses. Stepping back, I hold my hands up to shield my face from the heat, and for a moment I swear I can hear Bridger screaming before finally he falls silent. The flames are so strong, it's impossible to see what's happening at the center of the bonfire, but when I turn to Patricia, I realize that she's already carrying the can of gasoline back over to the farmhouse.

"Elizabeth," she says suddenly, turning back to face me, "I don't know if you've noticed, but the baby's crying. You really should give her a name, by the way. Even if it's just something you come up with on the spot." She reaches into her pocket and takes out the cigarette she showed me the other day, the one she'd been saving. With a faint smile, she walks over to the bonfire and holds the cigarette out until the end is lit, and then she takes a long drag. "God," she says eventually, "that felt good. You know what? Toad has some cigarettes in his basement. I think maybe I'm going to start smoking again. It helps me concentrate."

She holds the cigarette out for me, but I shake my head.

"You don't know what you're missing," she continues, taking another drag. "Don't spend too long out here. We've got work to do." With that, she turns and starts walking back toward the farmhouse.

Standing by the bonfire, all I can do is stare and imagine the bodies burning up in the inferno. I have no idea whether Bridger could have been saved, but he was still alive when the fire started and I'm certain he realized what was happening to him. With the baby staring up at me, I realize that there's no way I can just sit around this place with Patricia; she's clearly lost her mind, and it's only a matter of time before she decides that Toad and I, and maybe even the baby as well, are inconvenient. Then again, where else can I go? Eriksen was right when he said that I'm ill-equipped to go wandering off across the country, but if staying here isn't an option...

Glancing over at the barn next to the farmhouse, I spot Eriksen and Shauna's van, and I realize that maybe my best bet is to strike a deal with Patricia.

When I get back into the kitchen, I find Patricia washing her hands and arms in the sink. I watch her for a moment, trying to work out what must be going through her mind after she killed those three men.

"Was that the first time you've ever done anything like that?" I ask eventually.

"What?" she asks, as if nothing unusual has happened.

"Have you ever killed anyone before?"

She pauses. "Sure," she says after a moment. "I'm a doctor. People die around me all the time."

"But have you ever shot anyone?"

"No," she replies, drying her hands on a towel. "I know what you're thinking, Elizabeth, and I want you to try to understand this from my point of view. There's no place for sentimentality when you're dealing with life and death. Sure, I could have let those three guys live, but what would have happened? More arguing, more bickering, and then they'd have killed Toad and my specimen, and then things would have been tense and eventually there would have been deaths anyway. What I did, I did to ensure that the best possible outcome emerged from a situation in which death and conflict was already inevitable." She pauses. "If you think we could have sorted things out with a cozy chat around the table, you're wrong. And, I might add, hopelessly naive."

I pause for a moment. "What do you think about Toad?" I ask eventually. "Is he infected?"

She shakes her head. "Not with whatever's causing all of this. He's got a much more ordinary type of infection, although it's just as dangerous. He definitely could die."

"And there's nothing you can do for him?"

"I can't throw all my remaining supplies away on a long-shot attempt to save one guy," she replies. "Be sensible, Elizabeth."

"Let me take him away," I say suddenly. "I'll take him, and the baby, and we'll go in Eriksen's old van. We'll take enough gas to get us to Lake Ontario. I know some people who were headed that way, and I think it might be my best shot."

"You want to leave me here alone?" she replies.

"You can get on with your work," I point out. "No-one'll interrupt you -"

"I'll be alone," she says firmly. "What's wrong, Elizabeth? Are you scared of me or something?"

I pause, trying to work out what to say.

"Jesus," she mutters, "you're fucking scared of me."

"I've made my decision," I say, trying not to let my voice waver too much. "I'm going to load up the van -"

"Says who?"

"I need supplies for the journey."

"Not *my* supplies," she says, staring at me as if she hates me. "Why should I give you *my* supplies just so you can fuck off?"

"They're not yours," I reply. "Everything here is Toad's."

"Then let him come down here and make me give them up," she replies. "The world has changed, Elizabeth. Sure, all the supplies around here belong to Toad, but unless he can assert his right to them, it doesn't mean a damn thing. I need everything here." She picks up the gun from the counter-top. "The only way anyone's getting even a drop of the supplies around here is if they take them by force," she continues, fixing me with a determined stare that leaves me in no doubt that she'd shoot me if necessary. "This is how the world works now.

There's no legal authority to back up claims of ownership. You get what you can take, and you keep what you can defend."

"So you're going to shoot me if I try to leave?" I ask, trying to work out what to do next.

She pauses. "No," she says eventually, putting the gun back in the holster around her waist. Walking around the table, she comes closer, but it's clear that she's planning something. "There are four hundred and nine bullets left on this property, for various different weapons. If I shoot you, that's a waste of something like a quarter of a per cent of my ammunition." She pauses. "Put the baby down."

I take a step back. "Why?"

"Just put her down."

"Why?"

"For her sake," she replies, before suddenly lunging at me, pulling me across the room and finally slamming my head into the fridge, knocking me out immediately.

THOMAS

Missouri

"TOLD YOU," JOE SAYS as I enter the bedroom. "Isn't this fucking sweet?"

I stare at him. Or rather, at *her*. It's the old woman from yesterday, the same one whose decrepit, emaciated body seemed to have been left in this bed for so long. Her skin is gray and peeling, with yellow and green blotches, and her thin hair is hanging like cotton from her head. The difference this time, however, is that now she's got a grin on her face, and she's staring at me as if she finds this whole situation funny. Despite her appearance, there's something indefinably familiar about the whole thing, as if the old woman's face somehow has Joe's expression.

"Pretty cool, huh?" she says. "Don't worry about the fact that I look like some kind of mummified hag. The point is, I was able to move into her body. I can see through her eyes, Tommy, and that's basically how I found Martha, even though she's out in California. This old crone's already dead, and her body's no use, so I guess I won't stick around, but I just wanted you to see that I'm still out there somewhere. I'll be in the ether, going from body to body, looking for a way to bring this fucking asshole down. Maybe I can do it from the inside."

"Joe?" I say, unable to quite believe what I'm seeing.

"Sucks that she's such an old hag," he continues. "Maybe I should try to find someone a bit hotter some time, if you know what I mean. I wouldn't mind getting some action, maybe have a little sexy time with a mirror." He laughs. "Yeah, maybe that's what I'll do next. I'll go body-hopping through a bunch of fucking hot chicks and see what I can get up to. Maybe if I can occupy two bodies at once, I can..." He pauses. "I could occupy two hot women at once," he continues, with a sense of awe in his voice, "and make 'em do things with each other, and I'd be able to watch from both angles. Jesus fucking Christ, can you imagine how incredible that'd be? I need to do it, even if they're fucking zombies. Jealous?"

"Are you serious?" I ask, walking toward him.

"Hell, no," he replies. "I'm not serious about anything, Tommy. But it's real as all Jesus." He pauses. "You need to get going," he says after a moment. "Tommy, you need to go and meet Martha. She's pretty much the only family we've got left, so you need to go and help her and let her help you. Don't worry about anything else. Just get the hell out of here and come up with a plan once the pair of you are together. How long's it been since we saw Martha, anyway? Fucking years! She's pretty smart, when she's not being dumb. You can trust Martha. I mean, hell, she's managed to survive this long, so she must be doing something right."

"She can't be alive," I reply. "It's not possible."

"Would I lie to you?" he replies. "There are people out there, Tommy. Not many, but enough. A few million. Maybe if everyone gets together, they can do something about this cluster-fuck. These creatures, they're not so tough, and they're still rotting. Whatever this guy's plan is, I'm not sure it's going totally according to schedule, so there's still room for maneuver. He's panicking. He's getting more and more scared, and he's got less time to spend bragging and taunting us. He's racing from body to body, desperately hoping to find something. To be honest, it's kind of fun to watch."

"I can't leave you like this," I say, staring at him.

"What, stuck in some old hag's body?" He smiles. "I'm not stuck anywhere, kid. I can go to other bodies, other creatures. I don't know if the big guy even knows I'm doing it, but I'll try to stay all subtle and quiet, like. And then maybe, eventually, I'll pop out of another creature and say hi. I dunno, I'm getting kinda tired, so I think I need to rest, but I'll do whatever I can. As you can imagine, it's a pretty major mind-fuck right now. I just..." He pauses. "I just figured I show let you know that I'll be out there somewhere. I ain't dying, Tommy. Not yet. Maybe not ever, not now. I can go watch people all over the world, maybe even talk to them if I can summon up enough energy."

"So you'll come back?" I ask. "I'll see you again?"

"Reckon so," he replies. "You and Martha are family, so I'll find you somehow." He stares at me for a moment. "Tommy, how many fucking times do I have to tell you? Get the fuck out of here, okay? Do you really wanna leave Martha waiting for you out there? She's not exactly armed to the teeth, so make sure you get over to her and help her out, okay? I know she's older than you, Tommy boy, but there are some things she's better at and there are some things you're better at. You might make a decent team. Better than you and me, anyway." He smiles. "Go!"

"If I *don't* see you again," I continue, with tears in my eyes, "I'll come back to this place and check up on you."

"I won't be here," he replies. "Fuck, I'm already getting out. I'll seeya around, Tommy. Just promise me you'll find Martha. I set it up already, so if you don't go and meet her, you'll be letting her down. She was holed up pretty safe in San Francisco, so she's risking her life to go and find you. You'd better make damn sure that you don't let her down. This is a matter of life and death, kid."

"Yeah," I reply. "Of course."

"*Promise* me!"

"Of course I'll find her," I say firmly. "Even if it's the last thing I do. I'll go to that four corners place and if she's not there, I'll wait until..." I pause for a moment. "I'll wait forever if I have to. I'll find her."

"Okay," he replies. "That's good enough for me. See you around, Tommy. I'm off into the ether." He smiles, and then suddenly the old woman's body collapses back down onto the bed, landing in a dead heap.

"See you around," I mutter, before turning and running.

ELIZABETH

Pennsylvania

WHEN I WAKE UP, I realize I'm being dragged across the yard. It takes me a couple of seconds to work out exactly what's happening, but finally I twist around and see that Patricia has tied a rope around my arms. Before I can work out what to do next, I feel heat on my back, and I look over my shoulder to see that we're getting closer to the fire.

"No!" I shout, trying to struggle free. "You can't -"

Before I can finish, she drops me onto the ground, before unscrewing the lid of the gasoline canister and dousing me. With my arms tied to my sides, I try to scramble away, but there's gasoline all over my body now, running down my face and stinging my eyes so badly, I can barely even manage to keep them open.

"You're a fucking idiot," she says after a moment. "You know that? Things could have been okay here. You could have helped me, and we might have got some answers about that creature. Instead, you just showed me that I can't trust you, and if I can't trust you, then I can't keep you around."

"Stop!" I shout, getting to my feet. There's still gasoline in my eyes, and although I'm blinking furiously, I can't get it out. The result is that all I can really see is a faint blurry image of Patricia standing nearby, while the bonfire still burns behind her. If even the slightest spark or flame reaches me, I'll go up in flames.

"If you're worried about the baby," she continues, "then don't be. I'll do my best. It's ironic, in a way. I never wanted a kid, and now, through some torturous set of circumstances, I've been lumbered with one. Still, it'll probably be a good thing for me to have someone else around. If I was all alone, I might start to go a little crazy."

"Please don't do this," I say, as tears pour down my cheeks, mingling with the gasoline in my eyes. "Please. I'll do anything, but please, don't hurt me!"

"It's too late for that," she replies. "I'm sorry, but I can't let emotion enter it my decision. You've shown your hand, Elizabeth, and once you've lost my trust, it's gone forever. It's a shame, but there's no way back." Seconds later, I hear a match being struck.

"No!" I shout, trying to turn and run before something slams into my feet and I drop to the ground.

Before I can even try to get up, there's a loud bang, echoing around the yard, and I hear the sound of something landing next to me. I scramble to get away, terrified that at any moment Patricia's going to drop the match onto me and I'll burn, but as I get back to my feet, it's almost as if she's enjoying watching me struggle. I blink a few times, trying to clear the gasoline from my eyes, but my vision is still way too blurry. Spinning around, I try to work out where she is, but all I can see is the nearby bonfire. Turning, I stumble toward the farmhouse, before suddenly realizing that there's a figure coming toward me.

"No!" I shout. "Someone help me!"

"It's me!" a familiar voice shouts back, hurrying over and putting his hands on my arms for a moment. Realizing that it's Toad, I stand still as he unties the rope. "It's me," he says again, "don't worry. It's okay, she's not going to hurt you. Follow me."

Still not able to see properly, I let him take me by the hand and lead me across the yard, until suddenly he forces me to stop. My heart is racing and I can't see properly, so I don't even know what's happening, but I guess all I can do is trust Toad.

"Take your clothes off," he says, as I hear him moving what sounds like some kind of barrel.

"What?" I ask breathlessly.

"You're covered in gasoline," he replies. "Take your clothes off so I can wash it off."

Figuring that I need to just do what he says, I pull my clothes off as fast as possible, until finally I'm standing naked in the yard, covering myself with my hands as much as possible. Reaching up to my face, I try to rub the gasoline from my eyes.

"Not like that," Toad says, taking my hand and leading me over to the barrel. "This is rain water. Dip your face in here and open your eyes."

"It hurts," I say, feeling the stinging sensation in my eyes getting worse and worse. "It -" Before I can finish, Toad grabs my head and dunks me face into the barrel. I struggle for a moment, before finally opening my eyes. The pain is still there, but I finally realize that he's only doing this to help me. When he lets go of my head, I keep it underwater for a moment longer before finally coming up for air.

"You're lucky you're not permanently blinded," he says, placing his hands on my face and pulling my eyelids wide open. "Can you see properly?"

I nod. Although my eyes still hurt, I can see much better now.

"I thought you were dying," I say, looking at his bare chest and seeing the bandages on his shoulder.

"I'll be okay," he replies, still examining my eyes carefully. "The worst of the fever has passed. Now crouch down so I can pour the water over you."

Shivering and cold, I nevertheless do exactly what he says, and moments later he pours a deluge of cold water over my naked body. I let out a gasp, but finally he wraps a towel over my shoulders.

"What did you do to her?" I ask, looking over at the bonfire and seeing Patricia's prone form on the ground. Turning back to Toad, I realize that there's a rifle slung over his shoulders.

"The same thing she did to the others," he replies. "She was right about one thing. There's no law anymore, not really. We get what we can take, and she was going to take everything eventually. She couldn't trust you, and I couldn't trust her." He pauses. "But I trust you, and I hope the feeling's mutual."

I nod.

"You need to go inside and get warm," he continues. "I'll fix up the fireplace in the front room for you. Go and find some blankets and wrap yourself up. I'll take care of everything out here."

Half an hour later, I'm sitting by a roaring fire in the farmhouse, with blankets covering my body. Toad made me wash several more times, to make sure that the last of the gasoline was off my skin, and my eyes are still stinging a little, but for the most part I feel as if I'm okay. The baby is sleeping on the floor nearby, but although I know I should be holding her, I feel somehow frozen in place. I can't help replaying the past few hours over and over in my mind, first the way Patricia killed the others so casually, then the way Bridger called for help from the bonfire, and finally the moment when she poured gasoline on my body and lit the match; these three memories are just spinning through my mind, and I can't think about anything else.

"How are you doing in here?" Toad asks suddenly.

Turning, I realize that I hadn't heard him entering the room. He walks over to the baby and crouches down to take a look at her.

"Did you choose a name for her yet?" he asks, turning to me.

I pause for a moment. "Rachel," I say eventually.

"Nice name." Reaching down, he runs a finger across Rachel's chin. "Hello Rachel," he says after a moment. "I'm sorry things have been a little crazy. I can't promise there'll be much of an improvement in the immediate future, but I'll do my best to keep you safe."

"It was..." I pause again, wondering whether I should open up to him. "It was my mother's name," I explain, feeling a rush of relief. I don't know why, but it feels good to have someone named Rachel around again, even if she's just a baby. I guess I'm still in mourning for my parents. "She... She was Rachel. I guess maybe it's stupid. If you want to change it -"

"Rachel's fine," he replies with a faint smile. "I have no idea what kind of world she's going to grow up into, but at least she's got a good name."

"Patricia's dead, isn't she?" I ask after a moment. "You killed her."

"I had to," he replies. "She was going to kill you, so..." He pauses. "I put her on the bonfire with the others. I suppose that's poetic justice in a way. She was always so sure of herself. She kept talking about how important it was to make rational decisions, but at the end of the day, she was just out for herself, like everyone else."

"I thought I was going to die," I tell him. "I mean, I *really* thought..." I take a deep breath. "That's twice in, like, two weeks that I've almost died. Is it always going to be like this?"

"I have no idea," he replies, coming over and sitting next to me. "I guess the world is a pretty strange place right now, and no-one knows what's coming."

"What are we... I mean, what are *you* going to do next?"

He stares at the fire for a moment. "*We* have to decide whether we're going to stick it out here or head off somewhere else. I'm starting to think it might be smart to load the van up and get the hell away." He pauses. "Right now, however, I've got three things I want to do. First, I want to put some more logs on the fire, to keep us warm. Second, I want to change the bandage on my shoulder to make sure it doesn't get infected again. And third, I want to kiss you."

As I turn to look at him, I feel a strange tightening sensation in my chest, almost as if someone just reached in, grabbed my heart and twisted it around several times.

Without saying anything more, Toad gets to his feet and grabs some logs to toss onto the fire. It takes a couple of minutes for him to get the flames really roaring, and then he walks out of the room. I sit in silence, listening as he goes upstairs. For almost ten minutes, I just stare at the flames, feeling their warmth on my body and hearing the occasional creak of the floorboards as Toad moves around up there. He's sure taking his time, but I guess he needs to make sure his wound is clean. Finally, I hear him coming back downstairs and entering the room. He kneels next to me, with a new bandage on his shoulder, and after a moment he puts a hand on the side of my neck, gently pulls me closer, and kisses me tenderly.

EPILOGUE

HE'S DYING NOW, AND he knows it.

The television is still on full volume, its picture lighting up the room with patterns and shadows that change every few seconds. Joseph would like to turn the damn thing off, but he lacks the energy. All he can do is remain on the sofa and wait for the end. He finds it somewhat ironic that his final moments should be plagued by the sound of a bunch of news reporters, whose asinine gabble continues to flood the room with comment on matters that - as far as Joseph is concerned - don't matter at all. For Joseph, the television is one final representative of a world that is about to be snuffed out forever. The news anchors talk incessantly about things that don't matter, but when the real nightmare arrives, they'll be among the first to die.

He reaches out to take the glass of water from his nightstand. His tired, aching hand fumbles for a moment, and the glass is knocked off the edge. As he hears the smashing sound, Joseph realizes that he doesn't have the strength to go and fetch more water. His lips are dry and parched, but now he'll just have to die without enjoying even one last sip. Opening his mouth, he tries to wet his lips with his tongue, but this too is dry and withered. His eyelids feel tight, and when he opens his eyes, he can feel the skin pressing hard against his eyeballs. His body has surrendered, and the end is coming. As he lets out an involuntary gasp, he realizes that in these final moments he has lost control of his body.

And that's when he starts to cough.

Violently, painfully, his body convulses in a series of desperate attempts to bring up phlegm. The agony is indescribable, but he can no longer scream. As the coughing fit subsides, he waits for the pain to stop pulsing through his body. He never expected that his death would be like this. He thought he would die quickly, that he would pass easily and without pain into the next phase of the plan. Unfortunately, this is the one part of the plan that he got wrong. He knows now that he has to die in the same tortured way as the others; in fact, he believes that the others might even die more quickly, whereas he - as the originator, the one who reorganized the world, the one who is closest to assuming his position as the world's new god - has to suffer in this way.

Slowly, he starts to smile, cracking the dry skin at either side of his lips; as soon as the smile is complete, the last breath leaves his body, and finally the voices from the television are the only living things in the room.

***

No-one comes to move him.

For the first few hours, the television continues to fill the room with light and sound. Eventually, however, the signal is abruptly cut and the screen goes dark. There's still noise from the city, but this too fades over time and eventually it's as if the whole world has fallen completely silent. Later, there's the brief sound of rain against the window, but this doesn't last too long.

Silence.

Joseph's body remains absolutely still. He's on the bed, with sheets covering him all the way up to his chest. His dead face stares up at the ceiling, as if he was expecting something to appear above him as he died. There's still a faint grin on his face, but his eyes are dead and his body has started to stiffen. Already, his eyes appear to have sunk deeper into the sockets, and the skin on his face looks tighter.

Deep inside his torso, the process of decomposition has begun. He's the first, but not by much; soon, billions of people all over the world are going to follow him into death, but there's one crucial difference.

For Joseph, this is only the beginning. This is the moment when everything starts again, and soon the whole world is going to be remade in his image. Even as he drew his last breath, Joseph was absolutely certain that he would rise again in billions of new bodies, his conscious mine shattered and poured into all those new souls.

On the far side of the room, sets of notebooks are piled on top of a small desk. These are the notebooks that contain all his plans. If everything works out as he expected, the world is about to enter a period of necessary darkness that will pave the way for an eventual explosion of light. Joseph took a risk, and part of that risk involved his own death, but he was convinced - even up to the very last second - that the pain and misery would be worth every second. He knew that he simply had to get through these final moments and embrace the darkness, and he knew that there would be something else waiting for him on the other side. Something triumphant. Something beautiful and spiritual and real. He knew that he would wake up again one day. One day soon.

But not in this body.

This body, the original - the prime - is useless. In a way, it always had to end this way. By the time his body has fulled rotted away, however, he hopes to be back in the world. His world.

DAYS 9 TO 16

Continued in:

Days 33 to 36
(Mass Extinction Event book 4)

DAYS 9 TO 16

Also by Amy Cross

The Devil, the Witch and the Whore (The Deal book 1)

"Leave the forest alone. Whatever's out there, just let it be. Don't make it angry."

When a horrific discovery is made at the edge of town, Sheriff James Kopperud realizes the answers he seeks might be waiting beyond in the vast forest. But everybody in the town of Deal knows that there's something out there in the forest, something that should never be disturbed. A deal was made long ago, a deal that was supposed to keep the town safe. And if he insists on investigating the murder of a local girl, James is going to have to break that deal and head out into the wilderness.

Meanwhile, James has no idea that his estranged daughter Ramsey has returned to town. Ramsey is running from something, and she thinks she can find safety in the vast tunnel system that runs beneath the forest. Before long, however, Ramsey finds herself coming face to face with creatures that hide in the shadows. One of these creatures is known as the devil, and another is known as the witch. They're both waiting for the whore to arrive, but for very different reasons. And soon Ramsey is offered a terrible deal, one that could save or destroy the entire town, and maybe even the world.

Also by Amy Cross

The Soul Auction

"I saw a woman on the beach. I watched her face a demon."

Thirty years after her mother's death, Alice Ashcroft is drawn back to the coastal English town of Curridge. Somebody in Curridge has been reviewing Alice's novels online, and in those reviews there have been tantalizing hints at a hidden truth. A truth that seems to be linked to her dead mother.

"Thirty years ago, there was a soul auction."

Once she reaches Curridge, Alice finds strange things happening all around her. Something attacks her car. A figure watches her on the beach at night. And when she tries to find the person who has been reviewing her books, she makes a horrific discovery.

What really happened to Alice's mother thirty years ago? Who was she talking to, just moments before dropping dead on the beach? What caused a huge rockfall that nearly tore a nearby cliff-face in half? And what sinister presence is lurking in the grounds of the local church?

DAYS 9 TO 16

Also by Amy Cross

Darper Danver: The Complete First Series

Five years ago, three friends went to a remote cabin in the woods and tried to contact the spirit of a long-dead soldier. They thought they could control whatever happened next. They were wrong...

Newly released from prison, Cassie Briggs returns to Fort Powell, determined to get her life back on track. Soon, however, she begins to suspect that an ancient evil still lurks in the nearby cabin. Was the mysterious Darper Danver really destroyed all those years ago, or does her spirit still linger, waiting for a chance to return?

As Cassie and her ex-boyfriend Fisher are finally forced to face the truth about what happened in the cabin, they realize that Darper isn't ready to let go of their lives just yet. Meanwhile, a vengeful woman plots revenge for her brother's murder, and a New York ghost writer arrives in town to uncover the truth. Before long, strange carvings begin to appear around town and blood starts to flow once again.

Also by Amy Cross

The Ghost of Molly Holt

"Molly Holt is dead. There's nothing to fear in this house."

When three teenagers set out to explore an abandoned house in the middle of a forest, they think they've found the location where the infamous Molly Holt video was filmed.

They've found much more than that...

Tim doesn't believe in ghosts, but he has a crush on a girl who does. That's why he ends up taking her out to the house, and it's also why he lets her take his only flashlight. But as they explore the house together, Tim and Becky start to realize that something else might be lurking in the shadows.

Something that, ten years ago, suffered unimaginable pain.

Something that won't rest until a terrible wrong has been put right.

Also by Amy Cross

American Coven

He kidnapped three women and held them in his basement. He thought they couldn't fight back. He was wrong...

Snatched from the street near her home, Holly Carter is taken to a rural house and thrown down into a stone basement. She meets two other women who have also been kidnapped, and soon Holly learns about the horrific rituals that take place in the house. Eventually, she's called upstairs to take her place in the ice bath.

As her nightmare continues, however, Holly learns about a mysterious power that exists in the basement, and which the three women might be able to harness. When they finally manage to get through the metal door, however, the women have no idea that their fight for freedom is going to stretch out for more than a decade, or that it will culminate in a final, devastating demonstration of their new-found powers.

Also by Amy Cross

The Ash House

Why would anyone ever return to a haunted house?

For Diane Mercer the answer is simple. She's dying of cancer, and she wants to know once and for all whether ghosts are real.

Heading home with her young son, Diane is determined to find out whether the stories are real. After all, everyone else claimed to see and hear strange things in the house over the years. Everyone except Diane had some kind of experience in the house, or in the little ash house in the yard.

As Diane explores the house where she grew up, however, her son is exploring the yard and the forest. And while his mother might be struggling to come to terms with her own impending death, Daniel Mercer is puzzled by fleeting appearances of a strange little girl who seems drawn to the ash house, and by strange, rasping coughs that he keeps hearing at night.

The Ash House is a horror novel about a woman who desperately wants to know what will happen to her when she dies, and about a boy who uncovers the shocking truth about a young girl's murder.

Also by Amy Cross

Haunted

Twenty years ago, the ghost of a dead little girl drove Sheriff Michael Blaine to his death.

Now, that same ghost is coming for his daughter.

Returning to the small town where she grew up, Alex Roberts is determined to live a normal, quiet life. For the residents of Railham, however, she's an unwelcome reminder of the town's darkest hour.

Twenty years ago, nine-year-old Mo Garvey was found brutally murdered in a nearby forest. Everyone thinks that Alex's father was responsible, but if the killer was brought to justice, why is the ghost of Mo Garvey still after revenge?

And how far will the real killer go to protect his secret, when Alex starts getting closer to the truth?

Haunted is a horror novel about a woman who has to face her past, about a town that would rather forget, and about a little girl who refuses to let death stand in her way.

Also by Amy Cross

The Curse of Wetherley House

"If you walk through that door, Evil Mary will get you."

When she agrees to visit a supposedly haunted house with an old friend, Rosie assumes she'll encounter nothing more scary than a few creaks and bumps in the night. Even the legend of Evil Mary doesn't put her off. After all, she knows ghosts aren't real. But when Mary makes her first appearance, Rosie realizes she might already be trapped.

For more than a century, Wetherley House has been cursed. A horrific encounter on a remote road in the late 1800's has already caused a chain of misery and pain for all those who live at the house. Wetherley House was abandoned long ago, after a terrible discovery in the basement, something has remained undetected within its room. And even the local children know that Evil Mary waits in the house for anyone foolish enough to walk through the front door.

Before long, Rosie realizes that her entire life has been defined by the spirit of a woman who died in agony. Can she become the first person to escape Evil Mary, or will she fall victim to the same fate as the house's other occupants?

Also by Amy Cross

The Ghosts of Hexley Airport

Ten years ago, more than two hundred people died in a horrific plane crash at Hexley Airport.

Today, some say their ghosts still haunt the terminal building.

When she starts her new job at the airport, working a night shift as part of the security team, Casey assumes the stories about the place can't be true. Even when she has a strange encounter in a deserted part of the departure hall, she's certain that ghosts aren't real.

Soon, however, she's forced to face the truth. Not only is there something haunting the airport's buildings and tarmac, but a sinister force is working behind the scenes to replicate the circumstances of the original accident. And as a snowstorm moves in, Hexley Airport looks set to witness yet another disaster.

Also by Amy Cross

The Girl Who Never Came Back

Twenty years ago, Charlotte Abernathy vanished while playing near her family's house. Despite a frantic search, no trace of her was found until a year later, when the little girl turned up on the doorstep with no memory of where she'd been.

Today, Charlotte has put her mysterious ordeal behind her, even though she's never learned where she was during that missing year. However, when her eight-year-old niece vanishes in similar circumstances, a fully-grown Charlotte is forced to make a fresh attempt to uncover the truth.

Originally published in 2013, the fully revised and updated version of *The Girl Who Never Came Back* tells the harrowing story of a woman who thought she could forget her past, and of a little girl caught in the tangled web of a dark family secret.

Also by Amy Cross

Asylum
(The Asylum Trilogy book 1)

"No-one ever leaves Lakehurst. The staff, the patients, the ghosts... Once you're here, you're stuck forever."

After shooting her little brother dead, Annie Radford is sent to Lakehurst psychiatric hospital for assessment. Hearing voices in her head, Annie is forced to undergo experimental new treatments devised by a mysterious old man who lives in the hospital's attic. It soon becomes clear that the hospital's staff, led by the vicious Nurse Winter, are hiding something horrific at Lakehurst.

As Annie struggles to survive the hospital, she learns more about Nurse Winter's own story. Once a promising young medical student, Kirsten Winter also heard voices in her head. Voices that traveled a long way to reach her. Voices that have a plan of their own. Voices that will stop at nothing to get what they want.

What kind of signals are being transmitted from the basement of the hospital? Who is the old man in the attic? Why are living human brains kept in jars? And what is the dark secret that lurks at the heart of the hospital?

Also by Amy Cross

The Devil's Hand

"I felt it last night! I was all alone, and suddenly a hand touched my shoulder!"

The year is 1943. Beacon's Ash is a private, remote school in the North of England, and all its pupils are fallen girls. Pregnant and unmarried, they have been sent away by their families. For Ivy Jones, a young girl who arrived at the school several months earlier, Beacon's Ash is a nightmare, and her fears are strengthened when one of her classmates is killed in mysterious circumstances.

Has the ghost of Abigail Cartwright returned to the school? Who or what is responsible for the hand that touches the girls' shoulders in the dead of night? And is the school's headmaster Jeremiah Kane just a madman who seeks to cause misery, or is he in fact on the trail of the Devil himself? Soon ghosts are stalking the dark corridors, and Ivy realizes she has to face the evil that lurks in the school's shadows.

The Devil's Hand is a horror novel about a girl who seeks the truth about her friend's death, and about a madman who believes the Devil stalks the school's corridors in the run-up to Christmas.

For more information, visit:

www. amycross.com

AMY CROSS

Printed in Great Britain
by Amazon